The Hand
The Demise of the Neanderthal

Nick Meyer

Published by:

Nickaway Media   WWW.Nickaway.com
Corpus Christi, TX 78414
USA

1-6

ISBN:13:978-0615840574
(Nickaway Media)
ISBN-10:0615840574

DEDICATION

I dedicate this book to the Dalai Lama and these,
his words.
When asked what surprised him most about humanity
he answered,
"Man, because he sacrifices his health
in order to make money.
Then he sacrifices money to recuperate his health.
And then he is so anxious about the future that he does
not enjoy the present; the result being that he does not
live in the present or the future; he lives as if he is never
going to die, and then dies having never lived."

ACKNOWLEDGMENTS

This book was given to me in dream. Getting the concept into book form has taken a lot of work.
My friend, Rod McGregor, was able to take an idea and produce an image that portrays the concept.
Thank you, Rod.
A special thank you to all my friends who have taken time to read the manuscript, giving me suggestions and encouragement.
A special thank you to my stepdaughter, Alicia, who carefully read my manuscript and Texanised my writing.
Thank you, Alicia. X
A special thank you to my wife who has endured many hours of editing and correction. She was able to share the dream. Thank you, Brenda.

Author

Nick Meyer was born in England where he was a successful businessman. He immigrated to the United States in 1994 and is now a US Citizen. He is not aligned with any particular religion or tradition, but lives by the teachings of the Tao and Buddhism. He has written numerous articles for outdoor magazines as well as a children's book, <u>The Caterpillar Story</u>. The story of <u>The Hand</u> was given to him through dream, where he receives his inspiration. He is a successful entrepreneur and patented inventor whose ability to think outside the box keeps his internationally known fishing tackle company ahead of the curve. Nick also enjoys playing the guitar and painting.

Nick Meyer

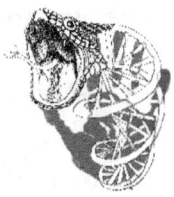

Chapter 1

It was totally out of context that Senator Peter Edward Shaw, now sixty-nine and bare foot, was sitting in the Travis County jail in Austin, Texas waiting to be processed along with the drunkards, druggies and hookers. The young punk sitting beside him said, "Old man, you're too old to be tagging." Peter ignored him, focusing more on the body language of the rookie DPS officer, Juan Espinoza, who had booked him and was now talking to the jailer sergeant, frequently turning and indicating towards the detainee.

Twenty-one year veteran of the Austin, Travis County jail, Sergeant Steve Madden immediately recognized the old man. Murmuring to himself, his right hand reached over and picked up the booking forms as his left hand reached for the IP, Important Person, documents that had to be filed and processed. This sort of shit would guarantee that the sergeant would have another extended shift, which is the last thing on earth he wanted. The sergeant was on his third marriage and nearing the end of an uneventful career that had left him with an acute dislike for the human race and his job.

The sergeant was telling Espinoza a brief background on the senator. "You would not believe how he's changed. He used to be the meanest son of a bitch on the planet. He knew everything about everyone and would not think twice about using it for his own benefit. He was dragged in front of several senate hearings over potential fraud, always getting off without a scratch. He was a total asshole and on top of the fucking world until the fateful day that a local lawyer, celebrating his 40% share of some freaking unjustified lawsuit, lost control of his BMW. He crossed the center medium, and hit his car head on, killing his wife and putting Shaw in a six- weeks coma," remarked Madden.

"Talk about fucking karma. Bring him over," said the sergeant.

The rookie, a bit too eager, moved quickly towards Peter. Reading the situation Peter stood up, his still painted red hand cuffed behind his back, making the maneuver difficult for Peter's old bones. "Slow down sir," said Espinoza, the word "sir" slipping out of Juan's mouth, pissing him off as he realized he was acting in a subservient way, the last thing he wanted to be seen doing. Every action he took or did in this microcosm of the booking office had a reaction, and he didn't want to be seen kissing the butt of a washed up senator.

Once Juan had passed Peter over to the Travis County Jail, his initial job was finished. Two members of the jail staff approached and, removing the cuffs asked him to place his hands on the table and proceeded to pat him down, at the same time asking him if he had anything in his pockets: weapons, drugs, needles etc. This was the same thing the DPS officer had asked when he caught him just as he removed his freshly painted hand from the sidewall of the Texas Governor's Mansion.

The processing was efficient and designed to intimidate. Instructions were given, and it was as if the jailers giving them were hoping the accused would mess up so they could show how much they were in control. The old senator was presenting no problems, but the fact he had some level of notoriety did require the officers to play the game slightly different from the normal perp. The basic booking of prints and pictures was quickly processed. He was then led off to the interview room, away from the gaze of the other prisoners.

Shaw was asked to take a seat next to a table with his back to the wall and was left unattended for about thirty minutes. Finally, Detective Jeffrey P. Granger entered the room. Granger was 6'2" with short salt and pepper hair. He was wearing a dark pair of Wrangler jeans; western cut shirt, a white cowboy hat, pointed-toe cowboy boots, and a belt buckle the size of two men's fists. He was ex-military and the daily routine of working out had never subsided. His slim frame made it easy to read the word Texas that was carved out of a gold and silver buckle. It was just another day at the office for the detective, and interviewing Peter should not have been a problem. Reading Peter his rights and taking a seat, the detective flipped on the recorder and again confirmed that Peter was clear about his Miranda rights and anything he said would be recorded and used against him. Peter confirmed his awareness of the consequences of anything he might say.

The detective started the interview. "Sir, you're here tonight as you have been arrested for an act of criminal mischief and in this state...." Before he could finish, the door swung open and a young lawyer, looking like the overworked trial lawyer John Grisham would portray, walked in dominantly placing his brief case between the officer and his client, purposely leaving his hand on the bag to form a barrier between the accused and the detective.

"Senator Sir, my name is Scott Nielson from Morgan and Morgan's. I am here to represent you and would prefer if you did not comment to any further question you might be asked until we have had time for me to advise you in private."

Nielson turned to the officer. Peter grinned and said, "I haven't had chance to say anything, but if the charge is defacing the Governor's Mansion my plea will be guilty as charged."

"Senator," the young lawyer said again, "I would prefer it if we could speak in private before you comment. It's very important." Turning to detective Granger he said, "Officer, I'd like you to leave the room so I can talk to my client in private." Granger, ignoring the lawyer, asked Peter if he would like to proceed with a statement or if he would like to be represented.

Peter paused before he commented and then

said, "I better hear what young Nielson has got to say." The officer stood up from the desk and proceeded towards the door, turning to the lawyer, "You've got thirty minutes."

He opened the door, then stopped and walked back to the table and turned the recorder off, pushed the eject button and removed the tape. The lawyer reached forward and placed his hand on top of the officer's. "I'd like a copy of that." The officer grinned at the lawyer, "You heard the senator. He's not said anything."

Granger pulled his hand from under the lawyers, hoping the lawyer would make one more movement that involved contact. This would allow him the opportunity to let the little pup know he'd consider it an assault, and Nielson might be requiring the services of one his partners, or a hospital. The game had been played, and Peter watched grinning as the two vied for control. Granger, hand on the door, turned to the young lawyer. "Thirty minutes." He then shut the door leaving Scott Nielson to earn his government retainer while trying to control the old coot. "Good luck," Granger thought, as he walked to get a much-needed cup of coffee.

No sooner had the door closed than the rumbling voice of Sergeant Madden was audible over the din of the booking hall. He was walking and gesturing with a wad of papers that detective Granger should follow him. "So much for that cup of coffee," he thought. About the same time that Granger caught up with him, the sergeant burst the door open on the shift commander. He walked up to his desk, simultaneously indicating to Granger to shut the door and dropped the paper work in front of the commander. "You're not going to believe this," he said.

The commander looked at the booking form in front of him and then looked up at the sergeant. He had no intentions of reading the document and wanted the sergeant to tell him what the hell all this was about. Looking right into the sergeant's eyes, he indicated he better start talking quick.

"A D.P.S. officer booked that crazy old fuck-of-a-senator Peter Edward Shaw. He witnessed him leaving red handprints on the Governor's Mansion. They caught him red handed, excuse the pun. They brought him in, and he is currently in the booking room with his lawyer. I was filling in the booking docs on the computer and entered the incident of complaint. The words red hands seems to have aroused plenty of interest. They have been looking for someone who has been putting handprints on state and federal monuments from Houston to Dallas, Goliad to San Antonio. In San Antonio, the tagger put red handprints on the door of the Alamo. It was all over the local news about six weeks ago. If it is him that's been doing this, you'd better call in the PR people. The shit will hit the fan. This is no longer a local incident. Some of those monuments are national, not state."

The commander quickly realized the gravity of

the situation and began rubbing his temples with both hands. "Who's his lawyer? One of those state employed boys?" he asked.

"Yes," replied the sergeant. "His name is Scott Nielson from Morgan and Morgan's. He was here within fifteen minutes of me contacting his office that we had a VIP here that needed a mouth piece."

The commander asked him to go over the arrest and how it went down. After listening to the story, he turned to the sergeant. "We need time. He's not a flight risk, so let's just book him for what we caught him doing, process him and get him out of here. If anyone puts the line between the dots, just tell them that we'll look into it. Detective, as soon as you can, proceed with the interview and keep your mouth shut. We need to keep a lid on this until we get a handle on it."

Sergeant Madden wanted to get the old man charged and the papers filed as soon as possible. He started to put pressure on the detective to complete the charge sheets and log all evidence that might be required. Already the word was out, and the local reporters started to arrive, becoming the normal pain-in-the-ass that a good reporter thinks he's got to be. As the first one arrived at the desk and asked for copies of the charge sheets, the sergeant opened the door to the office and shouted, "Which one of you pieces of shit popped the bubble? If I find out who it was, I will fire what's left of your ass after I'm done beating on it."

Back in the interview room, Scott was very aware that control was not an option. The old man's body language clearly showed that he did not care as to what the consequences of his actions might be. Scott thought a good start might be to hear what he had to say in his words.

He wrestled with what the man was telling him and again asked if he had signed any documents or admitted to any of the actions. Peter leaned towards Scott who had seated himself in front of him, far too close for comfort. "I assure you, I've not said or admitted to anything, but I'd like to remind you that the officer walked up on me while I was doing it."

"That's fine," said Scott. "I think they will be charging you with criminal mischief, but I really don't think anything will come of it unless you give them something to go on. If they ask anything, plead the fifth and give us some breathing room. I feel sure the media will be onto this, so I will prepare a statement. Do not say a word to them! Being the state capital, the local media love it when the righteous tumble. Your story fits that bill perfectly, and they will be after you. It would have been better if you were caught making out with some male intern in the public restrooms. As far as unique goes, an ex-republican state representative and congressman caught tagging does qualify for some quality airtime. The democrats are going to love it, and it doesn't matter that you haven't been to the house or on the floor in the last two years. Again, please don't make any comments; let me handle that for you."

Scott relished the thought of defending the senator on local and, potentially, national television. He was already going over how he was going to come off as caring, even concerned, and dwelling heavily on the subject of service Peter had provided for the people, as well as the tragic accident and loss of his wonderful wife. It is all about balance, and Scott felt he had plenty to say that would outweigh what might be considered an irrational act. Of course, he had no idea about the other incidents and just how big this might get.

Detective Granger reentered the interview room, ignoring the lawyer as he replaced the tape back into the recorder and pressed the record button. He again went over Peter's rights and laid out for him that he was being charged with criminal mischief and the possible consequences. It was not a serious charge, but the fact he was a senator gave it some gravity. He looked at Peter and asked him if he clearly understood what he was being charged with. He nodded but remained silent. The detective said, "Sir, I need you to say that you understand what you are being charged with and the potential consequences." Scott intervened, "He understands. Please get on with it."

Peter then said, "I understand." The detective, looking at Peter, slid the charge sheet in front of the lawyer and, without moving his gaze said, "Sign it."

Chapter 2

Alicia Fielder was sitting at her tiny corner desk trying to finish another mundane assignment when the editor of the Austin Statesman suddenly appeared. Her skin crept as the editor stood just a little too close behind her, enjoying that Alicia was feeling uncomfortable. John Kerr, who liked to be known as J.K., was a short, portly, middle-aged man of sixty. He had a mop of white hair and eyebrows that seemed to never end. His verbal language would appear he had no idea that he was standing inside her space, but he had been in the game long enough to read a situation and be very aware of boundaries.

Alicia's extended personal space was due to the fact that she was brought up in Red Rock, Texas, 35 miles southeast of Austin. Country people tend to have a larger personal circle than those from the city, and he knew that. Alicia had received an internship to the Austin Statesman by being on the Dean's List in Journalism at Texas A&M University. Alicia was tall and slender, with long blonde ringlets that accentuated her oval face. Pretty and smart was just the combination the editor despised, and he would use this to keep her in her place as much as possible. Being raised in Red Rock, Alicia was very aware of the farmyard bullying that somehow finds itself into the environment of the workplace, including the Austin Statesman.

Alicia pushed back from the desk, forcing the editor to step back. She apologized, but had in her own small way taken control of the situation. Alicia turned to face him and as she did he said, "I've got a job for you." The stale cigar smell mixed with sweat again reminded her of the farmyard she had left behind.

Since the advent of digital media, the Statesman had lost many of its best reporters and connections. The reduction in staff had been achieved mainly by not replacing personnel when people retired or left due to firing or illness. This allowed the paper to retain a bit of prestige as the inevitable demise applied pressure to its quality and shareholders worth.

John walked back to his desk with Alicia following. He seated himself behind the desk, his protruding belly overlapping the rim. Alicia stood before him, notebook in hand, awaiting instructions. Normally, a senator would demand the attention of a far more seasoned reporter than a twenty-four year old intern, but he had no option. As he started to talk, he halted himself to reflect on the decision to send her. He sighed in resignation and began his orders.

"I want you to go down to the Travis County Jail central booking office at five hundred West and Tenth Street. Get the inside on Senator Peter Edward Shaw who has been arrested. I got a call about ten minutes ago. Shaw is a colorful character. I have followed him for the last thirty years. He's as tough as they come. He was a straight talking southern politician with all its frills. He really could play the game and would hang anyone that got in his way or put him under pressure. He had the dirt, and, if you wanted it and could scratch his back, he would let you have it on anyone. He was one of the first to live by the rule, 'If you want a friend in Washington, get a dog.' All was well until a car accident put him in a coma for six weeks and killed his wife. He's never been the same. Rumor has it that he even pulled strings to get the drunk responsible out of the pen, but the M.A.D.D. group blocked any good intentions he might have had. He experienced a life changing moment all right. It cost him his wife and his job, and he would have hung that kid in the old days. Okay, we don't need much on this but a few lines. Find out what the charge is, and see if he will talk to you. Figure out his plea and what the hell is going on. Don't be long, and keep it short. Keep in touch. Use the cab account to get there and back. I've already made the arrangements." He waved her off not giving her any further chance for questions or uncertainty.

Alicia knew how to report. She had been around it for a long time. Her mother, a single parent, kept her in school and college working as an English teacher at Bastrop Middle School and as a contributing editor for the Smithville Times, a family owned newspaper that exposed Alicia to the workings of reporting. During her school holidays, she would go with her mother to all the council meetings and suitable newsworthy court cases that small towns thrive on. Her mother explained how the detail of the story and research would often lead in a direction you would not expect. Reporting was mainly putting down on paper both sides of an argument or story.

Alicia had experienced how difficult trying to stay independent and avoid bias could be as her mother had fallen on the wrong side of the paper's main advertiser, a local realtor company that was trying to develop an old landfill site. Her mother had found information that the developer was trying to cover up the fact that the site had been used for the illegal dumping of chemicals for years, and he was dodging the necessary cleanup expenses to make the land suitable for development. That's why the developer got the land cheap. Exposing this cost her mother her job with the paper, the paper lost the advertising, and the developer lost the project. The truth can be painful. A good reporter has to know what will sell and when to walk away from a story whose consequences are potentially too time consuming or emotionally too expensive.

At a young age, Alicia was shown the benefit of the coffee shop and small town gossip. Her mother showed her the art of teasing the story out from what, at first, seemed quite mundane. Much of the stuff that fills a local newspaper is not so much a news story, but a little dip into the life of the people who choose to share a zip code. It boils down to them and us, stuff to argue about, drawing a line in the sand, or who to vote for. She was finding out Austin was not that much different.

Alicia gathered her belongings: jacket, iPad, and notebook. Although she was very much computer savvy, she felt the ease-of-use of a notebook still gave her a slight edge. As she arrived downstairs, the cab was waiting outside for her and knew her intended destination.

As she arrived at the station, the cabbie dropped her off and informed her he had been instructed to wait for her. She thanked him and made her way to the station entrance. Two camera crews were hanging around outside as the talking-head reporter was inside getting the low down on the story. As she entered, she made her way through security into the charge area. The sergeant was handing out the legal size sheets of paper to three other reporters who were already in place and shouting questions at the sergeant that he did not appear to want to answer.

"Fuck you; phone the press office if you want any further information. I told you he was gone, now don't piss me off," she heard him saying as she entered the room. The reporter was asking why the senator was being allowed to walk out of the station after being charged with defacing a monument when other taggers were being treated far more harshly. The city of Austin had come down heavy on taggers of late, asking for the top punishment on every case. A fifteen year old had recently been given three years' probation and his parents were forced to pay the $10,000 cleanup costs for tagging a local high school football field.

The sergeant had reached a breaking point where you could clearly see he wanted to become physical. Instead, he leaned forward and shouted, "Fuck you!" He quickly regained his composure and went back behind the booking desk.

The reporter said, "This is bullshit. If you had caught a teen-aged gang tagger, you would have him in the back room and be scaring the shit out of him, not giving him a lift home and letting him out of the side door. This stinks."

"Was he drunk?" another shouted. Before the sergeant could answer, the third one was saying the charge sheet was incomplete. "Who was the arresting officer?" he asked.

Alicia stood back and waited for the mayhem to quell. Slowly they backed off, all three talking into their cell phones as they made their way out the door. The sergeant at first didn't look up, then with a quick shift of his head glanced up and then back down. Continuing to write, he asked her, "How may I help you, young lady?"

"I would like some information on Senator Peter Edward Shaw," she replied.

"Why?" the sergeant responded.

Alicia explained she was working for the Austin Statesman, allowing her strong accent to hopefully sweeten his response. Obviously not impressed, he didn't say a word or ask for any form of identification. He just reached with his right hand to a stack of papers, peeled one off and pushed it in her direction. He walked off before she could ask any of the questions that she had previously worked out during the drive to the station.

Over the desk and at the back of the room she could see the back of an elderly gentleman with no shoes being led out of an interview room and away from the entrance. She realized that it was Peter Shaw. She watched him curiously. He stopped walking, stood for a second, and then looked back over his shoulder directly at her. She felt a flush of warmth run through her as their eyes met. He then turned and continued walking out of sight. "That was weird," she thought. She made her way back outside to the cab. Two of the reporters who had been inside were doing their thing in front of the cameras.

As she sat in the cab, the clock ticking, she knew she had to get this story. This was her chance! She sat back and started to look over the charge sheet given to her by the jail sergeant and decided she had better run a Google search so she had some background. She unzipped her iPad case and waited for it to locate internet service. Within a few moments, she had the Shaw's address and was giving the instructions to the driver. This was beyond what the editor was requesting, but no way was she going back with just the charge sheet.

"Interesting," she thought as she read up on him. "The rise and fall of Senator Peter Edward Shaw," she mouthed and preened, looking at her reflection in the cab window; and now he is being charged with tagging.

As the cab arrived at the address, no other reporters were to be seen. The large iron ornate gates at the entrance to the enormous tree-lined drive were open. She instructed the cabby to proceed through the gates towards the house. She felt a desire to close the gate once they were inside. Her country upbringing and mother had engraved the shut-the-gate rule deep into her psyche. The lawyer's car, which had given Peter a lift home, passed the cab on the extended drive way.

Alicia couldn't help but think the drive was designed so that any visitor would understand the importance and power of the owner. She could see the lawyer slow and stare into the cab as they passed. The fact that no other reporters were to be seen was potentially a good thing, but also it could mean the story might be no more than a byline, and the editor would be pissed over the extra expenses of the cab. "The story has no legs," she imagined him saying and the exclamation "Oh, shit!" expelled itself from her lips as her mind played that scenario out. Not being totally put off by her observation, she alighted from the cab as soon as she could, shouting over her shoulder for the cabby to hang on, as she would not be long.

She stood on the steps that led up to the front door. There were eight steps and four marble pillars that framed the door. Alicia noticed they really could do with a coat of paint. The building was like a mini White House and must have been a wonderful sight in its hay day. Such impractical opulence scraped against her country upbringing. These same people would comment in disgust at the heavy gold chains some of the rappers could be seen wearing. She found the house no different and no more practical. "Bling," she thought as she closed the distance between herself and the front door.

She reached up and grabbed the antique doorknocker, as no doorbell appeared to be in sight. The knocker was rusted and she had to force it open and closed several times before finally managing a small knock at the weathered front door. That was all it took. The handle of the door turned, and the door started to open before she could even let go of the handle. It swung in, and Peter Shaw's head swung out to the side of the door as it still moved inwards. A very basic "hello" was how he greeted her, way friendlier than she had been led to expect.

She felt a strange warmth flood over her once again and quickly pass. "I'm here from the Austin Statesman," she said. "Would you give me some time? I would like to get your side of the story regarding your arrest over the Governor's Mansion tagging incident." She could not help smiling as she said this, and obviously the accusation struck him as humorous as well, as a grin covered his un-kept Santa Claus like face.

"My dear, it would be a pleasure to spend some time with you, and I look forward to that in the future, but unfortunately, tagging and being arrested has taken its toll on this old man. Would you care to come back tomorrow, and we will be able to go over it and see if we can get you a story? Call on my house phone," he said as he passed her his card. "You have a nice day dear." He closed the door, and she turned, clutching the somewhat dated business card that still had Senator Peter Edward Shaw, but the word Senator had been scribbled out with a pen. Gliding down the stairs to the cab, she felt more confident. She had the potential of an exclusive, she thought, and a reason for the extra time and expense.

Chapter 3

Leaning against the door, Peter felt every part his age, his body aching from the tiredness and apparent abuse the last few years had placed on him. He used his weight to snug the door locked. Turning to walk down the long hallway to the kitchen, he inspected the oil painting of himself and the way it followed him as he passed. He then looked at the mirror at the bottom of the hall near the kitchen entrance that showed his reflection. Even with a vivid imagination it was hard to concede that the image in the mirror was the same person as the one in the oil painting from three years earlier. The exterior image was different, but he thought it did not nearly reflect the changes the inner Senator Peter Edward Shaw had endured.

He opened the kitchen door and made his way to the fridge. Opening the door, he noticed it had also transformed compared to what it once had been. It now contained the basics: bread, peanut butter, jam, cheese, tins of sardines and cans of flavored water. Turning on the television, he placed bread, peanut butter and a can of water on the table in front of him. Sitting back, he started to make a sandwich while watching himself on the local news.

The reporter was going over the arrest and the

accusation of criminal mischief. It was not long before his mug shot appeared as the reporter outlined his arrest. "They must be short of stories," he thought. They started to go over Peter's history, talking about the car accident and showing old footage of him on a stretcher being placed into the back of an EMS vehicle. He sat staring at the image, slowly lowering his sandwich back onto the table.

For many months after the accident he could not remember anything, but slowly it all came back. Bit by painful bit, like a four-dimensional jigsaw, he was able to find the place in the time line that the memory fit. The timeline that led to the accident was something that intrigued Peter. How far back did it reach? His ancestors each playing their part, which would bring their sibling to that precise place at that precise point in time. It was this thought that made Peter feel sympathy towards the young lawyer, Henry J. Matthews, that was now forced to spend the rest of his youth behind bars. He was convicted of DWI and involuntary manslaughter. Had he been, in fact, just a pawn in a game? Had the conclusion been decided thousands of years earlier?

The day of the accident, he and his young wife, Serena, were heading into Austin for dinner. Serena was twenty-one years younger and what most people would consider a trophy wife, but Shaw loved her like no other woman in his life. He had finally fallen, but couldn't help but worry that she would tire of him and move on to a younger man.

Serena's phone signaled an incoming text

message. She flicked the screen and it was a reminder and confirmation from their favorite Italian restaurant, DaVinci's. The table would be ready for them and two guests at seven p.m.

The owner and his wife had become close friends, joining him and Serena on an all-expense paid trip to South Africa. This was just one of the several investigations by the ethics committee he had had to endure. At least twice a month, the Shaw's would dine free at DaVinci's, allowing for the reciprocal back scratching to take place. The fact the Shaw's would dine as regulars at the restaurant was a worthy investment, as the clients who needed to be seen with, or in contact with, the Senator were many and wealthy.

Serena told him who the text was from and faced the phone towards Peter so he could see the screen. He turned his head for what was only a second. As he brought his vision back to the road in front of him, the world slowed. Control had been taken from him as the inevitable started to unfold.

Henry J. Matthews could not believe his luck. He was thirty-one years old and he had just won a criminal injury case against one of the largest privately owned elderly care units in South Texas. Golden Years Elderly Homes had been in business for over twenty-five years. The owner, of Indian descent, had worked hard and diligently to build his empire on a strategic business plan and a caring environment for his customers. The monthly outlay for an elderly person wanting twenty-four hour a day monitoring was in excess of thirty-five hundred dollars. He had three homes, currently all filled to capacity, caring for eighty elderly people per unit. It was easy for Henry to work out that Golden Years was a cash cow with plenty of insurance and assets to boot.

Twenty-four months earlier, he had received a call from a middle-aged lady that said she had proof that her elderly father, Ralph Wade, had been abused at the Golden Year's facility in Corpus Christi, Texas. He was an eighty-four year old ex-marine and was suffering from advanced stages of dementia that had left him in an almost vegetable state and completely bed ridden.

It was on a visit with her son Brent, who owned a computer tech company in Austin, when she noticed bruises on her father's chest and back; small round bruises. She was going to have a word with the home management when her son told her not to do anything. He set up a remote-monitoring undercover camera in her father's room that they could monitor from Austin. She had no idea how this would work, but her son assured her that he could link into the home's network and have the monitoring system up and running early the following week. Within two days of the system being set up, the culprit of the bruises was filmed dishing out his version of care. The young male nurse could clearly be seen pinching the old man. You could hear Ralph crying out in pain as the young male nurse inflicted violence upon him. The nurse knew that the old man would not be able to remember or tell anyone what was going on; totally unaware that everything he did was being recorded and watched. Within hours, Brent and his mother were at the home with a Corpus Christi police officer that had seen the digital evidence. They immediately arrested the nurse and the family began the process of suing the nursing home.

The lawyers knew the case would be settled on the courthouse steps, but were surprised by the size of the claim and the greed of young Henry J. Matthews.

Henry had a mortgage, a maxed out credit card and a BMW that was costing him a fortune. He wanted to settle on this golden egg and he was not going to sling his hand until he had squeezed the maximum out of the defendant. Twelve point five million dollars was way over the top, but the good name of the home was an earner. The deal was struck with Henry walking away with just under four million dollars. This would ensure, for the time being, his extravagant life style and allow him to continue with his Henry J. Matthews ad that he had been running for the last twelve months on all the local channels. Not only was the advertising what got him the case, it had also procured him many society invites and dates with the local debutants.

No sooner had the handshake confirming the deal been made, Henry was on the phone calling his buddies and telling them to meet him at Sixth Street. Drinks were on him. The fact it was early afternoon had nothing to do with it; the party was on. As soon as Robert, one of his local lawyer friends, walked in, the Tequila shots were set up and Robert joined Henry in a test of machismo by showing who could slam them the quickest.

Robert was the only one of his three friends that received the call who bothered to attend, most knowing that the on-going bravado and free drinks would last for at least the next couple of weeks. Two hours of Shiner Bock's and Tequila chasers was all Robert could take. He told Henry, "I hate to do this to you, but I have got to get back to work." Henry reluctantly agreed and stood to shake hands with Robert. He showed a slight wobble and his left hand grabbed the bar for support. Robert warned Henry that he should get a lift or a Taxi. Robert only worked around the corner near the state capital and had lost his license a year prior for a DWI himself.

Henry assured him that he would be okay and made his way to where he had left his car, about two blocks away. He thought the walk would do him good and when he got to his BMW he convinced himself that he was now fine. He jumped in the car and did a very good job of getting out of the parking lot without hitting anything. As usual, he convinced himself he might be too drunk to walk but driving, he's okay. He laughed to himself, "I'm not drunk; I'm just full!"

He went out of the lot and down Fourth Street onto Interstate thirty-five. He accelerated up onto the freeway, enjoying the power of the five series BMW kicking him in the back. Shooting past all traffic and weaving his way into the left hand lane, he soon found himself cruising at a steady seventy-eight miles per hour, which in his mind was just slow enough not to attract the attention of any speed cops.

He exited Parmer Lane and turned right. "Just a few more miles and I'll be home sweet home," he thought. He accelerated through the second light, picking up speed quickly. In front of him in the other lane was a pickup truck loaded down with materials they had obviously picked up from Lowe's or Home Depot. Henry reached over for his iPhone when one of the sheets of plywood on the back of the pickup flew up in the air and made its way towards him. The shock made him pull hard on the wheel to the left, avoiding the piece of wood that had come loose. He found himself on the grass median doing seventy-eight miles an hour with the cruise control on. As soon as the tires lost traction against the grass surface, the computer sent the message for the five-liter engine to increase the gas going through the fuel injectors. The speed did not increase but the engine revolutions did. At this point, Henry realized what was going on and that he could not do anything about it. His hands were placed at eleven and two and he was gripping the wheel harder every second as the accident unfolded.

The BMW sprinted across the grass median, the tires spinning frantically, trying to find some grip. As soon as the tires hit the black top on the wrong side of the highway, the vehicle shot forward. Henry had no idea what was unfolding, but the slow dance that Peter Shaw and his young wife, Serena, were about to join him in would change his life forever.

Henry tried to avoid the accident but the best he could do was to try to veer left in the ever-decreasing distance between the two vehicles. As the right hand side of Henry's five series BMW hit the Shaw's Mercedes, the BMW air bags inflated. The initial inflation of the bags was an explosive shock that slapped Henry and removed all the wind from his chest. The impact speed of both vehicles was in excess of one hundred forty miles per hour. At the first second of impact, the Mercedes's air bags inflated also, pinning Peter and Serena firmly in their seat.

They were all now just along for the ride. The BMW rode up onto the hood of the Mercedes, and went through the windshield, avoiding Peter, but violently removing Serena's head from her pinned body. Both vehicles were locked in a deadly embrace, spinning across the highway to the safety rail. No other vehicles were involved.

Henry was totally unconscious and Serena was in the death throws of her headless body. Peter lay trapped, paralyzed and was suffering severe shock due to the bleeding and the fact that two vertebra in his lower back were smashed. The fire service worked frantically to free Peter. The inflated air bags had protected his upper chest region, but from his lower torso to his feet he was in a bad way. Finally, they managed to free Peter and have him helo-flighted to St. David's hospital. In the next two hours, Peter would be in and out of a morphine-induced consciousness, reliving the last few seconds with his wife, Serena.

Peter was lying on the stretcher waiting to be placed in the chopper. He looked up and noticed a hawk hovering above him, looking down at him. The beauty of the hawk carved itself into his mind. The pain was easing and the darkness growing. "Is this it?'" he thought. "Am I dying?" The hawk seemed to take over his mind as he slipped away into drug-induced unconsciousness. This was the last memory that he would have as Senator Peter Edward Shaw.

Henry had to be removed from the wreckage using the Jaws of Life, adding more misery to his devastated ego. He loved his BMW, which, prior to the Wade settlement, stretched his monthly budget to the limit. It was part of his young has-got-it-all persona he felt was vital to his position. He realized the seriousness of the accident and the potential consequences. If he could, he would have got up and walked away, but he lay there trapped by his injuries. The injuries he sustained in the accident were minor considering the damage he had inflicted on the Shaw's vehicle, but it was enough that the paramedics had him pinned to a stretcher, and the inevitable blood sample would be taken that would convict him of manslaughter. He mentally was kissing his windfall goodbye, knowing that every hotshot ambulance-chasing lawyer would be trying to prosecute him on behalf of the Shaw's. Jail and broke was the only outcome he concluded as he closed his eyes, retreating to his inner space and trying to forget.

Chapter 4

Hawk sat quietly on the floor of the cave, his legs crossed and his hands upturned resting on his knees, his head stretched backwards as if looking up, but his eyes were closed. He was deep in the cave away from the fire and the distractions of the group. The cold and the damp in the deepness of the cave did not seem to bother him. In his old age, Hawk spent many hours and sometimes days in the darkness in deep meditation. The children would sneak up on him to make sure he was still alive and breathing, his breathing barely audible, slow and deep. They would see if they could hold their breath as long as it took Hawk to breathe. One little girl, Water, would place her back against Hawk's, quietly sitting behind him. She did this just as Hawk had taught her how to feel the spirit of the Tree People. He would sit with his back to the tree and share the spirit of the tree. The young girl would feel the spirit and power of Hawk, which would comfort her.

Hawk was a powerful tenth-generation Shaman, a gift that was in his family bloodline. He was the second son, but the group recognized his superior powers over the first-born and it was he that became the tribe's Shaman at the passing of his father. The elder brother Cloud realized the superior powers of young Hawk, but he did not hold anything but love for him. The Seers did not have egos. The family members worked for the betterment of the group. They were all connected and acted as one.

Before the breakup of the tribe, only Hawk's immediate family knew the cave; its location being passed down and shown reverently by the elders as the chosen Shaman became of age. This secrecy was not to keep the cave from others, but to provide the stillness needed to be one with everything. The elders spoke of great ancestors who had used the cave to transcend presence and to share knowledge. Handprints of his ancestors could be seen on the cave wall and gave comfort to Hawk; when he was at the cave he was not alone. He had the strength and the combined knowledge of his ancestors with him. Hawk would love the seclusion and would meditate for many hours. He had earned his name for his ability to look down and pinpoint game, water and war parties that were in the tribal lands by becoming the spirit of a hawk. He would then transmit these visions to the other Seers, ensuring food and protection for all.

The three local tribes who shared this fertile land would fight as a group to defend their land from marauding war parties from the outside, but would go through display attacks where they would kidnap the tribe's young girls. The plundering and capture of the young maidens in the spring had become so normal the young girls would paint themselves and dress for the occasion. The attacks were more a show of aggression than an actual attack using weapons. They would sneak up to the villages under cover of darkness and when everyone had settled down they would feign the attack, running into the huts of the parents and pulling the young girls away screaming. This would be when the Seers were most verbal with screeches and body actions, simulating the stabbing actions with a spear to back the defender off. This method of outbreeding had kept the bloodlines pure, untainted by inbreeding.

The outbreeding had worked for many generations, but now the breeding base had become tainted and too small. Mutations were becoming more common. Thirty years prior, a hairless child was born to Cloud, the elder brother of Hawk. Hawk named the child Death Dog after a vision he had as the child was being born. The Shaman naming the children was the norm and his parents accepted it without question. This was not the first hairless child the tribe had seen, but this child was different. This child did not develop the ability to become a Seer, but did have advanced speech skills. His mimicry was amazing. Even as a young child he could mimic most of the animals they would come in contact with, on occasion fooling some of the hunters. He would hide, watching the hunters run past him in pursuit of game that did not exist, but could clearly be heard.

He was not a likable child. As well as his advanced speech skills, the child had an ego. He would act solely for himself and could be found hoarding weapons and food. At a young age, he would bully the younger ones, dangerously slinging stones at them or cutting them with skinning knives. At fifteen summers, he killed his younger brother in a rage of temper, jealous over a knife one of the elders had given the younger child. The younger child refused to give him the knife. Death Dog decided to take it from him, killing him in the process. He hid the body, but was caught with the knife he had taken. He admitted he had killed his brother and placed him in the river to be washed away. Hawk told Cloud that he needed to kill Death Dog or the tribe would regret it. Cloud could not bring himself to kill his only remaining son, so Hawk demanded Death Dog be expelled from the tribe, the hunters chasing him out and forcing him to leave the tribe's lands. It was a few years later that the other two local tribes had experienced the birth of more hairless ones, all very aggressive and ego-based individuals.

As the children developed, the tribes would ban them and it was not long before the Hairless Ones formed a tribe of their own. These hairless people were to be known as Non-seers and were now the biggest threat to the Seers. It was this threat that forced Hawk, and what remained of his tribe, to the cave. Hawk was aware of the eventual outcome and the inevitable demise of his people, but he wanted it on his terms. It was with all his power that he was now reaching forward. He needed to record his people in history. The Seers had existed.

Chapter 5

Alicia arrived back at the American Statesman and found the rest of the staff had already left for the day. Only the security guard remained. He let her in once she had shown her ID. "Quite impressive," she thought as the door to the elevator closed behind her. She pressed the button to the third floor and felt the jolt of the elevator motor as it engaged. She was still looking at herself in the mirror on the elevator wall as she arrived at her destination.

She walked from the elevator, past all of the cubicles and offices, to her desk, which was next to the copy machine, as far as you could possibly get from the elevator. It was not much, but it was her desk and in the quiet of the empty office she felt powerful to have her little place in what she felt was still a very powerful media outlet. She was meticulous and was immediately aware that someone had been going through her desk, just casually by the look of it as only the papers had been moved more fan like than when she had left them. "No problem," she thought, as she had nothing to hide.

She opened her laptop and started to report the details of Peter Shaw's arrest. She quickly scanned the charge sheet she had been given at the jail and double-checked what she had to report. In italic text and double-spaced, she noted that she had an appointment with the senator the next day. She emailed it to the head editor and the night editor who was on the next floor up and again tidied her desk, making the decision not to leave her laptop at the office like she had been doing.

She returned to the elevator and then to the ground floor, wishing the security guard good night as she vacated the building and made her way to the company parking lot. Her little Toyota Yaris made its way through Austin's downtown area where no matter what time of day you picked, it always seemed to be busy. Working her way south on Interstate Highway 35, she exited left onto Riverside Drive to Ben White Boulevard, and then proceeded southeast on Highway 71, also known as Bastrop Highway. Thirty minutes and she would be home and able to share her day with her mother. It was going to be fun to tell her that she had been on her first solo assignment.

As she unlocked the front door and walked in she could see her mother, Brenda, was in the TV room watching the local news and eating her dinner from a tray. As soon as she heard the key in the door, she put the food down and went to see Alicia. "Are you okay?" she asked. "I was starting to get worried."

"I'm fine Mom. I just got my first real assignment."

Before her mother could say anything else, Alicia could see her assignment being reported on the television behind her mother. "That's it!" she blurted, putting her things down and pushing her mother back into the TV room. Brenda automatically returned to her seat and started to sit while at the same time not taking her eyes off the TV screen. A mug shot picture of Sir Peter Edward Shaw was being shown in high definition before her eyes. It was a short teaser, saying the local bad-boy senator had again been arrested, and you would never guess for what, full story just after the break. As she watched, she was telling her mother that she was covering the story for the Austin Statesman. As soon as the advertisements came on, Brenda started to question Alicia about her day. Alicia briefly went over the outline of her day and said how she had been invited back tomorrow for an interview with Peter Shaw.

The news came back on and both waited patiently for the story. Of course, the anchor proceeded through what seemed like everything else before he got to the story. He briefly outlined what Shaw was being accused of and then went over his fall from grace since the accident. What made Alicia sit up and really take notice was the fact that they were trying to link Peter Shaw to other crimes around the state where someone had been putting painted red handprints on state and federal buildings and monuments. The link had been made and she was more than upset that she had not run a Google search on tagging, handprints, Texas, federal, and state. She realized she still had a lot to learn.

She was opening her laptop and was pressing

the on button as her cell phone rang. Putting the computer down, she raced to where she had put the phone as she came in. On the third ring she picked it up, looking at the screen before she pushed the answer button. It was her editor. He first asked how she was, and then quickly started to ask her about what had happened with the senator.

"Did you receive the email I sent from the office?" she asked. He confirmed the receipt of the email then proceeded to tell her that he had forwarded it to Jock Wentworth, the political editor for the paper. "I want him to appoint a more senior reporter as this story has got legs!" he explained.

'He loves that saying,' she thought. Alicia was deflated and expressed that Shaw had given her the appointment and she was planning on calling him in the morning.

"Have you got his telephone number?" asked the editor.

"He gave me his card, but I don't really feel that I should hand the number out. Besides, I left it at the office," she replied. This was not true, but she thought it would give her time to figure out what she was going to do. This was her story and she did not what to let it go.

"Fine then," he replied. "Be at the office by 8:00 a.m. so you can brief the reporter and give him the telephone number of the senator." He then added, "And don't be late!" as he put the phone down.

Brenda called her from the TV room telling her to sit down and eat her supper. As Alicia played with her food, Brenda asked about the story. Alicia laid out the events in more detail ending with the recent phone call from the editor. Her mother agreed that the telephone numbers and card were given to her and not to the newspaper.

"You really should not give up the card information. A reporter has a loyalty to their contacts and your editor will understand that." Alicia had not been in the game long, but she knew better than to think the editor would have any understanding about her wanting to keep her contact information private.

After a restless night, Alicia awoke early and headed for a hot shower, the day's possible events still playing over and over in her mind. She realized that it was not going to be good. Her mother's reassuring words over breakfast were not stopping the recurring image of a very negative outcome.

Two hours soon passed, the elevator doors opened and she stepped out feeling like a condemned criminal. No one seemed to pay her any attention as she proceeded towards her desk, but she felt the attention of the editor. He rose from his desk and paced himself so he would arrive at her desk at the same time she did, a speed-over-time calculation that Alicia pondered and considered playing with as the distance to arrival shortened.

"Morning Alicia," he said as they both arrived at her desk. "I will call Jock and we can have a meeting in my office to go over the senator's story." She noticed that her desk had been gone through and again her papers had been disturbed.

She squeezed between him and her desk, pulling the chair out and taking her place behind the desk. She opened the top left hand draw and pretended to look for the card. She then returned her gaze to the editor and said, "Someone has been through my desk and I think they must have taken the card." She feigned a pissed-off look and then said that the card had Shaw's personal number on it. The editor knew this was a ruse. He had been through her desk and he knew she was aware of that, so he had to play along with it.

"Are you sure Alicia? Why would someone go through your desk?" he asked, countering the bluff. "Did you not write down the details of the card?" Alicia was not good at lying and with the perceived pressure of the situation her face started to redden.

"I'm pretty sure I left it in this drawer. I could check my car, and I guess it could be at home." The editor immediately spotted her weakness.

"Alicia, why don't you go and check on that," he said. "We need that contact information. When you get back, come to my office and we will have a conference with Jock and his reporter."

She went back to the elevator and returned to her car. The pressure of the situation was building and she had to face up to it. She pretended to search the car in case she was being watched. "Time to let Mr. Editor know that the card is mine," she thought. "If I am not doing the story, I am not going to reveal the information that was given to me in confidence, Peter Shaw's personal home phone number."

The head editor, J.K., was nicely seated behind his desk with Jock, the political editor, and his seasoned political reporter, Tim Green, seated evenly around the walls of the office. She felt very exposed as she closed the door behind her. She turned, recognized the vacant chair and proceeded to sit down before being given any instructions from J.K..

He opened the meeting, not bothering with any introductions, by asking the reporter, Tim Green, "Okay, what we got?"

Tim Green was a tall, lanky man in his early thirties. Alicia had seen him around the office and often wondered how he had gotten to be one of their top reporters, as he seemed disheveled and awkward. She had heard others refer to him as nerdy and she could see how he fit the bill. To her surprise, he was able to lay out in far more detail the background of the story than she had been aware of from her quick research. She quickly recognized how good Tim was at his job. He had even interviewed the owner of Da Vinci's restaurant; an ex-friend of Peter Shaw's who had been mentioned in a senate enquiry over abuse of funds. Apparently the senator had taken the owner and his wife on a free holiday to South Africa, compliments of the taxpayers of Texas. The owner of the restaurant explained that since the accident Peter was not the same as he was before and that he had not been back to the restaurant since. He went on to explain that from what he had heard Peter had lost it and was apparently mentally unstable, at best. Then Tim went on to explain how the story was developing because the handprints Shaw had been caught putting on the Governor's Mansion had been appearing on several of the state and national monuments throughout Texas.

"My phone has been ringing off the wall with people wanting this story," J.K. interrupted. "The word is out and we need to get in front of the pack." Turning to Alicia, he asked her to go over what she had. Alicia felt intimidated at this point and could feel her face getting red once more.

"I picked up the arrest sheet from the police station and saw the senator briefly as he was escorted out the back. I decided to see if I could get an interview and drove out to his mansion on the outskirts of town. He let me in, said he would give me an interview, but that he was very tired. He gave me his card and said to call him today."

J.K. immediately butted in. "Did you find the missing card, Alicia?" he asked. Alicia, feeling outgunned and realizing how good Tim was, gave the card to J.K. against what her original intentions had been. As she handed the card to him, she began her plea to stay in the process.

"Shaw gave this card to me," she said. "I should be the one to make the call for the appointment."

Before J.K. could object, Tim said, "That's right. You make the call and make sure we get this interview."

J.K. stared at him for a moment then turned to

Alicia and said, "Get the interview as soon as possible. If it can get done this morning, we will then be the first to network the story. Jock, who had been quiet up to this point, agreed and said he would make some calls for some background. "Let's all get back together before lunch," he finished. Alicia was intrigued how this was all playing out, but realized the benefit of working a story with a group. She even started to appreciate how J.K. was conducting the process.

She had been at her desk only a few moments when Tim was standing across from her asking her to call Peter Shaw. She looked at her watch. It was 9:04 a.m. She opened her diary and called the number off the card. The phone rang several times before he answered. "Good morning, Sir. This is Alicia Fielder with the Austin Statesman. We spoke yesterday."

He answered, "I know who it is. How are you this morning?"

"I'm fine, Sir. Would it be okay to come and see you today?" she replied.

"That will be fine," he responded. "Give me an hour to freshen up. I'll expect you around 10:00."

"That's perfect, thank you!" she said. She did not mention the fact that Tim was coming with her. She thought it was best left for Tim to explain when they got there.

Before long, they were on their way over to Peter's mansion in Tim's Nissan Pathfinder. Alicia was pleasantly surprised at his choice of vehicles, as she had expected something more on the lines of a Volvo, or a mini-van. Tim explained that he had interviewed Peter Shaw before and that in the old days he could be a real prick. "I'm really not looking forward to this," he said. Alicia was searching the Internet on her phone for any other updates on the case, making it very apparent to Tim that she was trying to concentrate. This allowed her the privilege of not needing to talk, as she felt intimidated by him.

As they arrived at the open gate they could see they were not the first reporters to arrive. One of the local TV stations was in place and taping a report. As they drove past and onto the auspicious driveway, Tim commented, "This is way over the top. No wonder you called it a mansion. He must be frigging loaded." Alicia just stared out the window, taking in the scene for the second time.

As they arrived at the house, Tim again asked, "Are you sure we have an appointment?" Alicia grinned, stepped out and made her way to the door. She waited by the door for Tim to catch up before she again fought the old rusty knocker. They both stood staring at the door, waiting for it to open. Finally, it slowly opened and Peter popped his head around the wedge of the door.

"Ahh, Alicia, I see you have someone with you," he said without opening the door any further. Alicia quickly turned her head to Tim and introduced him. There was a silence as if Peter was thinking about his next move. Then his head popped back behind the door and the couple waited in silence. Finally, the door started to open, Peter remaining behind the swinging door. It halted, and still out of view, Peter told them to come in.

Tim started to go first, but then his upbringing got the better of him and he stepped backwards to let Alicia take the lead. They found themselves behind Peter walking down the entrance hall. Peter told them to shut the door behind them and indicated, without turning his head, for them to follow. It was then that Alicia realized how damaged Peter was. She was looking at his portrait hanging on the wall at the end of the hallway and comparing it to what she was following now. Peter was shoeless, longhaired and unshaven, jeans and a sweater being his choice of clothes instead of a three-piece suit and tie. He had a sliding gate, his feet not leaving the ground. His hips were pushed forward; obvious was the pain that Peter was suffering with every step he took.

He led them to a small reception room off the left of the entrance hall. They walked in behind Peter and he took his place behind a nice Georgian desk. Slowly and carefully, he lowered himself into the chair behind the desk and then slid it forward. He indicated for Tim and Alicia to take a seat, which they did. As they started to sit, Alicia opened her iPad and Tim flipped open his note pad, making clear that anything that Peter said would be on the record. Peter started the conversation saying, "How can I help you?"

Alicia introduced Tim and explained that he was

a senior reporter from the Austin Statesman. Peter said he knew Tim and remembered talking to him before. Tim realized this was his opening and proceeded to take control of the interview with some questions directed at Peter about the arrest and charges he was facing. It was clear that Peter was not too concerned about the apparent charges he faced and proceeded to take the line he had been given by the appointed lawyer, Scott Neilson. "The truth is," said Peter, "At this moment I am not at liberty to discuss the details of my arrest or what led up to it."

Tim responded, "Can you comment about the apparent link between the painted hand that you were caught putting on the Governor's Mansion and the apparent identical painted handprints that have shown up on other state and national monuments, for example the red handprints on the doors of the Alamo?"

"Tim, I did see that it was something the local police were looking into. I, again, am not in a position to comment."

As if on cue, the outdated phone to the left of the desk burst into life with a ring tone that matched its appearance. Peter looked at the phone, which was now on its third ring, apologized and answered. It was Scott Neilson, who quickly asked, "Good morning Sir. How are you today?" Peter then explained that he was giving an interview to two young reporters from the Austin Statesman. Shaw could clearly hear Neilson's gasp prior to him saying, "Sir, do not say another word. The situation is getting worse and the police want you back at the station. If you value your freedom at all, please ask them to leave."

Peter put the phone down and re-centered himself with Alicia and Tim. "I'm sorry to have wasted your time, but I have been advised not to talk to you further at this moment. I will have to bring this meeting to an end," he said. He pushed his chair back from the desk and using the desk and one arm of the chair he slowly and painfully stood. Tim and Alicia, without being instructed and in unison, stood up. Ahead of Peter, they made their way to the exit. They stood by the door, waiting for Peter to arrive and open the door before they excited. Peter again apologized and Tim again quickly asked, "Have you any comments about the linking between the other handprints that are very similar to what you are being charged with?"

Peter smiled, chose to ignore the request, remained silent and opened the door for them to leave. They squeezed past Peter thanking him as they made their way to Tim's car.

Tim started to open the door to his side when Peter called out to Alicia and he indicated he wanted her to come to him. She went back up the stairs and said, "Yes, Sir." He leaned forward and said, "Alicia, I would like to have another meeting with you, off the record, just you. When you get a chance, call me and let's set up a meeting."

Alicia was surprised and flushed. She said, "Okay, I will. Goodbye." She returned to the car where

Tim was buckled up, engine running and waiting for her. "What did he want?"

Alicia knew there was no point in trying to lie. "He wants a meeting with me, off the record."

Tim thought about it for a moment in silence and then said, "Alicia, you keep that to yourself. I did not hear it, and no one at the paper needs to know. I am intrigued why he wants to talk to you. Will you tell me if you need any help or advice? Just let me know and I will do what I can."

"Thanks Tim," she said, with a lot more respect for him than she had going into the meeting that morning.

Chapter 6

Detective Granger was lying back on the rear two legs of his chair, his feet up on the desk and holding a plastic cup lined with a paper towel, spitting tobacco juice into the cup and staring at the computer screen. He had samples of the handprints analyzed and it had been determined that the paint had been made from Red Ochre in all instances. The paint on Peter's hands when he was arrested by DPS officer, Juan Espinoza, appeared to be of the same consistency. However, no one at the time had the presence of mind to take samples. The slam-dunk was still in play, however, as the handprints of the right hand clearly showed a damaged ring finger, with the top third missing in all prints. This was an injury that could not be denied, and Shaw just happened to have lost the top third of the same finger in a car crash three years ago.

Kicking back from the desk, the chair rocked forward. Granger stood up and pressed the print key at the same time. Taking one last spit into the cup, he placed it next to the keyboard and made his way towards the communal printer and then to the chief's office. The chief was on the phone as Jeffrey arrived and he soon established it was the governor on the other end. The chief assured him that he would be kept in the loop and updated. The governor owed Peter, as it was Peter who had been the king maker that had actually got him the opportunity to run for governor. Three years prior, Peter's blessing was all that was needed to unlock the political clout of the Texas Republican Party. It had not been cheap, but it was effective. Even though the consensus was that Peter was no longer competent, the governor could not afford to have Peter as an enemy. The governor was advising the chief not to be heavy handed with Peter as he had done so much for the state of Texas. The chief explained that he had to be seen as being fair and was not in a position to just drop it.

Putting the phone down and mumbling, "Politics," he turned to Jeffrey. He asked, "What we got?" Jeffrey laid out the case against the senator. After a very brief review, the chief pushed back from the desk and explained the politics and the lack of value in the case for dollar spent, and at the same time said, "We must be seen to be pursuing this or we will get the sort of heat we don't want."

Jeffrey had been around long enough to know the signs that this case was going nowhere. The chief told Jeffrey to make a call to Peter's lawyer. "Let's have them in and go over what we have with them. Make them feel uncomfortable, Jeffrey. All this case needs is time. The media will forget all about Sir Peter as soon as something new comes along. Keep the PR boys up to speed. I will have a word with them myself."

As Alicia and Tim were driving off, Peter closed the door. As he did, the phone started ringing. It would not hurry him as he proceeded the painful walk down the hall towards the kitchen. After the sixth or seventh ring the phone stopped. "No problem," Peter thought, and felt confident that whoever it was would call back. He had only just got inside the door of the kitchen when his prediction was fulfilled. That loud, dated ring designed to get attention and aggravate was on its third intention when Peter removed it from its wall mount and greeted the caller with a very low-key and tired sounding, "Hello."

"Peter, this is Scott again. How are you feeling?" Scott said.

"Okay," Peter responded.

Scott, not holding back, proceeded to outline the fact that the police had been on to him and wanted Peter to come down to the station so that they could go over the other handprints that had been placed illegally on monuments throughout the state and appeared to have a very similar M.O., or Modus Operandi. Scott then said, "We need to get to the station as soon as we can, but we need about thirty minutes together before we go in. The media are also on to this and have managed to link the tagging's. If you could get yourself ready I will pick you up and we can go over everything and then go to the station." Peter agreed, and before Scott finished the call he made Peter promise not to talk to anyone until they had time to talk.

Peter looked down at his bare feet. "Not too

pretty," he thought as he wiggled his toes. Then he said out loud, "But that's about as ready as they will get."

Since Peter had been released from the hospital he refused to wear shoes. The contact with the earth was very important to him, giving him a feeling of belonging and connection. Scott was soon tapping on the door, fighting the resistance of the old rusty knocker as Peter started to open the door. Scott was disappointed that Peter had not readied himself any more than when he had last seen him sixteen hours ago. Same old jeans, what appeared to be a cleaner t-shirt, and still no fucking shoes!

"Don't you think we should cover those feet of yours," said Scott as he followed Peter to the small office. Peter did not comment, preferring to let Scott just hang. Lowering himself into the chair behind the desk, he signaled with a wave of his hand for Scott to take a seat.

Peter opened the meeting. "Well, what do we have?"

Scott put his brief case on the floor and proceeded to tell Peter that detective Granger had called him and wanted them to go downtown to the station. "He would like to go over the charge and also ask some questions about other painted handprints that have been placed onto other state and national monuments. You have obviously seen the reports turning up on the local news and we need to be coming up with some answers."

Scott continued with his summing up of the

situation, trying desperately to ensue upon Peter the seriousness of the charges and the consequences that could put Peter behind bars. Peter did not seem at all disturbed by the apparent threat of having his liberty removed. Scott did not know if this was because it was not Peter's first rodeo as far as being accused of something that potentially could remove his freedom, or that he genuinely did not care. Scott then went on to describe how he had looked into the possibilities of them linking the crimes. "It does seem quite possible, even with the limited information I have been able to get off the Internet about the hand prints. They do, in fact, seem very similar in application and it might lead one to assume that they were done by the same person."

Peter just sat looking at Scott, not saying a word. An extended uneasy silence hung in the air as Scott waited for Peter to start talking. It did not happen, and Scott proceeded to explain how the detective had contacted him and the fact that they had not arrested Peter was a good sign. "But let me assure you, Peter, they could lock you up for this. Austin has had a lot of problems with taggers and you cannot expect any sympathy from the public or law enforcement." Scott then turned to Peter and asked him directly, "Was it you? Did you put those handprints on those monuments?"

Peter, without any explanation or defense, answered his question, "Yes."

Scott responded, equally short. "Why?"

Peter, with a slight grin on his face, responded, "I felt the need to."

Scott placed his elbows on the table, his hands in front of his mouth, palms tight together, staring above Peter's head as if praying for an answer. He did not talk or move for a good thirty seconds and then said, "If you value your freedom at all, you must let me handle this. Do not admit what you just said and if asked, plead the fifth. To the media, tell them you are not at liberty to discuss the accusations and they need to speak to me, Scott Neilson of Morgan and Morgan's, as we are handling the case for you."

It was early afternoon when they arrived at the station, pulling around the back of the station as instructed by the detective. Scott identified himself and was let into the car park area and shown where to park his car by an elderly gentleman wearing a well-worn police-style uniform, even a badge. He was obviously a retired cop or a cop's relative. Scott pulled his car neatly into the parking spot making sure to leave plenty of room on Peter's side, as getting out of the company Nissan Maxima was not going to be easy for Peter.

At least Scott had managed to get Peter to put a pair of flip-flops on his feet, but that was as far as getting dressed for the occasion Peter had gone: same jeans and same t-shirt. "What the fuck?" Scott thought, offering support to Peter as he first slowly lifted his legs out of the car, then grabbed the door and Scott's arm for support.

The slow cadence of Peter did draw attention with one of the local officers who asked if Peter needed a hand or a chair. As they walked up the ramp towards the large iron door it electrically unlocked and then opened. Desk Sergeant Steve Madden was waiting for them and beckoned them both in. He then led them to a vacant interview room. He walked in and held the door open as Peter was still having problems trying to keep up. The sergeant told them to take a seat and the detective would be with them shortly, as he himself left the room. Both sat quietly waiting, Scott indicating with a raised index finger to his lips not to say anything.

Sargent Madden went to Granger and told him they were in interview room two. Granger thought he would let them stew for a while. He remained checking emails, chewing and spitting. "I need some time for them to feel the gravity of the situation," he thought.

Scott asked Peter, "You okay?"

Peter assured him he was fine. Scott reached to the clip on his belt that was holding his iPhone. He checked and noticed he had service. 'Great,' he thought. Both hands holding the phone, he started checking emails and texting. Peter made himself as comfortable as he could, straightening his back and removing his flip-flops; his bare feet now on the floor in front of him. He then placed his hands on his lap, palms upturned, rolling his head back as if looking up. He closed his eyes and started a slow rhythmic breathing.

Scott looked at him, concerned at first and then thought again, 'What the fuck?' He proceeded with a descriptive text to his girlfriend about the situation and the fact that Peter now appeared to be in a trance, ending it with LOL.

Forty-five minutes passed before Granger graced Peter and Scott with his presence. As he walked in Scott stood, putting his phone down on the table and expecting Peter to show some signs of awareness. Peter's head was still back as if looking at the ceiling, eyes closed, breathing slow.

Granger went for a vacant chair, and then he turned to Scott asking, "Is he okay?"

Scott reached forward and shook Peter's knee. Peter's body started as his spirit climbed back in. Bringing his head down, it was as if he was awakening from a sleep.

Detective Granger welcomed the senator and thanked him for coming in, almost ignoring Scott and certainly not making him feel welcome or wanted. Placing a brown folder on the table he removed a stack of about thirty papers. Most of them appeared to be pictures of painted handprints and text. Not saying a word, he laid them neatly in order making sure that each picture had the relevant text next to it so it was easily visible to Scott and Peter. He then removed a tape from his pocket, reached for the recorder that was on the table and placed the tape in it and pressed the record button.

Neither Scott nor Peter said a word. Scott was aware of the protocol and Peter was very much aware of the old adage, 'He who talks first is the weakest.'

Detective Granger grabbed a chair that had been against the wall and dragged it towards the table, turning it at the same time so the back of the chair was facing Peter. He cocked his leg over the seat and sat with his arms resting on the back of the chair. "Okay," he said. "Let me first explain to you your rights one more time." Jeffrey then again went over the rights of the arrested and asked Peter to clearly state that he understood that this conversation was being taped and would be used against him. He then appeared to relax, asking Peter if all was well. He then said, "I see you have made the local news. What do you think?"

Peter replied, "Must be looking for a story."

"It seems like you have been linked to the other handprints that have appeared on monuments throughout the state," said Granger.

Scott leaned forward, told Peter not to answer, and then turned to the detective saying, "That comment is nothing but hearsay and assumption."

Granger stood, grabbed the chair by the back, spun it around, sat down and shuffled to the table. Relishing this moment, his hands reached onto the table and squared the papers, looking into Peter's eyes for any sign. Peter returned the stare, giving no signs of emotion, very much aware of the papers being organized by Granger in his peripheral vision.

Expecting Granger to start going into the detail

of each pile, Peter was surprised when Granger played a move to hopefully get Peter to open up and hang himself. He ignored the documents and asked Peter directly to admit putting the handprints on the Governor's Mansion. "Peter, I am not going to charge you with these other instances at this moment, but instead of wasting time I would like you to explain in your own words why you left Red Ochre handprints all over the Governor's Mansion."

Peter waited before answering. "I would prefer not to answer that question as it might be used against me."

Granger shuffled in his seat, nudging even closer to Peter and the table. "You do realize with the evidence we have against you, and the fact that DPS officer Juan Espinoza caught you in the act, make it pretty easy for us. I am just trying to save time. Also, the court will look upon your circumstances more favorably if you come clean and show some kind of remorse."

Peter sat stone-faced, letting detective Granger build what was becoming pretty obvious, overwhelming evidence. Remembering Scott's directions, he was not going to say a word. Scott rebuffed the accusation. "The fact is Sir; your officer caught my client with his hands, actually his right hand, with red paint on it. On the side of the Governor's Mansion were two handprints. Apparently, the officer then assumed it was Peter who was responsible; nothing but assumption."

"Look Neilson, I said I was not going to charge

Peter yet with the other hand prints, but if you keep being a prick about this, I will. You will love the other assumptions I have linking Peter that could change this from a minor misdemeanor into something with a heavier consequence," said Granger. Peter looked at Scott. Scott's head dropped, signaling that he needed a few seconds to regroup. Granger rested back in his chair. 'Check,' he thought.

Sargent Madden was at the front desk when Tim Green walked in, having been tipped off by his insider. Madden raised his head from the desk and realized who it was instantly. Without saying a word, he turned his back on Tim leaving him unattended and walked into the main office; closing the door behind him, blocking Tim's view but not his hearing. Madden began coming unglued because, again, the press had been alerted. Madden knew someone had called in the fact that Peter Scott was in the building. "Who the fuck called the Statesman? I will find out who it is and I promise you I will personally kick your fucking ass," he shouted, as he walked between the detective's desks towards the chief's office.

The chief was sitting behind his desk shuffling papers. No one else was in his office and Madden walked straight in. Without asking to talk, he blurted out, "Some fucker has told the press we have Shaw back there."

The chief replied, "Okay, I will call the PR group

and see how they think we should play this." He was on the phone for only a few seconds outlining what was going down. Putting the phone down, he turned to Madden and explained they were coming down. "Time to get the PR boys to earn their money and get these press jerks of my back," said Madden.

As it was, the PR boy was actually an attractive young woman named Marie Davis. She was a four year veteran Police PR officer and was well used to handling far worse scenarios than a bit of paint on the Governor's Mansion. She was well aware of the situation and the requested kid gloves she had been asked to wear when dealing with Sir Peter Edward Shaw.

Marie listened to the chief and asked for twenty minutes. She would then have something to work with. As she was about to leave, Madden asked if she could do a favor for him. "Yea sure, what do you want?" she replied.

Madden responded, "Someone, or should I say some shit, keeps contacting the press every time anything goes down. It's one of the detectives, but I am not sure which one."

"Do you think they are doing it for money or what?" she replied.

"If I was to take a guess," said Madden, "Knowing how those egotistical self-promoting turds think, it's so that they can make sure anything written about them is favorable."

"Okay, let's see if we can use it to our

advantage," said Marie. "Let's see if I can come up with some misinformation. It won't take long for that well to dry up and in the meantime we get to play. Give me those twenty minutes."

Back in the interview room Scott turned to Granger, "Let's see what you think you have." Scott felt sure this was just bravado on Granger's behalf and it would be handy to see what hand Granger was holding. Scott had a meeting with his senior partners prior and all agreed this case was going nowhere. Peter had been a very powerful political figure and no one with ambition would risk the exposure over such trivial charges. Although considered nuts, you never knew what strings Peter was still capable of pulling.

Granger repositioned himself at the table, placing his hand on the first of four piles to his left. Pulling it towards himself, he paused, and then turned the papers around so that Peter could clearly see them. Granger then went on to explain that the pictures were of the east wall of the Alamo taken Monday morning, January 12, 2010. The picture clearly showed eight random hand prints plastered on the east wall. "We feel that we can link these prints to the ones your client put on the Governor's Mansion," said Granger. He paused, enjoying the discomfort Scott's type A personality was inflicting upon him. He continued, "If you have a look at the prints furthest to the right of the picture, which are clearly the best, you can see the person who placed those hand prints on that wall had the tip of his ring finger missing."

Peter, without thinking, slid his hands off the table, placing them on his lap out of view of Granger or Scott. Granger then went on to explain that the paint used in all incidents was a mixture of egg and Red Ochre. "That happens to be a paint you just can't get at Wal-Mart or Sherwin Williams," said Granger. "No, the person who used this paint made it themselves. They also had an in-depth knowledge of ancient native pigment paint techniques."

Scott interjected that he himself had seen handprints in a cave in north Texas, which had been placed there over 3000 years ago. "Are you going to be charging Peter with that also?"

"No," said Granger. "I will let that one slide. I am more interested in the ones we can prove have been done in the last two years and possibly using pigments purchased at Natural Pigments on Sixth Street on two separate occasions. The first in November, 2009, and again in June, 2010 and both using Peter Shaw's American Express ending in number 5007."

'Checkmate!' Granger thought to himself, unaware that Peter was able to pick up on this. Scott, both hands open, as if begging a favor, asked if he could have a few moments alone with his client. This pleading brought a smile to Granger's face. He pushed himself away from the table, stood and stretched. "Sure," he said. "Ten minutes." He then left Scott and Peter alone.

Marie was just leaving the chief's office when

she could see Granger heading her direction. The shit-eating grin on Granger's face obviously had a story to go with it worth her delaying. She stood holding the door open for Granger as he arrived. This led to an uneasy moment, as Granger's southern manners would not allow him to let pretty Marie hold the door open for him. He paused; Marie got the message and passed the door holding to Jeffrey and she proceeded back into the chief's office.

Closing the chief's door behind him, Granger remained standing and started to address everyone in the room. "Okay, I have them ready to admit the Governor's Mansion deal by letting them know we also have them bang-to-rights on the other tagging events. Everyone knows Senator Peter Shaw is guilty of all of it. His lawyer is trying to play hard ball, but he really has found himself down a blind alley."

"How is the old man handling it?" asked the Chief.

Granger responded, "He really does not seem concerned. I feel sure if he had been left without a lawyer this case would have been tucked up and forgotten long ago. I am halfway through trying to sort out some leads on the vagrant killings case and this bullshit is taking far too much of my time. We all know it is not going anywhere." This all jumped out of Granger's mouth before he had time to edit it. This kind of bluntness was why Granger had remained just a detective, and one of the best in Austin. His cowboy upbringing would not allow him to pander to the politics that was necessary to climb the ladder inside the department.

He re-answered the Chief's question with a reassuring, "He don't seem to give a damn. I am ready to formally charge him with the Governor's Mansion tagging event." confirmed Granger. "I could pass it up to the prosecutor and let him go over it, but to be honest, it's a small crime and the lawyer knows he has no way of getting Shaw out of this mess, and the old man don't care."

Marie interjected, "Okay Jeffrey, what about the other instances?"

Granger was quick to answer. "It was him. I honestly think he wanted to get caught. Think about it. I want to commit a crime and the crime is leaving my handprints all over the scene of the crime while not taking anything or doing any damage apart from leaving the prints. Most criminals will go to extremes to remove prints, but Peter Edward Shaw leaves them purposefully. THAT IS THE CRIME! No, he wanted to get caught. The question is why."

Marie came back at him, "Motive?"

"Now you got me," said Granger. "I really don't think we have to prove motive in this instance as we have so much pinning him to the crime. The thing is, this was not just a random act. It was well planned out. The paint he made himself. It's the same consistency and makeup as that used on cave walls sixty thousand years ago. It's a red ochre pigment mixed with egg white. He purchased the pigment on two separate occasions from a small art shop in town. It's the only shop that sells it. I have a copy of his signed credit card slips." This was the sort of detail that made Granger such a good detective, thought the captain. Granger finished, "If I had to guess, I would say he was trying to attract attention. I really think the motive might be something better answered by a shrink. If I can get him to confess, I will sure as hell ask him why. It is a question that has intrigued me."

It was agreed that the charge should be made official and passed upstairs to the state prosecutor's office. "Give the old man the opportunity to come clean, but really it's not necessary. We have plenty enough to pin him on the Governor's Mansion paint job," said the chief.

"What are we going to do about the other cases?" asked Marie.

The chief said, "We are not going to charge him with them. If we do, we potentially could lose control of the case. Some of those monuments are federal. Let's just say we are still investigating those crimes."

"Okay," Marie interjected. "I will work up something for the media. Now is our opportunity to get the grass to work for us. What has been decided in here must remain between us. Outside of this door, we will inform everyone that we will be charging the senator for the Governor's Mansion incident, but we will add that we will continue the investigation as we feel we can link him with the other crimes. And, just for the benefit of the leaker, we will add that we will be requiring a complete psychological analysis of Shaw. We feel sure he will end up either behind bars, or in a hospital."

"Nice!" said the chief. This gave him something to show he was working with the governor and it should be enough not to have people accusing the department of letting the big boys slide. "Jeffrey, go and finish up with Shaw and his lawyer. When you have him charged, we will get Marie to give a press release to those reporters hanging around outside."

Sergeant Madden excused himself, deciding to make himself a coffee and see if he could be the first to call his friend, the editor of the Austin Statesman, and let him know how the Austin PD were going to handle Sir Peter Edward Shaw.

Chapter 7

Alicia arrived home and even before she got to the front door she could smell the cinnamon, indicating her mother had made some cookies. She unlocked and opened the door. As she entered, Brenda could instantly see Alicia's woe-is-me posture. She leaned forward; twisting to make sure her floured hands didn't dust Alicia's dress, and kissed her cheek. She asked, "And what sort of day have we had?"

"Not good," Alicia responded.

As her mother took Alicia's handbag, she said, "Well, let's hear what happened."

"J.K., the editor, has put me into telephone sales," said Alicia.

"What? Your internship was to learn about reporting, not telephone sales," her mother responded. "Come into the kitchen and I will get you some dinner. I want to know exactly what happened."

Alicia explained how the meeting went and that Peter had cut the meeting short.

Her mother asked, "Was it because you had someone else with you?"

"I don't think so. He invited us both into his study and just as we got started he received a phone call. We think it was from his lawyer. What was interesting was Shaw called me back as we both were getting into the car. He told me to get back in touch with him and to not bring anyone else. Tim, of course, asked what he had said. I told him and he told me not to tell anyone at the paper. "Keep it to yourself," were his exact words.

"Do you think you can trust him?" Brenda asked.

"Yes, I think so," replied Alicia. "All was well until we arrived back at the newsroom. We went straight to the Editor's office to debrief. Tim was great. He could sense my uneasiness and proceeded to go into the detail of the short interview we had with the senator."

She went over what Tim had said for her mother word for word. "Tim started with how he was surprised at how the mansion has gone downhill since the accident. He explained that it is obvious that, mentally, Shaw is not what he used to be. Apparently, he has aged terribly and physically he appears to be in pain. He said he had not had time to see if he is on any pain medications as an addiction might explain his lack of concern for his appearance. J.K. chimed in, wanting Tim to go into more detail over his assumption. I remained quiet as Tim responded. He explained how he had nothing to do with Peter Edward Shaw since prior to the accident, emphasizing the Edward.

He had been reporting on the misuse of funds, which was being investigated by the Senate; in fact, it was one of the first assignments J.K. had put him on.

J.K. sneered and grinned at that point, saying, 'Trial by fire.' Tim responded that the senator was as quick and slick as they came and told him that when referring to him in print, not to forget his middle name, 'Edward,' which was the family name of his great grandfather and southern Civil War General Edward Shaw, who incidentally had been the largest slave owner west of the Mason Dixon line.

His wife was several years younger than him, but he was in good condition and pretty much had control of Austin politics. In most instances you had to go through his press officer if you wanted to talk to him, but if you did get the opportunity you had better stay on script with your questions if you valued your job.

Now, it's all different. He appears to be a slow moving, beaten man. Tim thinks we should maybe get an opinion from one of our experts as to his mental state. J.K. said it might be something we could run with and chimed in that it could it be a form of Post Traumatic Stress Disorder and that it would be a worthy side line as there's a lot of interest in that syndrome.

J.K. then asked if we were able to get anything out of him as to why he was doing the tagging. Tim told him we barely got into the interview. He was friendly enough then got a phone call, probably from the lawyer, and the interview was terminated and we were led out. J.K. asked what time that would have been and I chimed in that it was about 11:00. He said that would tie in with the fact that they were planning on taking Shaw back down to the station, and he had inside information that they are going to charge him. Then he told Tim to get back to the station and see what he can find out. That was when he told me to go over to the advertising department and see if I can help out, maybe to help with some canvassing of advertisers, adding that it's the backbone of the paper. As we left the office, Tim reassured me not to take the move personally, and that J.K. can be a real ass."

Alicia turned to her mother and said, "I really don't understand what I have done wrong."

Her mother reassured her and told her, "That's politics. In the career path you have chosen and the fact that interaction is an important part of the life of a reporter, you will find out that often you will get on a lot better not by what you do, but by what you don't do. It's a fine balance and a lesson that most of us learn only with age. You have done nothing wrong. The problem is J.K.'s. Unfortunately, the consequence is what you have got to deal with."

As her mother finished her sentence Alicia's cell phone rang. It was Tim. "Alicia, I have been to the station and also I called a doctor friend of mine and done some background, checking on the senator's health." Alicia was surprised Tim had called, but felt really pleased that he was keeping her in the loop. "They have charged him with tagging the Governor's Mansion. He has only just been released to go home. None of us could get at him as they let him out the back door again."

Alicia chimed in, "I tried to call him and left a

message on his answer phone with my cell number. That explains why he has not got back to me."

Tim continued, "On the way home, I called a doctor friend of mine at the ER who worked on him after the accident. The doc told me that he is amazed that he can even walk. He had severe damage to his lower back. He was so badly damaged in the accident they put him into a coma to allow him to recover. When they brought him around and he was able to take control of his recovery he had refused all medication, including pain pills. He said it made him sleepy and unable to focus. He spent hours meditating; 'self-healing' were his words. Apparently, he was the talk of the unit. He did recover quickly and amazed them all by walking out of the hospital. A lot of the doctors were betting he would never make it."

"That's sad that he is in so much pain," said Alicia. "I hope he gets back to me soon. I am really interested in what he has to say."

Tim responded, "When he gets in touch with you," emphasizing the word when, "I would love to know what he has to say." He then casually asked, "Would you like to join me on Saturday evening for a drink and to go and see Bo De Pena at Antonlo's? He is a local artist, great to see live, and a good friend."

It seemed like ages since Alicia had been out with a boy. Her first long-term relationship had ended three months ago when her first love started dating her best friend. She responded quickly. "Yes, that sounds like fun," hoping that she did not appear over enthused.

You could clearly hear the smile in Tim's voice as he confirmed he would be in touch at work to arrange times. He then added, "Great, great. Okay, I'll see you at work," he confirmed and then hung up, not giving her time to change her mind.

Alicia turned to her mother with, "Things are moving faster than I thought. I will give Shaw a call tomorrow and after thinking about it, getting away from the editor in advertising might be just what I need. I will have plenty of time to call and make an appointment; the interview is what is important now."

Her mother confirmed, "Let the story lead you, Alicia. It will take you where it needs to go." Her demeanor changed as she sat down to the table to tell her mother about her conversation with Tim and her date.

Peter opened his eyes to the phone ringing. The day was already brightly shining through his bedroom window. He could feel the heat of light on his old legs and it felt good. The phone continued to ring. Peter had no intentions of answering it, thinking it might be his lawyer or the police. After the fifth ring, the answer phone kicked in as he lay listening. To his surprise, it was Alicia leaving a message and making clear it was the second time she had called. She would call again later that morning and then again left her cell number.

He could not move quickly enough to answer the phone and thought it would be best to let the answer machine do its' business and he would return her call when he had got himself ready. He slowly raised himself, sliding his legs off the bed and gently lowering them to the floor. He assumed the standing position, and holding the foot of the bed, was able to maneuver himself into a position were he could slide on the same jeans he was wearing the night before when he was released from the station. Two hours and four cups of coffee later, he was finally ready to return the call to Alicia. He used the same number she had left and was surprised it was her personal number and not the number of the newspaper. Alicia picked up immediately as she could see it was Peter Shaw.

"Good morning, Sir. Thanks for getting back to me," she said.

He replied, "Alicia, you don't have to call me Sir. Peter will do just fine."

She responded, "Oh, Okay. I was wondering when it would be possible for me to come around and continue with the interview. I promise I will come alone, like you asked."

Peter showed no signs of hesitation. "You can come around whenever you want. Just make sure you call first to make sure I am not busy."

Alicia wasted no time in committing Peter to an appointment with a confirmation. "Would this evening be okay, like late afternoon? I could call in on my way home from work."

"That will be fine," Peter confirmed.

As soon as Peter hung up, Alicia made her way

to the coffee machine via the long way to make sure Tim could see her and join her. Tim noticed her immediately. He had been waiting for this opportunity and, without making it too obvious, pushed back from his desk and followed her to the coffee machine.

Alicia opened the conversation. "I've got the meeting tied up with Peter Shaw for this afternoon on my way home."

"That's great," confirmed Tim. "Any idea as to why he wants to talk to you so bad and no one else?" He leaned forward to the machine and started to feed the quarters in and at the same time asked Alicia what she wanted to drink.

"No, I did not have a chance to ask him any questions on the phone. I thought I would leave it until we were face-to-face. Coffee with milk, no sugar, please. I am planning on leaving a little early," Alicia answered.

"Getting excited are we?" said Tim with a smile on his face.

"You bet!" responded Alicia. "I can't wait to see what he has to say and also why he wants to talk to me."

"You let me know as soon as you come out of the meeting," said Tim.

"I will," responded Alicia.

At 3:30 p.m., Alicia informed her department head, Susan Burke, that she was about to leave. She had told Susan earlier that she would be going, but she did not give an excuse; she just said that she had to leave early. Susan did not ask for a reason, which pleased Alicia, as she hated not being able to tell the truth, but she couldn't help but add one remark as Alicia turned to leave. "In the real world, you have to let people know if you are not going to be able to do what you are expected to. You can't just up and leave whenever you want," she said.

"It won't happen again. I just can't miss this appointment," Alicia replied as she stepped onto the elevator and pushed the button.

On reaching her car, she unlocked it, got in, and started it so the air conditioning could kick in. The 100 plus degree temperature inside the car soon dropped. As it did, Alicia made her call, hoping that Peter Shaw would answer. Five rings had gone by and Alicia was about to hang up. Then, just before the answer phone kicked in, Peter picked up with what appeared to be a very sheepish, "Hello."

"Hello, Senator Shaw. It's me, Alicia Fielder from the Statesman. Is it okay for me to come around for our interview?" Alicia asked, trying not to sound too anxious.

"Oh, yes, that's fine," responded Peter. He sounded a little bit slow and groggy, as if he had just awoke. Alicia picked up on this and reconfirmed that all was well.

"Are you sure?" she asked.

Peter confirmed, "Its okay. I've been meditating. I'm looking forward to seeing you."

As soon as Alicia arrived at the front door to the

mansion, before she had even attempted to fight the old doorknocker, Peter opened the door. He invited her in and she followed Peter down the hall into the kitchen. "Would you like anything to drink?" he asked. "The choices are limited, but you are more than welcome to anything I have."

"No, thank you. I am fine," said Alicia, who was already laying her stuff out on the kitchen table and starting up her iPad.

Peter slowly lowered himself into one of the chairs and turned to Alicia. "Okay, where do we want to start?" he asked. Alicia still felt a little uneasy, but thought the best bet would be to go over the fact that he had been charged with the tagging.

"Well," she replied. "I understand the police have officially charged you with tagging the Governor's Mansion."

"Yes," Peter replied. "They finally got around to it. I would have let them charge me on the first day, but my attorney had to make them jump through hoops before they arrived at exactly the same point we were at before he got involved. Still, I suppose it is in my best interest to follow his instructions."

Alicia asked, "Was it your lawyer that called and cut our meeting short yesterday?"

Peter replied, "Yes, that was him. 'Don't talk to the press,' was his advice." He smiled and let out a little chuckle.

"That sounds like good advice," Alicia grinned. "So, why are you talking to me, Sir?"

"The name is Peter, Alicia. I dropped the 'Sir' and any pretentions that went with the title after the accident," Peter commented.

"Okay, Peter, but why is it you will talk to me? Tim is a seasoned reporter and could do a much better job than me. I'm just learning."

Peter leaned forward as if about to tell a very personal secret. "Alicia," he stated. "I have a very important story to tell. I need someone to listen and write it down. I think you are the person."

"Why do you think I should be the person?" she asked, taken back by his intensity.

He replied, "I just do, and as the story unfolds I think you will understand why I chose you. Since the accident, I am not in the great shape I used to be. I get tired easily these days, so we are going to have to keep the interviews short and frequent. I'm not quite sure how much time I have left to get this story out. I don't really suppose any of us are sure of our time left on this earth. I think I have become quite an expert in the unpredictability of future," he concluded with a grin.

He continued, "I don't really feel we have to go back prior to the accident. My life before that day is pretty well documented. I think a good starting point for you would be the accident. The last thing I remember as Peter Edward Shaw, the Senator, I was laying on the gurney. I was realizing I had just lost my wife. The medic was reassuring me I would be okay as he was filling me with morphine. I was transfixed on the sky. It was the most beautiful blue sky I had ever seen.

As I started to drift in and out of consciousness, a hawk came into view and was hovering directly above me, looking down. He was looking at me, and in me, as I drifted into the blackness. Over the next six weeks, I was kept in an induced coma. They did the breathing, eating and drinking for me. Slowly, my body started to heal, fixing itself, so that I could return to it. It is barley usable, but considering I have a further use for it, it is acceptable." Again the grin swept across his old face.

"During that period of apparent near death, I experienced a time leap," he explained. "It is the only way I can explain it. I was taken back in time to the beginning of our species, a time before speech. I say taken, because I did not just go back, I was taken by a being, a person from the past that I became part of. I was him, and he was me."

Alicia again felt very uneasy, but because of his demeanor she did not feel threatened. She remained silent, letting Peter tell his story. At worst, she might have wasted some time, but the thing that came to her were the words her mother had told her, "Let the story take you to where it needs to go. Your job is to report."

Peter could judge her uneasiness. "It really does sound like the ramblings of a crazy old man. If someone had told me what I am asking you to believe before I was in the accident, I would not have believed it. In fact, when I first came out of the coma, I laid for many days wondering if it had been a dream. It was so vivid. Then I realized I had changed. First, I noticed I had brought back with me some of the gifts of early man. My sense of smell is far more powerful than it has ever been. I am now not only able to catch the scent of something; I can also judge the well being of a person, their mood and their intention. I have other gifts too, for example, I want you to think of something that you want to tell me. Think of it and will me to receive it. It can be anything. Think of a picture or a situation. Open your mind and tell me about it. Add a color or a scent to your thought."

Alicia was thinking it was some sort of party trick, but went along with it. She thought about Lady Gaga and her dress made of meat, imagining how it would smell and look. The thought repulsed her vegetarian leanings, but she focused on it, convinced Peter would never get it.

Peter looked at her and said, "Who is Lady Gaga and why would she wear a meat dress?"

The answer cut Alicia's breath short. Making a gasping noise, and after a brief moment, the first, "Wow," popped out of her mouth, followed by a more pronounced, "Wow. You must have read my mind!"

Peter realized that he now had her interest and confidence. "Alicia," he began. "Like I said, I have an amazing story to share with you."

Alicia was unable to focus on the reporting side of the story. She was still trying to understand what she had just experienced. "Can you read people's minds?" Alicia asked again. The thought of spending time with a person who knew your every thought was unnerving, almost like conducting the interview with out your clothes on.

Peter reassured her that a person's thoughts had to be transmitted to be shared, but that the person's demeanor and smell tell a lot of a person's information as well.

Alicia chimed in, "Smell?"

Peter answered, "A person's smell changes with stress and aggression. Lying, for example, can be stressful. Also, you can tell a person's health. It's amazing. I would never have believed how much information you can get from a person's smell. Put that together with the ability to transmit thought and you have a very powerful way to communicate and comprehend."

Alicia asked, "Peter, can you just go over what you are telling me again? Are you saying the day of the accident, which you remember up to the point of being put into the ambulance, you then went into a coma; when you came out of the coma you had these powers? Is that the story?"

"No," replied Peter. "Well, yes and no. What happened, Alicia, is that I was taken back in time to witness the demise of the first true humans; our ancestors: egoless, speechless, gifted beings. Alicia, I know this is not what you expected, but I am already starting to feel tired. Would you mind if we continued another day?"

Alicia could see the tiredness on Peter's face. She let him know that she totally understood and immediately started to stand and pack her stuff. "Just one more thing," she asked. "How far back do you think we are talking when you say you went back in time?"

As Peter stood, he said, "I think, from what little research I have been able to do, I went back about 40,000 to 45,000 years ago. I have read of cave art they believe were done by the Neanderthals in Northern Spain from around that period. Also, this is the time when the first Homo-sapiens, modern humans, started showing up."

"Okay," Alicia responded. "I will do some research on that time period and see what I can come up with before our next meeting."

Peter responded with a smile. "That will be great." Still attempting to stand without holding onto the table, his head again bent with an apparent grimace, and he carefully let go of the chair. He proceeded to the hall to lead Alicia back towards the front door. Alicia picked up all of her belongings and slowly started to follow Peter down the hall. As he went past the door next to the kitchen, he said, "That's my library, where I used to do a lot of reading and research." He stopped and opened the door.

Alicia said, "Do you mind if I have a look?"

"No, of course not; help yourself," Peter responded.

She eased herself past Peter into a room that had three large walls covered in books on seven shelves from the floor to the ceiling. "Oh, my God," she commented, as her eyes scanned what must be a priceless collection of books. On an antique desk sat

Peter's computer, still switched on but looking almost as dated as some of the books on the shelves. It's surprising what five years does as far as technology is concerned. Peter could see Alicia eyeing the computer and commented, "It still works."

Alicia's eyes went to an open book laying on a separate antique stand, just a little bit bigger than the leather bound book it was holding. The book was open, and lying on top of the book was a white pair of cotton gloves, as if dropped. Peter commented, "Thomas Jefferson, Collective Papers, 1829. I think that was one of the last books I purchased before the accident. I used to love spending time going over early American books. I have quite a collection."

"Yes, you do!" confirmed Alicia.

She quietly stood looking close at the books on the shelves, reading the undamaged spine of a leather bound book by Alexander Hamilton titled The Federalist Papers. She then stood back and cleared her mind. 'Can I bring my mother to show her this collection?' she transmitted. It was a test and a question.

Peter picked it up instantly and responded with, "Of course you can bring your mother. That would be fine."

Another 'wow' made its way from Alicia's lips as she thought to herself, 'They are never going to believe this!'

She turned to Peter and said, "Amazing, Peter. When do you think I will be able to come back and continue the interview?"

Peter slowly continued towards the front door, at the same time inviting Alicia back whenever she wanted.

Alicia then asked, "Would mornings be less stressful for you?"

Peter thought about it and agreed that the mornings would be better and then asked, "How will you work that into your schedule?"

Alicia replied, "Tomorrow is Saturday. I could meet tomorrow morning if that would be okay with you."

"Sure," he answered, "But let's do it after 10:00. It takes me a while to get moving."

As she left Peter's house, she speed-dialed the number for Tim. As the blue tooth transmitted to the car speakers, she put the car into gear and headed home. Tim's voice came across the speaker, cheery and inquisitive.

"Hi, Alicia," he said. "How did it go?"

Alicia responded with a curt, "Fine. He really is nice. I have to be carful though, as he is in a lot of pain. The interviews have to be kept short as he finds it too stressful and tiring.

Tim, not missing the reporter's chance, asked, "Well, did he tell you why he tagged the mansion?"

Alicia did not want to go into too much detail at the moment. The story needed editing in her mind before she could discuss it. "No, but he admitted he had been charged. It did not seem to bother him at all. He did not get into the detail of the tagging and I did not push the point. I think he has a story that he will share with me, but it will be in his time. This is going to take time to get the whole story."

Tim chimed in, "Talking of time, what time do you want me to pick you up tomorrow evening?"

Alicia smiled to herself, responding, "About 7:30 would be fine."

Tim asked, "Could you send me your address? I would hate to get lost."

"I will," said Alicia. "I have another appointment with Peter tomorrow morning and will let you know how it's going when you pick me up."

"Great. See you tomorrow," said Tim, as he hung up the phone.

Alicia immediately turned her thoughts back to Peter Edward Shaw and everything he had told her, and shown her, in that short meeting. She wanted to get home and begin the research she had promised Peter she would do. For some reason, she wanted to please the old man.

Chapter 8

Alicia spent the evening researching cave art. It was apparent where Peter had got the idea for the handprints. What was strange to Alicia was that no one at the paper had done any research into painted handprints. It might have helped them track down why, or at least been an interesting insert, into the governor's tagging incident.

One thing she was able to dig up at http://trove.nla.gov.au/ndp/del/article/4400765 was an interesting article on Australian Aboriginal telepathy. On Thursday, August 6, 1931, Mr. David Uniapon, a full-blooded member of the Naninjeu tribe, gave a talk on how Aborigines sent messages over long distances. Uniapon said in his report, "When an Aborigine wishes to appeal for help or to send any other message to a member of his tribe, he would first attract attention by a smoke signal. The person seeing the smoke then strives to do a very difficult thing, to clear his mind of every thought and so become fully receptive to the message sent." The fact that telecommunication had been documented as a method of communicating certainly gave credibility to Peter's story. Alicia was really excited about being able to let Peter know what she had found.

As her mother prepared breakfast for Alicia and herself, she could hardly contain her excitement. She had been thinking all night of the potential of the story. The brief outline of the interview she had been given by Alicia was amazing. Alicia found her mother's enthusiasm for the story very supportive.

Alicia left the house at just after nine and was again at the doorstep of Peter at just after 10:00 a.m. She did not have to knock. Peter opened the door just as she arrived.

"Good morning, Alicia," said Peter, sounding rested and cheery. "Sleep well?"

"Yes, fine. Once I was able to get Sir Peter Edward Shaw out of my mind," Alicia responded with a smile.

Peter picked up on her humor and responded, "Sir Peter Edward Shaw out of your mind. Hmmmmm, you sure Alicia?" joining her in the joke. He directed her, "Come on in. We'll go to the library. I think it will be more practical and comfortable."

Alicia walked into the library and Peter told her, "Use the desk. I will take the more comfortable couch so I can stretch out this old back of mine if I have to, if you will excuse my recumbence?"

Alicia made her way behind the desk and unfolded her iPad. As she fired it up, she found that Peter still had an active connection for his home network. "Would you mind if I logged on to your server?" she asked.

Peter responded by making his way behind the

desk and producing a piece of paper with a fifteen-digit code. 'The code must be another thing left over from when he was a senator,' thought Alicia. Most personal WEPs now days are six digits. Alicia typed the code into her iPad and linked into the network. "That's it," she said. "Now we can check stuff online if we need to."

Peter proceeded to tell her, "I had a call from my lawyer, Scott Neilson, telling me that detective Jeffrey Granger would be coming over for me to sign a statement. The lawyer said he had checked it out and it was okay, and it will save us a trip to the station."

Alicia asked, "What do you think will happen over what you have been charged with?"

Peter showed his lack of concern with his answer. "Not too sure. I'm not losing much sleep over it."

It was clear to Alicia that Peter did not want to go any further talking about the tagging incident, as Peter followed with his own question. "Were you able to find anything out with your researching last night?"

"Yes I was," Alicia confirmed, and went over what she had found out about the Aboriginal telepathy.

Peter was pleased she had found the article and confirmed what David Uniapon had said about the difficulty in silencing one's mind. He said, "I spend many hours meditating. Not only does it calm me, but also it really helps to relieve some of the pains I still have. When I really get into a deep meditation, I pick up what I call noise. I was aware some of the ancient peoples still have the gift today. I bet a lot of the noise comes from them."

"So you can hear people when you meditate?" asked Alicia.

"Yes," he replied. "I pick up random transmissions. That's what I call noise. You'd be surprised at how much is out there."

"Awesome," said Alicia.

She leaned forward and passed the article that she had printed to Peter. She needed to proceed with the interview and decided to refocus back to the time of the accident. Pulling a document up on her iPad that outlined where she had left off, she began. "You said that you remember laying on the gurney and looking up at the sky and a hawk. What do you remember next?"

Peter leaned back and began. "As I closed my eyes that day, it was if I was spinning in darkness, much like you would experience as a child when you made yourself dizzy. I had a desire to steady myself, to open my eyes and get my bearings. My eyes were heavy and I was unable to open them. A bright light started to tear through the darkness. I thought I would not be able to look at it due to the brightness. Although it was amazingly bright, I was able to look directly at it, and as I looked at the light the spinning sensation eased. The light slowed the spinning sensation and gave me a focus, which was reassuring. I looked deep into the light and started to drift towards its' base. I was drifting towards it, into the light, without any effort of movement. I could feel myself accelerating towards the source.

I picked up only the sound at first; it was the cry of a hawk. As I stared into the light, I was able to identify what became the same hawk I had seen before I closed my eyes. It was reassuring to have recognized something from consciousness. The desire to head towards its cry was becoming very important, and as I did I had a sensation of speed, moving faster and faster. I was accelerating towards the hawk that was leading me deeper into the light.

Suddenly, there was a blinding flash, and it was as if I was awake, but I was now a consciousness inside another being, in another time. I had become an observer only. I had no control over the body I occupied and had no desire to have control. The body I was inside of was Hawk, a Shaman. It was apparent from the beginning that he was aware of my presence. He had reached across time and brought me back. At first I had no idea what the purpose was, but he welcomed me. We sat quietly, breathing deeply, eyes closed. His breathing was slow and deep. His focus was on the stillness of the meditation. 'Welcome,' he thought, but no sound was transmitted from him, but I could clearly hear and feel his comforting welcome."

A loud knock on the door finished the interview and brought both Alicia and Peter down to earth with a shock. Alicia had been recording what Peter had been saying and as Peter stopped and opened his eyes she leaned forward and hit the red record button on the screen of her iPad, stopping any further recording.

Peter started to struggle to relieve himself from the grip of the couch. Alicia intervened, "Would you like me to answer the door for you?"

"Yes," said Peter. "I think it will be the detective. Bring him through to the library and I will sign his documents for him."

Alicia opened the door, surprising Detective Granger. He collected himself and asked, "Is Peter Shaw in?"

Alicia asked, "Who shall I say is calling?"

Granger responded, "Detective Granger. I have some documents for him to sign."

Alicia confirmed that Peter was expecting him as she swung the door open to let the detective in. She walked into the hall, leaving it to the detective to close the door. She then beckoned him to follow her down the hall to the library. They walked into the library and Peter was still sitting on the couch. Granger noticed instantly that he still had no shoes on and was wearing the same clothes he had been wearing at the station the day before.

Granger said in a friendly tone, "Good morning, Sir. I have got some documents for you to sign. Sorry to bother you on a weekend, but I wanted to get this wrapped up."

Peter smiled and said, "No problem. Scott, my lawyer, has been in touch and told me it was okay to sign the papers." He then turned to Alicia and asked, "Would you be so kind as to pass one of the large books from the corner of the desk so that I may use it on my lap to sign the documents?"

Alicia passed a book to Peter and placed it on his lap. He turned to the detective and introduced Alicia. "This is Alicia Fielder. She's an intern with the Austin Statesman. She is interviewing me."

The detective turned to Alicia, nodding and saying, "My pleasure ma'am."

'A true Texan,' she thought.

Peter asked if the detective wanted a seat. Granger declined and remained standing over Peter, placing each paper in front of him as he explained what it was and where to sign. Peter again confirmed that his lawyer had already told him to sign the documents and he realized he was signing his life away. The detective grinned and continued sliding the papers in front of Peter one at a time and holding his finger on the papers where he wanted Peter to sign; a silent instruction. Thirteen papers in all, and on the last one the detective asked him to sign and date it. Alicia was impressed by the neatness and boldness of Peter's signature, another relic of his past.

"That should do the trick," said Granger, who then excused himself. "I have got to get to my oldest daughter Zoe's birthday party, and before that I have got to drop these documents back to the office." He again thanked Peter.

Alicia stood up to lead the detective to the front door. As she reached the door, the detective again thanked her and asked for her name. "Alicia Fielder," she confirmed as she opened the door. "Have a great day," Alicia said, while hanging onto the door until the detective's car had started moving.

Returning to the library, Peter was ready to continue with his story. The detective and the signing of the statement did not faze him. He laid back into the couch saying, "Now where were we?"

Alicia quickly returned to her place behind the desk and referred to her hand written notes. "You found yourself inside someone as an observer," said Alicia.

Peter confirmed. "Oh, yes, our man Hawk. I was not sure where I was at first. I thought I was dead. The only way I can describe the sensation was that I felt an overwhelming calmness; like a child in pre-birth, still in the womb. It was a reassuring sensation. Hawk was allowing his mind to comfort me, making me aware of our presence and the deep calmness as he meditated. I became aware of the fact that I was inside of another being, and the more aware I became, any fear or apprehension I had was removed. One way to describe what I was experiencing was that it was like being at a movie, but I was in a situation where I controlled how the movie proceeded. I was able to wind it back if I needed, but I could not change the outcome of a situation. I could witness everything that had brought us to this point. I was able to dive into his memories including the feelings that went with them."

Alicia asked, "Were you observing from the outside, watching as a separate third party, or are you saying you were inside Hawk? Were his memories given to you much in the same way I would think about my own past? The memories, are they in mental pictures, with smells and feeling?"

Peter confirmed he was observing from the inside. "It was as if thinking back on a memory, like looking at a movie in 4D, with smell and emotion. It was soon apparent where I was. I was inside Hawk. The first conscious observations I had was of Hawk's breathing, very slow and deliberate. Then Hawk's breathing began to shallow and the focus moved from the internal tranquility that had greeted me to an awareness that Hawk was starting to open his eyes. It was the crying and wailing of a female that was bringing Hawk out of his meditation. As he opened his eyes, the light from the entrance of the cave was brilliantly dazzling. Hawk had been meditating away from the entrance; seeking the seclusion the darker parts of the cave gave him.

I became aware of other beings, people, inside the cave who were highlighted by the light from the entrance and a small flickering fire they gathered around in the middle of the cave floor. The air was heavy with smoke, warm, sweet smelling smoke; the sweet smell from strips of herb covered meat drying in the smoke above the fire. They were heavy, powerful beings; their bare arms covered in hair. They were covered with layers of skins wrapped around them and bound with a sinew twine. Their feet were also covered and bound by skin and twine, helping and protecting them from the cold damp cave.

Hawk walked towards the fire. The people

around the fire shuffled to make room for him to join them. Stepping into the circle, one of the children, Water, reached up and touched his leg. Hawk looked down and reached for the child's head and placed his massive hand on it. She then rested her head against his massive calves.

The woman who was making the noise again attracted Hawk's attention. Moving the child's hand from his leg, he made his way towards where the woman was being supported by two women holding her by her arms as she squatted over a fur in what I soon came to understand was the birthing position. A woman was crouched behind her like a catcher in a football game, her hands supporting a newborn, the umbilical cord still attached. The new mother gave one last moan and relieved herself of the afterbirth and what was left of her waters. She was straining now to turn her head and look behind herself at the child she had just birthed. The catcher quickly covered the child in a fresh skin, her large face showing concern. She stood and brought the child towards Hawk, uncovering the child and holding it for him to inspect. The child was hairless and pale in color, like a modern human.

I felt the sadness of the situation, as it was apparent that Hawk had to make a decision that saddened him, but one that had to be made. Hawk spent very little time inspecting the child before he wet his hand, and then slipped it into a pouch around his waist smearing the sweet, dry powder onto his index finger that he presented to the lips of the newborn. The child eagerly started sucking on his finger, ingesting the potion. Hawk then mentally called for Wolf, one of the four hunters the tribe still had with them. "Come," he requested. Wolf arrived quickly. He knew why he had been called and immediately reached forward for the child, now bundled in the soft skins the midwife had swaddled it in.

The mother started whimpering. Hawk crouched down and placed his arms around her, holding her head on his shoulder and transmitting calmness to her. She responded, receiving his thoughts that comforted her. She was saddened, but understood why Hawk had made the decision. Wolf then came forward, uncovering the child he held so she could inspect it herself. It was the first time she had seen it. She could clearly see the child's lack of hair and instantly understood. She turned from looking at the child and re-buried her head on Hawk's shoulder.

Wolf walked off with the child. Holding it in one of his massive arms, he went to the fire and picked up a burning log to show his way deep into the cave. This is where he would place the child on a ledge, away from the tribe and the light. Wolf had walked a good distance back into the cave and the walls of the cave started to close in. He then turned in a separate tunnel that was lower and smaller, his massive frame barely able to stand or walk without his shoulders rubbing the walls. After a while, he held the flame and could see what he was looking for, a shelf protruding from the side of the tunnel wall. He laid the bundle up on the shelf and then left the newborn to the cold and damp of the cave. It would be here that the child would soon pass.

Hawk gently stood, passing the care of the new mother back to the two women that had been supporting her during the birth. The new mother's name was Star. The Hairless Ones had captured her in her second year as a woman. Young and vulnerable, she had been repeatedly raped and injured by her sadistic capturers. Her face and young body was terribly injured, the bite scars very apparent on her young face. She was able to escape after six weeks of hell. She was clever and her jailers had grown to trust her, asking her to go to the river with the skin water bags to fetch water, not believing she would dare try to escape as it would certainly mean death if she was recaptured. She made her way to the river and on the way she contacted Hawk with her mind. Hawk had been waiting for this and had his hunters go out to get her. Hawk was able to guide them to where she was. This they quickly accomplished without being detected, returning her to the safety of the cave. As she recovered, it soon became apparent she was pregnant. Star was aware that the child could be born hairless and the consequences if it was.

Hawk walked alone to the entrance of the cave looking out into the light. The entrance of the cave was high above the fertile land that was once his homeland. He was heavy of heart. The beauty in front of him was a stark reminder of what once had been. Standing at the entrance in the cold light of day reminded him of the reasoning for his decision, helping relieve him of his guilt and of the suffering of the child in the back of the cave.

He breathed the fresh air deeply and then returned to where he had been meditating. He again assumed a cross-legged seated position, facing the painted bare wall of the cave. He started breathing, slow and deliberate, dropping his head backwards as if staring at the ceiling. He closed his eyes and his breathing deepened. Hawk cleared his mind and reached back to the mind of the child to help it pass. The killing of the child was a very personal thing for Hawk. He would be needed to guide the child so its passing was quick and with understanding. He would appear as a light for the child to focus on, a pure white, warming light that would attract the attention of the child and remove any concern for the cold and the natural desire to survive. Hawk's potion and guidance would quickly help the child to peacefully pass, allowing its spirit form to return prematurely to the permanence of its source.

Wolf returned to the fire, replacing the burning log. He slumped down heavily, and without further motion or sound, he stared in the embers. He was questioning the situation and why the once-powerful Middle people now found themselves in this desperate situation.

Wolf's tribe was the holder of the fertile lands skirting the river to the mountains in the west. The tribe was one hundred plus, consisting of twenty fine hunters that found it easy to keep the tribe in protein. Now the survivors numbered less than twenty in total and with only four hunters, which included him. The duties of providing the tribe with good protein and protection were the responsibility of the hunters. This weighed heavy on the heart of Wolf, as he was their leader. He had proven himself many times in battle and for his ability to track and hunt. He was also a prized flint knapper, able to produce a powerful Clovis style point from a suitable mother stone that had been heat-treated in a matter of minutes. These large powerful spear points mixed with his courage and ability made him a very valuable asset to the tribe.

His courage and skills were not enough. The rules of the game had changed. The Hairless Ones were more cunning; they did not abide by the rules of combat that Wolf and his hunters did. Mutual respect for your foe did not exist in their game plan. The first sign of this was the near total destruction of the lower tribe. They left only one survivor who was able to tell of how the hairless beings had attacked at night. This was a cunning and deadly change in tactics. The tribe had been sleeping, no guards were posted, and any of the tribe that was awake was quickly dispensed and silenced. They used fire and screaming to instill fear and to confuse, brutally attacking the women and children as they slept, putting the tribe's hunters into total confusion. The Hairless Ones enjoyed the surprise and zero resistance. They feasted on the corpses of the lower tribe, mainly the large muscle areas, but also the cheeks and eyes leaving terribly mutilated corpses. Having no respect for the dead, they left remains scattered as carrion for scavenging animals. They also would take body parts, which they would proudly hang around their necks: hair, ears, and teeth. The mutilation of the dead spread fear amongst the Seers.

It was not long before the Middle tribe became the focus of the Hairless Ones. The deadly night attacks, which had been so successful to eliminate the lower and upper tribes, would now be used to wipe them out. Wolf relied upon Hawk for intelligence that would pre-warn of any attack, but the dark hours veiled Hawk's eyes, leaving the tribe vulnerable. Hawk, however, was watching the Hairless Ones on the move during the day, and he was able to observe their preparations, a harbinger that would allow him to pre-warn the tribe of a planned attack. Hawk held council and it was decided that he would move the women and children to the safety of his secret cave, leaving the hunters and the male elders to defend against the attack.

He personally led the women and children the five miles towards where the river narrowed. The pathway, which meandered beside the river, appeared to end into a deep blue pool, radiant with depth surrounded by large smooth boulders, with a backdrop of a two hundred foot waterfall. It was here that Hawk led the women, children, sick and elderly away from the river. It was off the path. He had to forcibly make his way through the undergrowth. This would lead them to a small cave entrance that he had to uncover. Tall vines and a few head size rocks had to be moved before one could find the entrance, even if you were standing next to it. He left the group standing by the entrance of the cave and went back to make sure he covered any tracks, being very careful not to break any of the plants or brush he had to move to camouflage the group's direction. Hawk then pulled from a pouch a leaf covered fungi, which he carefully unwrapped, making sure it did not touch his hands. Today we call these fungi Stinkhorn, and this was used to cover the scent of the exodus. The smell of the Stinkhorn would successfully mask the scent of the tribe, its obnoxious odor repulsive to the sensitive nose of early man.

Arriving back at the cave, he motioned for the group to go inside. It was small, dark and very damp. The cave floor had a covering of running water trickling towards the entrance. Hawk moved in behind the group and then replaced the rocks that would cover the entrance. Many of the children were scared of the claustrophobic darkness they found themselves. Hawk squeezed past them and again took the lead. The cave made its way upward, all the inhabitants holding hands in a long chain. Slowly, a glimmer of blue light started to comfort the young ones and it led them to the other end of the cave, which exited behind the waterfall.

The cave had, at one time, been the flow channel of the river. Hawk had been shown this cave by his grandfather, who had himself been shown it by an earlier descendant. The children were in awe standing behind the waterfall. One of the younger males ran forward to touch the water. His mother ran forward also, grabbing for him and dragging him back from a twenty-foot fall and a certain drowning. The curtain of water hid them from the outside. A shelf, wide and safe, would lead them to another entrance that would then lead them away from the fall, bringing them out on the other side of the fall, but over one hundred feet up. Again, the entrance was covered and led one hundred feet more, through the bush, to a small path.

The path wound its way around the cliff face and upwards at quite a severe angle. It was barely wide enough for one person. The angle and the width of the path made some of the children petrified, sliding along the cliff face in front of their mother. The group soon arrived at a plateau, a wide flat area that opened up into a massive cave. They filed in. Hawk went to the wall and quickly had a torch alight, showing the size of what was to become their sanctuary. It was not long before a fire was lit and the children had enough light to reassure them and so they could explore."

Peter broke Alicia's submersion in the story with a very painful sounding, "Aaahhhhhh," as he tried to move himself to a position that would stop his back muscle from contracting. He slumped sideways on the couch, stretching his legs out. He let out a slightly less aggressive,"Aahhh," as he straightened himself once again, pushing himself upright with his left hand. Alicia quickly stood, thinking she was going to be needed and quoting that well used sentence when one human encounters another who is clearly in distress: "Are you okay? Can I do anything?"

Peter raised his head, smiling and reassuring Alicia that all was well. He then said, "I think we had better call it a day. My old war wounds are starting to play up and I need to lie down and take a rest; meditate for an hour or so. It's the only thing that really relieves the pain."

Alicia said, "That's awesome you can do that."

"That's another gift Hawk gave me," Peter confirmed.

Alicia returned to the desk, stopping the recorder and making sure she had saved her notes before she shut her iPad down. She noticed it was already 2:30 and was amazed at how quick the time had passed. She looked at Peter. "The story is amazing. I have a thousand questions, but they can wait until you can give me some more of your time. I know its Sunday, but will tomorrow be okay with you Peter?"

Peter responded with a grin, "I will have to check my diary. Yes, of course it will be okay."

Alicia added, "Will 10:00 a.m. be all right again?"

Peter replied, "That will be fine. Alicia, I want you to feel at home here. You don't have to go. You can stay if you want and use the library for any research, if you think it will help." Peter slowly started to stand, and then he turned to Alicia as he walked towards the door.

"Let yourself out. I will see you in the morning Alicia."

Alicia continued loading her iPad into her bag. "I hope you feel better. I will see you tomorrow."

Peter, going out through the door, turned and said, "See you tomorrow Alicia," leaving Alicia to let herself out.

Chapter 9

Alicia closed the massive front door as she left the mansion, skipping lightly down the stairs while pressing the remote to open the door on her car. Putting her bag on the passenger seat she turned on her iPhone. She placed her foot on the brake and pressed the start button, quickly checking the controls to make sure the air was on high to fight back at the hundred degree temperatures you could easily get in a parked vehicle in Austin most times of the year.

She sat waiting for the car to cool and her phone to switch on the blue tooth. The phone's success was confirmed by the monotone female voice saying, "I-Phone connected." Looking down at the screen she could see she had several calls and a string of text messages. One call got her attention; it was from the editor. He had left a message so she pressed the play button to retrieve it.

"Alicia, when you get this message, give me a call at the office," boomed across her speakers.

"What the heck does he want?" she thought. "Probably wants to move me to the mail room." She pressed the screen and started a call to the editor.

After two rings, he answered. "Good afternoon, Alicia. I understand you have been with Peter Shaw."

He stopped his sentence at that point, forcing Alicia to reply.

"Yes, he wanted to see me," Alicia responded, leaving it just as short.

"Why?" he asked.

The conversation played out like a tennis match: short returns demanding attention. Alicia was intrigued how the editor knew everything and was a little pissed off that he had the nerve to call her on her free time and interrogate her about something she believed had nothing to do with him. The Editor had put her in advertising and Sir Peter Edward Shaw was not buying.

She responded, "He wanted to talk to me in private."

"While you are working for, and if you want to continue working for, the Austin Statesman, private does not exist. You need to tell me right now what is going on and what the senator wants to talk to you about in private," he bullied.

Alicia remained quiet for a few seconds.

"Well?" said the editor.

Alicia was evaluating the power of the story and the value of her unpaid internship trying to sell advertising before she responded. "Private to me means it has nothing to do with you," she finally replied. "I would like to remind you that it's Saturday. I am on my own time and selling advertising is not what I envisioned when I accepted the internship with your paper."

After a few seconds, the editor replied, "Okay, Alicia. I will have the security empty your desk and you can collect your belongings from them at the entrance. You, young lady, are fired."

Alicia quickly responded. "I had nothing of any value in my desk because someone, as you know, has been going through my desk when I'm not around. Therefore, I have not left anything for them to steal. Whatever is there, keep it!" she said as she put the phone down.

She was glad to be rid of her internship, but she was disappointed and saddened that it would end with being fired. She looked at herself in the mirror. Sadness and bewilderment stared back. "I was so excited to get that opportunity! But how did he know I was with Peter Shaw?" Her sadness turned to anger as she realized the probable culprit. "Tim you bastard!" she said with total indignation.

She flicked to her favorites in her iPhone and dialed Tim. Tim answered quickly, "Let me call you back," and he put the phone down. This did not help, and only fueled the fire in Alicia. Several minutes went by before Tim returned her call and Alicia was seething.

"Hello," she answered curtly.

Tim quickly picked up on her mood and started talking. "Sorry about that. I was on the phone to the editor. He called just before you did. He told me he 'had to let you go' because you went behind his back and was working independently on the Peter Shaw story. How the heck did he know you were talking to Shaw? I don't get it. I promise you I did not tell a soul."

"Well, how did he find out then? There was only you and my mother and Peter that had any idea where I was. My mother certainly wouldn't have talked to anyone about my interview. I was in the middle of the interview when the editor called the first and second time, according to my phone log. That leaves only you, Tim. No one else knew that I was at that meeting."

Tim sighed, "Honestly, Alicia, I haven't told anyone. I swear to you."

Alicia thought for a moment, and then said with a raised voice, "Well, do you think that sicko bastard would have had me followed or something? How did he know?"

Tim responded sadly, "I have no idea Alicia. Did the senator take any phone calls or did anyone stop by his house while you were conducting the interview?"

"Yes, actually! His lawyer called and then a detective came around to have him sign some documents; a statement about the tagging incident," said Alicia.

Tim jumped in, "That's it! The editor has a personal secret insider at the station. He's been getting the jump on news stories for years. I bet it's the detective."

Alicia said, "That's terrible. I liked him, and honestly I find it hard to believe that he would do such a thing. He seemed like such a gentleman. Fucker!"

Tim was surprised by this comment, but

couldn't blame her and secretly smiled and added that to the list of all the things he liked about her. "Are you going to try and get your job back?" he asked

"No." Then after a short pause, she added, "Never!

Tim then asked, "Well, how did the interview go? Did you find out what this is all about?"

Alicia kept the answer short. "Awesome," she said.

"Tell me about it," Tim said, realizing the untimeliness of his question. Softening the assumption, he quickly added, "But I understand if you decide not to."

Alicia responded, "I really think that I must honor the privacy of what Peter is telling me. It will become public when he decides the time is right. I will tell you this. His story is amazing. I have a million questions and tons of research to do. It's hard to get your head around. Everything he says leads to more questions."

Tim replied, "If you need any help with research, just let me know. I promise I will not tell a soul." After a moment of silence, he added hopefully, "Are we still on for tonight?"

Alicia was feeling comfortable again with Tim's sincerity and confirmed, "Pick me up at 7:30. Check your email for my address and a map. See you later." She put the phone down and sat for a few minutes more before shifting into drive and heading home.

Brenda could hear the key enter the lock of the front door. She moved from the kitchen sink, picking up a cloth and wiping her hands, to watch Alicia come through the door, close it behind her and walk down the narrow hallway towards her. She could tell instantly that Alicia was upset; her shoulders were forward and her head was down. She had a Kleenex in her hand and was wiping her eyes as she looked up and quoted the obvious, "I'm home!" Alicia had held her tears until she pulled into the driveway. Then, the flood of tears and emotion overtook her, forcing her to sit in the car a full fifteen minutes before she pulled herself together to face her mother.

Brenda dropped the dishtowel as she went forward to comfort Alicia and find out what was wrong. Before she could voice her question, Alicia put her bag down and started sobbing on her mother's shoulder. "That bastard editor fired me. My first job and I got fired!"

Her mother was confused as she realized Alicia had not been at work. She asked, "What do you mean he fired you?"

Alicia explained how the editor had called and was angry over her private meeting with Peter Shaw. As she explained, her phone began to ring. She removed her head from her mother's shoulder and looked at the phone's screen. It was Peter Shaw. Still holding onto her mother, she sniffed, wiped her face with her forearm, and then brought the phone to her ear pressing the answer button and saying, "Hello."

"Alicia, are you okay?" Peter asked.

Alicia responded with a very unbelievable, "I'm fine."

Peter, sounding fatherly and concerned, said, "I know you are not okay Alicia. What's happened?"

"I got fired by the editor for having a meeting with you and refusing to tell him what it was about," she replied.

Peter breathed in a very audible breath. "He fired you? Who do you think told the editor you were meeting with me? Who else knew?"

Alicia was quick and careful with her answer, not wanting to cause any problems.

"Well, the only person I can figure that could have told the editor I was with you was the detective. My mother, you, and Tim, the reporter that was with me the first time I came to your house, are the only people that knew I was with you. I initially thought it might have been Tim, but he has assured me he hasn't said anything. He told me the editor has an insider who is always giving him information. Honestly, I trust him, Peter."

"Let me ask you this, Alicia. Would you like your job back?" asked Peter.

Alicia was quick with her response. "Hell, no. That editor is a creep and I have got a far more interesting assignment working with you, Peter."

Peter was pleased with her response and let her know. "I appreciate that, Alicia. I need you, but I will get to the bottom of this, as it should not have happened."

Alicia then asked, "Peter, do you mind me asking why you called? Did you know I had been fired?"

Peter responded, "No, I was meditating and felt you were upset about something. I felt the need to call and check on you."

"That's wild," said Alicia. "You are awesome! Thank you."

"I'm glad your okay," he replied. "See you in the morning, Alicia." He put the phone down, not waiting for her to respond.

Peter stood, pushing on the receiver and waiting for the familiar click indicating a clear line. At the same time, he began going through his address book looking under the H's for Thomas William Haynee, Mayor of Austin. If you want to stir things up, trickle down works. Go to the top and give them hell. They will pass the problem down far more effectively than trying to have the problem passed up. Confidently, he called the mayor's private number even though it was late on a Saturday. He knew he still had enough clout to be a problem to most Austin politicians and to get the mayor to answer his call on a Saturday afternoon. A female who had an accent from south of the border answered the call quickly. "Good afternoon. This is the Haynee residence. How may I help you?"

Peter coughed, clearing his throat, then responded. "Good afternoon. Could you inform Thomas that Peter Shaw would like to talk to him?"

The maid repeated his name and waited for

confirmation that she had pronounced it correctly. She then informed Peter she would go and see if Mr. Haynee was available.

Haynee was watching college football with his son-in-law, both supporting opposing teams, when the maid interrupted. "Sir, you have a gentleman on your private phone line who would like to talk to you. His name is Peter Shaw. Would you like to talk to him?"

Haynee was surprised to hear that name and wanted it confirming as he pressed the pause button on the Tivo. "Who did you say it was?"

The maid responded, "Peter Shaw."

Jumping up, Haynee turned to his son-in-law. "I need to take this call in my study." As he walked away, he muttered under his breath, "What the fuck does he want?"

As he left the room, he grabbed a handful of popcorn from the coffee table, dropping a good percentage of the kernels onto his massive antique Persian rug as he left the room. As he walked towards the entrance of the study, he reflected on his relationship with Peter. It was Peter who had funded his campaign, which led to the silent partnership for Peter in Haynee Commercial Development, a real-estate company responsible for much of the commercial development on the north side of Austin. He seated himself behind his desk, grabbed the phone and pressed nine, opening the line to Peter. He quickly opened the conversation with a sickly and overripe greeting. "Peter, how are you old man? I have been meaning to call you. My schedule has been ridiculous lately, leaving me very little time for old friends. How have you been?"

Peter had no time for his pandering and felt no need for any ass kissing, going straight into the reason for the call and to his concerns. Peter wanted action, which was apparent to Haynee. Haynee confirmed the name of the girl and the details. "Alicia Fielder, and she was an intern with The Austin Statesman. Let me get this right, Peter. You're saying that detective Granger leaked her meeting with you to the editor which led to her getting fired?"

"You got it," Peter responded. "I let that detective into my home. I believed he would have the decency as an officer of the law to protect my right to privacy. What he did by contacting the editor has cost the young girl her job. I want you to get an apology from him to Alicia Fielder, and Granger should face some form of reprimand."

"Peter, leave it with me and I will see what I can do," assured Haynee as he flipped his Rolodex to Peter's old senator card. "Is your home number 267-9333 still the best one to reach you?"

Peter confirmed the number, thanked Haynee for getting involved, and then put the demanding close on the conversation. "I will be waiting for your comments Thomas." He put the phone down before any return from Haynee could be transmitted.

Haynee heard the handset disengage and

turned his head to stare at what now had become just another object. Refocusing, he replaced it back into its holder. He stood and started to walk towards the door to return to the game and then the power of Sir Peter Edward Shaw refocused him, and in an exaggerated comical circle he returned back to the place he had just left, picking the phone up and looking at his Rolodex for the number of the police commissioner.

Jeffrey Granger was on the lawn enjoying his daughter Zoe's birthday party. Standing behind the stainless gas operated Weber grill, he flipped and recoated the ribs with his version of BBQ sauce, which he assured everyone was an old family secret. In reality it was mainly Heinz ketchup, garlic powder and brown sugar. The kids loved the secrecy of the sauce, and the flavor. He closed the lid to let the ribs suck up the apple woodchip smoke that had moments before been soaking in a pan on the table next to his Shiner Bock beer. The three girls were playing in a small pool enjoying each other. Jeffrey grabbed the hose that had been used to fill the pool and turned it on them. They all screamed with excitement as they slipped and tried to get out of the pool and out of range of Jeffrey's deadly aim.

His wife appeared at the door, phone in hand, indicating with no sound to Jeffrey that he had better take the call. As he approached her, she pushed the mute button and at the same time placed her other hand over the phone as she mimed, " It's the chief."

Granger walked into the house taking the phone off his wife as they passed in the doorway. She went into the garden to be with the girls. Granger seated himself, placed his sneakered feet on the coffee table, and stared at the ceiling as he pushed the un-mute button and started the conversation. "Good evening Chief, what's going on?"

"We've got a problem, Jeffrey," he began. "I just got off the phone with the commissioner who gave me hell over our department leaking information to the Austin Statesman. When you met with Peter Shaw today so he could sign papers, there was some young girl intern there named Alicia Fielder. The paper had not sent her to the meeting and when the editor found out, he fired her over it. Apparently, the only way the editor could have found out she was there was through you. Shaw is pissed and wants heads to roll. Your head!"

Jeffrey was shocked by the accusation, realizing that the finger of evidence clearly pointed in his direction. If asked, he would have called himself 'a person of interest'. He had not talked to the Austin newspaper and was trying to connect the dots. How they found out about Alicia being at the Shaw's was beyond him. What he knew for sure was that it wasn't him. He responded the only way he knew how. "Chief, I can assure you that I never leaked to the paper about the meeting. I went straight from the Shaw's house to the station. I logged my time and scanned and filed the statements that I had him sign. I have no idea how they found out. The only person I talked to was shift Sargent

Madden. I am helping with my daughter's birthday at the moment. Can you let me get back to you with some answers? I have some questions I need to ask certain people before I can work out how the hell the Austin Statesman got that information. Leave it to me and I will have some answers for you by Monday."

"Jeffrey," said the commissioner "You need to take this very seriously. That old bugger Shaw still has a lot of clout in this town. We need to get him some answers, and quick."

Jeffrey volunteered, "Chief, let me give him a call and assure him that I did not leak or compromise his privacy to the Statesman. I will let him know that we are taking this very serious."

The commissioner confirmed that would be a good idea. "I will start putting out fires from my end. Get back to me Jeffrey as soon as you have something, and wish your daughter a happy birthday from me."

Jeffrey placed the phone down and at the same time pressed the end call button. He went to his jacket hanging in the hall, removing his black Moleskin notepad, flipping it to the entry that had the senator's number. He dialed the number and waited. The phone rang three times before Peter Shaw answered with a firm, "Hello."

Jeffrey began, "Good afternoon, sir. I'm sorry to bother you, but it has been brought to my attention that the Austin Statesman has fired the young lady that was with you this afternoon when I had you sign those statements. I can assure you, sir, that I did not leak that information to the Statesman."

Peter chimed in before Jeffrey could finish his sentence. "Detective," Peter retorted, "I am not sure how they got the information that Alicia was here. What I am confident about is the fact that only you, Alicia and I knew she was here when you had me sign those statements. I am confident that Alicia or I did not call the Statesman and inform the editor. That seems to leave you."

Jeffrey defended himself. "Sir, I assure you it was not me that called the Statesman. I have a bit of research I need to do to find out how this happened. I did mention her presence casually at the station and I need to find out who heard my comments and leaked the information. Give me some time to narrow it down and I will get back to you on Monday with some answers."

Peter could sense the sincerity in Jeffrey's voice and eased up his tirade. "Jeffrey, I honestly trust you. I am upset that my privacy has been compromised and Alicia getting fired is not acceptable."

Jeffrey seized this moment to apologize. He felt that the editor finding out about Alicia was somehow his responsibility. "Sir, I am so sorry this has happened. I take your privacy, and our relationship, far more important than anything the editor of the Statesman can do for our department or me. I will get to the bottom of this. Would you like me to call Alicia and apologize?"

Peter was confident that Jeffrey would find out

how this happened. He realized that he was unintentionally responsible, and that was enough to get him on the hunt. Guilt would be the motivator for Jeffrey and Peter was comfortable with his apology and sincerity.

"No, that's okay Jeffrey. I do want you to get some answers, as I don't think this sort of thing should be allowed. Don't worry about Alicia just yet. Let's find out who was responsible for the loss of her job and then that would be the time for you to talk to her." With that, Peter told Jeffrey to return to the party and put the phone down.

Jeffrey felt anger well up inside him. He had his integrity brought into question and for the first time in his career he had to apologize to a person he was investigating. He promised himself that he would find out who had leaked the information and quickly. For now, he had to clear his mind of the speculations and focus on his family and his daughter's birthday.

Alicia donned her cowgirl boots and pranced in front of the full-length mirror. Standing with her back to the mirror, she strained her head over her left shoulder first, and then reversing looked over her right shoulder. She was satisfied with her look, the dress was not too short, but short enough to show off her shapely legs. As she checked herself out in the mirror, the chimes of the doorbell let her know that Tim was at the door and on time.

"Mom can you get the door for me?" she asked.

Her mother went to the door. Looking through the spy hole she could see Tim outside, looking down at his shoes and holding a bunch of flowers. Tim offered his hand, which Alicia's mother accepted. "Tim," he said, making sure not to apply too much pressure to her mother's hand, yet enough pressure to make sure it was a confident handshake.

Her mother smiled and said, "Brenda. Nice to meet you, Tim."

Tim walked past her, heading in the direction of her loosely pointing arm, past the stairs and into the open plan kitchen adjoining the small but comfortable living room. Alicia's mother pointed for Tim to take a chair and told him to make himself at home. Tim gave the flowers to Alicia's mother saying, "Brenda, these are for you."

"How nice," she responded. She took the flowers and presented them to her nose with a deep inward breath and a satisfying, "Mmmmmm," which let Tim know that his gift was accepted with approval. She took the flowers to the kitchen and reached to one of the higher cabinets above the sink for a suitable vase to put them in. She arranged them carefully. "I love fresh flowers. Thanks!"

Alicia made her entrance. Tim stood, admiring what he was about to be seen with downtown. Her mother told her to come and look at the flowers Tim had got her. "They are for me!" she preened.

Alicia was pleased that Tim was so considerate and thought, "What a slick one you are, Tim, to get my mother flowers. A very nice touch." This was a part of Tim she had not expected and it surprised her.

She kissed her mother and at the same time clearly laid the time scale for her date. "We won't be late mom. I have got to be at Peter's by 10:00 a.m. tomorrow."

Tim grinned as he repeated, "Peter? Good for you, girl."

Trying to find a place to park on Sixth Street on a Saturday night was no small feat. Tim had to park about a mile from where Bo was playing. As they parked, he opened the door for Alicia and placed his arm around her in a very natural and acceptable way. The walk down Sixth Street was part of the fun. Austin blues music and people were spilling into the street. The Austin logo 'Keep Austin Weird' had no need to worry. The weird was very much evident and the carnival atmosphere made it a fun place to be.

As they arrived at Antone's it was still pretty early. Bo was on the stage setting up, but as soon as he noticed Tim he stopped what he was doing, jumped off the stage and came over to say hello and be introduced to Alicia. Bo was short, good looking and friendly, offering his hand to Alicia as Tim introduced them to each other. Tim kept his arm around Alicia's shoulder as Bo repeated his name, shook Alicia's hand and kept the conversation going.

"Well, even a blind hog finds an acorn sometimes," said Bo. "What's a good looking girl like you doing with Tim?" he continued, grinning and accepting the friendly punch Tim placed on his shoulder. He led them to a table he had some of his gear at and told them to take a seat. Alicia sat down and Tim asked her and Bo if they wanted a drink.

Alicia accepted, "Just a light beer."

Tim asked, "What brand?"

Alicia said, "It really doesn't matter as long as it's light." Alicia had not acquired a taste for beer or any other alcohol. She did not mind people drinking around her, but she personally only drank to be sociable.

Bo declined, explaining he already had a drink and needed to get his gear ready. Tim went to the bar and Bo excused himself to continue with his set up. Alicia sat looking around and studying all the pictures of past stars that had played the venue. She was concentrating so hard she missed that Tim had returned with his hands full. Placing the drinks down he made himself at home beside her. She sipped the cold beer and Tim asked if the drink was okay. Alicia finished swallowing, wiped her mouth and nodded her approval. "It's fine, thanks."

Tim asked, "Do you like dancing?"

Alicia leaned forward to take another sip and confirmed she enjoyed dancing and at the same time returned the question to Tim. "Do you like to dance?"

"I'm not bad, but I would not call myself good at it."

Alicia laughed, saying, "I did not ask how good you are. I asked if you liked to dance."

Tim laughed with her saying, "To be honest, I

am a bit self conscious, but if you want to dance, we will dance." he smiled. Alicia liked this and made a mental note that they would dance once the music got going.

Bo opened up his set with a blues number he had written that focused the audience and let them know they had a quality performer on stage. Tim smiled and shouted over the music so that Alicia could hear. "He's good, isn't he?"

She shouted in agreement. "Yes!"

It was Bo's fourth number before Tim felt confident enough to attempt dancing. Alicia thought Tim's dancing was not that bad and was secretly pleasantly relieved. She told Tim he was good as they returned to the table.

Bo joined them during his break and Alicia told him how good he was and asked where she could get hold of his music. Bo explained he was selling his music online and gave Alicia a card with all the web details for her to download his songs.

Bo again started playing, the time flying by. It was soon time for Alicia to remind Tim she had to be heading home. They mouthed, "Bye," to Bo, and he acknowledged it with a nod in their direction, not breaking a beat. The drive home was fun. Tim stopped at a late night taco shop that he swears was the winner of some unheard of Best Tex-Mex Taco in Texas competition. He laughed at his own stupidity for bringing it up. They both enjoyed the over filled tacos in the car park of the taco stand. Alicia realized she was beginning to like Tim more and by the time she arrived at her house the first goodnight kiss was not as intimidating as she had expected, converting the relationship from friendship to boyfriend and girlfriend easily.

As she exited the car, she again turned and thanked Tim for a great night. "I hope we can do it again soon." The door closed and Alicia headed towards her house door.

Tim admired how fit she looked as she walked away, then he shouted, "Give me a call after your meeting with Peter Shaw."

Alicia shouted back, "Will do. Night," as she kissed her hand and held it high over her right shoulder and continued her progress to the door.

Chapter 10

Leaving the house slightly later than she planned, Alicia pointed her car west, placing the low morning sun behind her. Her mind drifted back to the previous night: Tim, Bo and 6th Street. She was glad she had gone and looked forward to spending more time with Tim. The memory of his lanky, loping dance brought a grin to her face. She looked at the clock on her dash. It was only 9:30 a.m., a bit too early to call and thank Tim for a great time. She decided to leave that until the evening.

Arriving at Peter's, she was surprised to find him sitting on the porch next to the front door sipping coffee. The door was ajar and Peter was enjoying the morning air. She closed the door of her car and approached Sir Peter Edward Shaw. How uniquely strange he had become; so different from the Peter before the accident. She warmed to the casualness of the situation and joined Peter, sitting next to him.

"Beautiful morning, Alicia," Peter said as he slid over so she could lean against the wall rather than the frame of the door. "I have been watching and listening to that Mockingbird. He has a wonderful vocal range. I often see him going after a cat that likes to stalk the neighborhood, absolutely fearless. He flies in, pecks the cat on the rear end, always keeping just out of reach. The cat will run for cover across the lawn, under that low bush." He pointed with his hand towards the Privet on the side of the drive. "Such confidence for such a little bird," he remarked.

"I have one at our house," Alicia responded. "He starts his day off on top of the gable of the roof, singing at the top of his voice; just letting everyone know that he is."

Peter laughed at her understanding and went straight into her dismissal from the statesman. "I'm so sorry your visit yesterday cost you your job."

Alicia shrugged her shoulders. "It was not a job, it was an internship. The editor had demoted me to telephone sales and I was not getting paid. Getting fired did me a favor. Now I can concentrate on your story."

"Well, I want you to know," Peter responded, "I have been in touch with several people and let them know that I am not very happy that a confidence in my privacy has been compromised by the Austin Police Department. I talked to Detective Granger. It was definitely leaked through him. Was it intentional? I don't think so. He called me from his house during his daughter's birthday party and assured me he would find out who leaked this and why. He asked if I could give him a couple of days and promised he would get back to me with answers. I do trust him. He sounded sincere and upset." He paused, and then added, "I do trust him."

Their attention was demanded once again by the Mockingbird. It landed on the uppermost branch of a massive Live Oak, flicked its tail high pointing down with both wings, and opened its lungs to exude a song to match that of any Nightingale. Alicia and Peter sat silently, both enjoying the warmth of the morning sun as they watched, spell bound, enjoying the company of each other and the attention demands of the Mockingbird.

Peter broke the moment as he attempted to get himself up from the porch. "I love sitting here watching the day unfold, but I think I have done a bit too much sitting. Would you mind helping this old man get up?"

Alicia quickly put down her iPad and note pad, sprang to her feet and offered Peter her hands to try and help him stand. Peter accepted one of her hands, turned so he was kneeling, and then with as much effort as he could muster tried to stand. Alicia pulled with all she had, but both realized it was not going to happen. Peter started laughing and Alicia was soon affected by the humor of the moment, sharing in the laughter and quieting the Mockingbird. He released his hand from her grip and returned to the kneeling position, still laughing. Bare feet, old jeans, long hair, and stuck to the floor; for sure not the Peter of old, Alicia pondered.

Peter finally controlled his laughter. "Would you be so kind to go to the kitchen and get a chair?" he asked.

Alicia returned quickly with a chair and placed it in front of the still-kneeling Peter, making sure the chair was planted firmly. He placed one hand on the chair and with Alicia helping, managed to stand enough so that he could turn and place himself on the chair. He thanked Alicia and explained, "Getting old is tough, not for the weak of heart."

Once he felt rested enough to attempt to stand and separate himself from the support of the chair, Alicia picked up her laptop and note pad, linked arms with Peter, and arm-in-arm they made their way through the large front door, then down the hall towards the library.

Peter took his place on the large sofa and Alicia took her place behind the desk. She switched on her iPad and connected to the Wi-Fi, which the iPad remembered from the previous day. He turned to her and asked, "Alicia, where were we?" She reviewed the previous day's story and Peter picked up from where they had left off.

"As it happened," Peter explained, "Hawk's prediction had been just in time."

The Hairless Ones attacked as predicted that night. Wolf had moved all of his hunters out of the huts. The village consisted of about twenty huts made from wood and flora collected from the area. The hut's construction consisted of six large beams locked together at the top with animal sinew, much like a teepee, but exposed enough to let out smoke from the cooking fires inside.

Large palm-like leaves were laid around the structure from the ground to the apex and covering it all were large treated animal skins which were laid over the outside of the leaves and locked in place with twine made from plants and vines. This construction provided a warm, dry environment that protected the tribe. The entrance to the hut was an area that had animal skins loosely hanging over the un-thatched entrance. Outside of each hut were drying racks holding skins, and also pallets, which held roots and edible plants. Each hut could sleep up to ten people; most holding the immediate family, grandparents through to the children, sleeping and eating as one. In the center of each hut was an area to hold the fire. The fire was used for warmth and also to dry and smoke meats and fish, a major part of the high-protein diet these large-boned and massively muscular beings required.

The village's topography was on a hillock surrounded on three sides by trees. The fourth side faced east and fronted the river and the row of dugouts used to fish and to transport the women to hunt roots and herbs. The small hill the village was on protected it against flooding from the river, which happened every rainy season.

Wolf realized that to gain an advantage, he needed to give the village the appearance of normalcy. A large fire was built in the center of the village and small branches were collected and wrapped in skins to give the appearance of young hunters sitting around the fire. When everything was in place the elders that still had some fight in them took up positions inside the huts, armed and ready. Wolf told them when the signal was given to stay inside and make noise like they were panicking, drawing the attention of Death Dog's troops. This would give Wolf time to get his troops close to the Hairless Ones undetected.

Wolf positioned his prime troops outside the village. When hunting large animals, the hunters would bury themselves beside a pathway that they knew the large animals would take. The ability to camouflage was vital to make this technique successful. It also required the courage of the hunter who had to lie perfectly still while the large animals were sometimes only inches away. The hunters would wait for the opportune moment, then carefully position themselves to thrust a poison-coated stabbing-spear deep into the heel of the animal, then quickly retreat to safety. They would then follow the animal, sometimes for two to three days, before the poison would take effect, dropping the animal and allowing the hunter to move in and finish off the wounded prey. This could still be very dangerous, as often the young or mate of the fallen would hang around and protect the fallen animal. Also, the wounded animals would focus whatever energy they had left to kill or maim their tormenter.

Wolf personally checked that every hunter was in place and was well hidden. They all knew that they had to wait for the non-verbal instruction from Wolf to attack. They had been given an advantage because of the pre-warning Hawk had given to them that it was time.

Wolf's Neanderthal rock and stick clubs and

short heavy stabbing spears were no match for the long throwing atlatls the Hairless Ones were using. Wolf had seen the Hairless Ones hunt using these throwing spears, bringing game down at sixty paces. Their weaponry was superior at long range, but Wolf's hunters were more powerful and superior when the combat was at close quarters. Wolf had to get the combat hand to hand if he was going to be successful in destroying Death Dog's attackers.

Once all of Wolf's troops were in place, he dug himself in and then carefully covered himself and cleared his mind. He felt the spiritual presence of Hawk, which he found comforting. He let Wolf know that the women and children were all safe at the cave. The fact the women and children were safely hidden removed a burden from Wolf, allowing him to focus on the battle that was about to commence.

The sunset and the darkness of the night matured. The night sky was clear, alive with stars, and the moon, being in the first phases, finally appeared, a mere slither in the night sky.

Death Dog brought his troops under cover of darkness into position one mile to the south of the village. His physical appearance was fearsome. On his head he wore the upper part of a wolf's skull, the fur matted and stinking around his neck. The lower mandible of a massive male Neanderthal hung on his bare painted chest, the large perfect teeth pointing outwards. Both of his arms were painted blue to the elbows. From his waist hung a belt made of finger bones, dried ears and other body parts ripped from the corpses of his fallen enemies. His powerful body was large for a Hairless One. His father, Hawk's brother, provided the Y chromosome that gave him the welcome Neanderthal traits. His feet were covered in fur and bound with twine made from sinew. He was an evil, sadistic killer who controlled with fear.

He enjoyed killing and torturing his captures, skinning them alive; seeing how long he could keep them alive as he removed their skin. It was his pleasure to make them watch him as he devoured their flesh. He had developed great skills at skinning and could remove the lids from the eyes without damaging the eye itself, so the person being tortured could not escape his gaze.

His sadistic traits were not restricted to his enemies. If he felt he had been failed or his orders had not been successfully completed, he was quick to employ the same techniques on whoever, in his sick mind, had failed him. He enjoyed the fact that his subordinates hated and feared him.

For Death Dog, this was his day of redemption. He hated Hawk with a passion and held him responsible for his expulsion from the tribe. He also felt that his father, being the elder of the family, should not have allowed Hawk to be the tribe's Shaman. He wanted Hawk taken alive. The time had come for payback.

Hawk was quiet in the back of the cave, deep in meditation. His head was bent back, his eyes were closed and his breathing was deep. The vision he was witnessing was troubling, but one he had to witness. The sun was setting; the women were at the river playing with the children and preparing for another day. One young mother held her child who was not enjoying having the water of the river poured over its head, then rubbed hard as it fell away. The hunters were gathered by the large community fire, which had been built in the middle of the village. It was much like the ebb of any other day. This peaceful vision was broken with a woman screaming, which quickly got the attention of the hunters.

From the trees emerged a massive wolf with filthy fur, red eyes, a mouth full of massive, drooling teeth. It was running at the children and grabbed one by the leg. The mother of the child ran at the dog, attempting to stop it from dragging away her screaming son. The dog stopped, releasing its grip on the child's mangled leg, and moved its attention from retreating and dragging the child to the trees to killing him. He repositioned himself over the screaming child, biting into the neck and shaking its massive head from side to side, quieting the child quickly in death. The wolf then turned its attention to the mother who stopped her forward momentum, still screaming and holding her leather water sack above her head, trying her best to scare the dog from her now silent, lifeless child.

In three large bounds, the massive dog brought the now-retreating mother down and proceeded to tear into her, removing large threads of her intestines hanging from its blood covered mouth. It turned and made its way back to the child, leaving the mother helpless and mortally wounded.

The hunters were closing the gap but the dog did not seem to be in a hurry. They were running in slow motion, unable to get within effective range to kill the dog. The dog arrived at the fallen child. Looking at the hunters as they attempted to reach him, but were nightmarishly slowed as if running in thick toffee, it raised its leg and pissed on the motionless child, tainting the meat, which it left and retreated back to the forest. This was not a good vision. It disturbed Hawk, but it was one he felt he had to keep to himself.

Death Dog primed his killers with his plans for the attack and started to move them forward. Two separate groups of six were instructed and left separately, taking the southerly and northerly entrances respectfully. Four of his best joined him by skirting around the village and approaching it along the edge of the river. The effect was a pincher movement. He expected the two troops of six would scare the tribe, and the enemy would try to escape to their dugouts into the river and freedom. However, he would be waiting for them. When all of his troops were in position, Death Dog would signal with a scream; a sign the attack should begin.

The three groups stealthily maneuvered into position. Wolf could hear them approach as he lay silent, calming his breath so it would become almost inaudible. He hid under an overhanging shrub next to the path as the hairless soldiers maneuvered only inches away. Their steps were soft and chosen wisely. If any one of Death Dog's troops should forewarn the tribe with a misplaced step or breaking of a twig it would cost them their life.

Wolf's keen sense of smell picked up the Hairless Ones' scent as they approached. He lay silent and hidden as they passed. He cleared his mind and communicated the amount that had passed him and with the intelligence his other troops gave him through thought, he was able to establish the amount of troops Death Dog was bringing against them. He reassured his troops, telling them to stay hidden.

The total, including the six that had taken the southerly path, did not seem an overwhelming force to Wolf. He felt confident that he would be able to attack their flank and get within striking distance. He needed to get the fighting on a hand-to-hand basis before they were discovered, giving his troops the edge they needed.

His troops remained silent and hidden as the Hairless Ones maneuvered into the village and as quietly as possible placed themselves within range of the hunter mannequins apparently asleep near the fire. They approached, crouching and silent, the throwing spears loaded into the atlatls; excitably awaiting the signal from Death Dog for the mayhem to commence.

Death Dog's troops were in position. They lined up in front of the dugouts, their atlatls cocked and loaded. He could make out his hunters in the shadows; he waited patiently until he was sure. He then raised both his arms into the air and let out a screaming yell, which was the signal that his troops had been waiting.

Wolf heard the scream and in unison all of his troops raised from their hiding places, synchronicity apparent in their movement. When hunting, they would run all perfectly in sync, much like a shoal of fish or flock of birds. Now the synchronization had a more sinister motive. To the observer, their massive form rising up from the ground was zombie-like. The Neanderthal's had a heavy lurching gate as they moved unseen, each one of them selecting a separate target.

As Death Dog's soldiers unleashed the first volley, each spear easily found its target. The thirty paces between the mannequins and the throwers was an easy range for these seasoned killers. The spears landed, but the reaction of the fake hunters gathered around the fire was not natural. Death Dog's soldiers moved forward towards the fire, confused. One of the younger soldiers, Ape, ran forward attacking one of the mannequins, ripping the skin from the twig structure revealing the hoax. From the huts began a loud wailing, which again confused Death Dog's attackers. They realized the mannequins sitting around the fire were not the young hunters, so they turned their focus towards the huts. The killer's began moving toward the hut the noise was coming from. Death Dog could clearly see the confusion of his troops, but remained in position excitably awaiting the arrival of the first runners. The gap between Wolf's Neanderthals and the Hairless troops narrowed and they remained unseen.

Death Dog was the first to notice the movement in the shadows and realized his advantage was slipping away. He started to run forward, screaming at his squad to follow him. Running at full speed, he was able to get within atlatl range. Still at a full run, he unleashed a throwing spear, which found its target.

The young Neanderthal stopped dead in his tracks, dropped his weapons as both hands stiffened and opened. Not understanding what had happened, he looked down at his chest at the shaft of the spear buried deep and unmoving as he pulled at it to remove it. Dropping to his knees still confused he rolled on to his back and looked up into the darkness as the adrenalin flowed out of his body, leaving him with an overwhelming desire to close his eyes and sleep. He could feel the presence of Hawk as he drifted towards the light that now filled his world. Comforted by Hawk's presence, he accepted the light without fear.

Wolf saw his young soldier fall and was able to quickly identify Death Dog who had stopped running and was standing with the light of the fire flickering on his deathly image. His soldiers were running headlong to attack the young Neanderthals who were about to attack the flank of Death Dog's soldiers. This was a mistake. As they clashed, the massively boned Neanderthals attacked with skill using the heavy clubs and stabbing spears. Death Dog remained out of range of the clubs and picked off two more from a distance of thirty steps. He screamed at his soldiers to fall back. He had to regroup, as the close combat with the large Neanderthals was a battle he couldn't win.

Those that could broke free, but three were caught and were noisily dispatched by the Neanderthals. They screamed, trying to escape the bone crushing clubs. Wolf went to assist one of his soldiers finishing off a wriggling, screaming Hairless One. Placing a powerful foot on his back, he raised the massive stone and wooden club and then delivered the blow to the head of Death Dog's soldier. The head now misshaped, broken and silent, allowed Wolf and his soldiers to refocus on the retreating Death Dog's force.

The Hairless Ones were much lighter and faster, moving quickly in the direction of Death Dog and passing the advantage back to Death Dog's soldiers. They were now out of range of the clubs and stabbing spears, but close enough for the atlatls to devastate the closing, lumbering Neanderthals.

Death Dog moved forward and started to unleash spears, finding his targets and dropping the Neanderthals one after another. His retreating soldiers regrouped and joined him in stopping and devastating the diminishing defenders.

The elders had come from the huts and joined Wolf in the defense of the village. They were throwing their heavy stabbing spears and clubs, but Deaths Dog's soldiers were out of range. In very short order the number of Neanderthals still standing and able to put up a fight was not enough. The Hairless Ones were taunting them, trying to go around the sides of what remained so they could encircle the group and finish them off.

Wolf realized they were done for and was preparing to launch a final attack when Hawk communicated loudly in his mind that they must retreat. Wolf was confused, but quickly transmitted the order to his troops. Those that were able started to back away from the huts and take cover. Wolf and four of his soldiers were able to make it to the thick forest.

The cover of the trees and undergrowth made the atlatls not as effective and the pursuers knew the odds were not in their favor, returning quickly to the exposed Neanderthals still in the village. The Hairless Ones focused their aggression on the remaining Neanderthals. They would not close in on them, but ran around them unleashing well-aimed spears, which easily found their target. The last five Neanderthals, which consisted of four elders and one young hunter, tightened their formation, dropping their weapons and submitting to the inevitable. Standing with their heads lowered and surrounded by screaming Hairless Ones, they were removed of their weapons and corralled by their capturers.

It was immediately apparent to Death Dog that Hawk was not amongst the captured or the fallen. He quickly instructed two of his troop to hunt down the runners. They immediately picked up the spoor of Wolf and his four hunters, tracking them into the forest.

Death Dog ordered the burning of the village. His remaining soldiers pillaged the huts before setting them ablaze. Wolf could smell the burning and hear the screaming of the Hairless Ones as he retreated deeper into the forest, still under cover of darkness, with what remained of his force. He was devastated by the loss of the village, but he could not take the time feel sorry for himself as he and his troops continued away from the village.

The two pursuing Hairless Ones were able to follow the tracks and could smell the Neanderthals as they retreated. They realized they did not have the advantage in the thick forest, so they had to pick the perfect place to attack. They needed a clearing where they could pick them off safely. Wolf kept his troops moving silently through the thick undergrowth and continued for the next two hours to remain protected by the forest. The dawn was slow to come, its red glow piercing the forest from the east. The light was behind Wolf and welcome. He knew that Hawk would now be able to guide him and warn him of any forces that might be in pursuit of him. Hawk was watching and as the light raced across the canopy of the forest, he was able to pick up the two Hairless Ones who were pursuing Wolf. Hawk guided Wolf through the forest to a natural ravine, which led to a small subsidiary of the river. The deep tree covered sides would be the ideal place to trap the pursuers who did not know that Wolf was aware he was being pursued, or that the hawk flying high above was watching.

The Hairless Ones knew they were close. They could smell Wolf and his Neanderthals. They could also see the fresh damage to the undergrowth, apparent by sap seeping from the wounded flora. They wanted to make sure they did not come upon them too early, so progress in the direction of the signs was deliberate and contrived. As they approached the ravine, they could see the tracks leading down and the clear signs that one of the escapees had ripped a handful of flora as he had tried to support himself from sliding downwards uncontrolled.

Wolf led his team down through the ravine. Then he and one other soldier backtracked up the ravine to take cover and wait for the Hairless Ones to spring the trap. The other two troops left tracks along the ravine in the opposite direction.

The Hairless Ones confidently inspected the signs and proceeded down into the ravine. When they had passed, Wolf loudly dropped in behind them while the two below closed off the escape.

The Hairless Ones realized instantly that they had walked into a trap. The one nearest Wolf was holding on to a large sapling with his left hand to steady himself as he unsheathed a flint knife from his belt with his right hand to fight off Wolf. The Hairless One further down the ravine broke and started to run.

One of Wolf's hunters leapt from the side of the ravine, surprising both Wolf and the Hairless One as he landed heavily into the fight; breaking the sapling and smashing into the Hairless One, making him drop his knife and forcing him to the ground. As they rolled, the Neanderthal started striking with his heavy club and before the pair had stopped rolling, the killing was done.

Wolf could clearly hear the shortened scream as the one who attempted to run ran headlong down the slope into a club that appeared from behind a tree and smashed into his face, killing him instantly.

Alicia stopped her recording, dropped her hands to her sides, leaned back against the back of the chair, and without saying a word straightened her legs and stared at the ceiling. She remained silent and deep in thought, mulling over the savagery and consequence of what she was hearing.

Peter remained silent and watched until Alicia refocused her gaze from the ceiling to him. She asked why Hawk had not killed the Hairless Ones when they were born. Peter explained, "When the mutation first appeared, they did not realize how different these Hairless Ones were. In the first instance they were accepted, much like a handicap child today. They were loved as all children were loved. It was not until the child reached adolescence that the aggression became dangerously apparent and a problem. The hairless children's vocal abilities developed and they started to communicate between themselves using voice. The ability for them to communicate using thought was much limited; this sense had weakened with the loss of hair. However, with voice came ego and self-betterment.

It was soon learned by the tribes not to trust the hairless children; they would steal and hide food and tools for personal use. They had no concept of working for the betterment of the family and would aggressively go after things they felt they needed, often just hoarding for no other reason but to prevent others from having it. When the tribes made a decision to expel the Hairless Ones, they had no idea they would group together and become such a threat.

The mutation was not a slow process. The Hairless Ones, by using aggression and ego, found themselves in a situation where they could take advantage, as in Darwin's observations: if the mutation gives the individual an advantage in the environment it finds itself, it will dominate and eventually wipe out the weaker variant. We, Alicia, are mutations of the Neanderthals, caused through the small breeding stock. This led to inbreeding, causing certain markers in the DNA strand to be turned off."

Alicia responded, "I thought evolution meant new and improved. Losing the ability to communicate through thought and develop aggression is a devastating step backwards."

Peter responded, "I agree, but you have to understand how aggressive the desire by an individual to procreate is. That is the main motivator in nature and it is extremely aggressive. You can watch lions kill the young of a mother to prevent the spread of an intruder's DNA. Mix that desire with the cunning of ego and you have the Alpha Male syndrome, which our society has always respected in life, business and war. It's what they call being the winner."

Alicia reluctantly agreed, commenting, "I still see it as a step backwards."

"As a group species, the mutation was devastating and costly for the betterment of a few. However, in today's competitive environment, you will see it will be an argument where you will find many who will pick up the gauntlet saying how that aggression and win at all costs attitude has improved society. Society today is moving further away from the benefits of a tribe or group; they want self-promotion and independence. They retreat to their little box to enjoy the spoils of their personal success."

Peter then asked Alicia to help him up, explaining that he had better go and lay down, again telling Alicia she could stay if she wanted. She declined, helped Peter up from the sofa, and then made her way home.

Chapter 11

Alicia headed down the long drive from Peter's massive house and voice-dialed Tim using the blue tooth. "Call Tim."

The phone went through its process then confirmed it was dialing Tim. "Calling Tim, mobile." Then the phone started to ring.

Tim answered. "I was wondering if you were going to call today."

"Well, I would have called you earlier as I was on the way to Peter's, but I thought it would be a bit early for you. I wanted to thank you for last night. I really enjoyed it. Bo is awesome."

This made Tim's day. "He is great. I have known Bo for a long time. I'm really pleased you enjoyed his music. Are you going to do anything this afternoon?"

Alicia looked at her watch; it was only 1:30p.m. "I was thinking of going for a walk with my mother around the Bastrop State Park. I could do with the exercise. You are more than welcome to join us."

Tim was glad she had asked him and confirmed that he would join her. "That would be great. I have been lying around the house and could do with the exercise myself. What time?"

"Let me get home and change; let's say three

o'clock at my place?"

"That will work." Then, clearly wanting to drag the conversation out, he asked, "Well, how did the interview with Peter go?"

Alicia said, "It is really deep and absolutely enthralling. I could listen to him all day, but he is not in the best of health, so he can only do so much before he feels tired and needs to rest. His story is awesome. I will go over it with you on the walk if you want."

"Sure," responded Tim. "I will let you go and get ready myself. See you at your place."

Tim arrived at Alicia's house on time, but before he could get out of his car, Alicia and her mother, Brenda, appeared and headed towards the car. He quickly started to sling stuff around to make room for them in a vain attempt to make the car look respectable. Note pads, laptop, and other tidbits were quickly placed on the driver's side back seat. They climbed in, Alicia moving to the back seat and her mother riding shotgun.

Alicia started to give Tim directions when he informed her he had been there before. He then asked, "How often do you walk the park, Brenda?" He was curious as she still looked good for her guestimated age of forty-five.

Brenda ran the park three times a week to keep in shape, but replied with a simple, "A couple of times a week," and left it at that.

"Alicia, what about you?" Tim asked as he physically maneuvered the mirror and his head so he was looking directly at Alicia in the back seat. She picked up on his grin that accompanied the question.

"Don't you worry about me, Tim-O. You won't have to hang around for me."

They arrived at the park gate. Brenda showed her pass to the state-employed gatekeeper who recognized her although she was not in her car and waved the vehicle through, not checking her pass for the expiration date. Tim parked the car and they all piled out. Tim asked, "Well, what way do you want to go?"

Alicia responded, "It really doesn't matter to me."

Tim responded, "According to nature, it does."

"Really?" said Brenda.

Tim answered by quoting, almost verbatim, some trivia he had researched in the past. "We run counterclockwise because everything in nature tends towards a counterclockwise motion. The list of natural phenomenon that runs counterclockwise is amazing. For example, the molecule structure of amino acids, the shape of seashells, the rotational direction of all the planets, except Venus, and the orbital direction of the earth around the sun. As for manmade events, you have carrousels, windmills, except in Ireland, revolving doors, cable operated airplanes, the usual direction in which people spin Hula Hoops, baseball runners and Elvis' hips all move counterclockwise. So, one could assume, Alicia, it is important." He finished, grinning from ear to ear.

Brenda again chimed in, joining in the humor. "Well, in that case we had better go this way." They started on the three-mile walk around the state park in a counterclockwise direction. "By coincidence, I do tend to feel more comfortable going around the park this way. Strange!"

Alicia joined arms with her mother, and Tim, not wanting to be left out, linked arms with Alicia and made sure he was in step, skipping to adjust his stride to comply. After making sure he was in step he said, "Unicity."

Alicia gave his arm a comforting squeeze and at the same time said, "Tim, you are such a nerd."

Tim answered, "Nerds are cool."

After a few moments, he asked, "What did Sir Peter Shaw have to say today?"

Brenda also confirmed her interest. "Yes, how did it go today, Alicia?"

Alicia remained quiet for a moment, thinking deeply about whether she should let Tim in on what was happening. It was then she felt the presence of Peter. "It's okay, it's okay." She could feel him telling her that it was okay to share the story. She mumbled "wow" under her breath, marveling at Peter's ability before she began to share his story.

They walked arm in arm counterclockwise around the meandering path, through the stoic pines, going over the story. Brenda and Tim were quiet and focused, both realizing the importance of the story to Alicia. Two miles quickly passed, as did the story. Tim had some questions about the inbreeding and he wanted more details about the Neanderthal tribes. Alicia was able to explain better than she had realized, telling of how they lived.

"Imagine a small village with a few people. They have weapons that they use to hunt with, not using them for war. They enjoy the labor of their hands, they do not waste time inventing laborsaving machines, and they have reached a very practical knowledge level, which they share via thought and dream. They do not travel far since they dearly love their homes. Although they have boats they are not used for travel, they are used for fishing and gathering food. They are content with healthy food gathered locally. Their clothing is practical and useful. They really are satisfied and content. It is an egoless society, each individual being content to be part of the tribe, sharing in the joys and losses of the individuals within the unit. This contentment was ultimately to become their downfall. The bloodline lacked variety and mutations started to appear."

"It's almost like the bible," said Tim.

Brenda wanted clarity. "What do you mean, Tim; like the bible?"

Tim answered, "It sounds like the Garden of Eden."

Brenda added, "As in the Book of Genesis?"

Tim then asked, "Have you studied the bible, Brenda?"

Brenda replied, "Oh, yes. I was brought up in

rural south Texas by loving, God fearing, and strict southern Baptist parents. Attending Sunday school and bible study on a regular basis when I was young was not an option; and when I was young I enjoyed it. In my late teens I started to question some of what I was hearing. In my early twenties, I rejected the church and its teachings, mainly because of the long-standing prejudices held in the south. In the eighties and nineties, the N-word was common, conflicting with what I would hear as the words of Christ on Sunday. It seemed as if the congregation had missed the point. Then I had a young preacher try to convince me that whites and blacks were different. Not just in color, but at every level different. He literally did not see them as human. It was the final straw and not the message I was getting in church. I did not like it and refused to attend the church again. My parents were devastated, especially when I married a non-practicing Catholic, Alicia's father, but eventually they accepted it." She paused a moment, then added, "It does seem similar to the story in Genesis."

As they walked enjoying the waning afternoon, the pines were starting to come alive with flocks of marauding starlings filling the air with movement and noise. They returned to the car, piling in with an agreed destination and purpose. They were all going to enjoy some of Brenda's spaghetti, one of Alicia's favorites.

The piping hot spaghetti was soon on the table and, with Tim leading the gathering in a very short prayer of thanks, a common practice in Texas, they began enjoying their dinner. As they filled their plates, the conversation again returned to Peter's story. Tim wanted to dig deeper into the Garden of Eden similarities. Tim was a seasoned reporter and was expert at digging for the story, as were all three gathered around the table. Tim floated a hypothesis. "Let's assume for a moment that the people who wrote or told the story of the original sin and the Garden of Eden received it as a dream. For the sake of discussion, and please correct me if I am wrong Brenda, Eve was from Adam, I think from his rib. This would make them have the identical DNA strand. If we can imagine a Shaman or Seer dreaming this vision and seeing the DNA, he could interpret it as a snake. The story in Genesis would be a warning against inbreeding."

Brenda stood and went to her bedroom to retrieve her family bible, which was beside her bed. Alicia got up and fired up her iPad. Both returned to the table with the research tools necessary to remove the speculation. Alicia started to type into Google the words Serpent and Garden of Eden, and then placed her finger over the search button. It quickly downloaded the result. She finished her mouthful of spaghetti, wiping the sauce the uncontrolled tails left on her chin.

"Okay, in the Book of Genesis, the serpent is portrayed as a deceptive creature or trickster who promotes as good what God had forbidden. The serpent appears in the Garden of Eden who tempts Eve to eat the fruit of the Tree of Knowledge and denies that death will be a result." After a short pause she continued. "Check this out. The Hebrew word nahash is used to identify the creature that appears in Genesis three, in the Garden of Eden. God placed Adam in the Garden to tend it, but he warned both Adam and Eve not to eat the fruit of the Tree of Knowledge, 'or you will die.' The serpent tells Eve that this is untrue, and that if she and the man eat the fruit they will have knowledge and will not die. So, Adam and Eve eat the fruit, but the knowledge they gain is loss of childlike innocence, and they are banished from the Garden. According to the rabbinical tradition, the serpent represents sexual desire."

Brenda interjected, "The serpent is desire to sin? I have never looked at it like that before. This does tie in nicely with Peter's story."

Alicia said, "Yes, it does. I wonder if Peter has looked at the possible correlation between the Book of Genesis and his story. The serpent in Genesis represents the DNA strand and the inbreeding is the original sin. The consequence: removal from the Garden of Eden, as in the Hebrew version; the loss of childlike innocence."

Brenda added, "I am not sure where I heard it, but I understand that ego starts developing in a child around the age of three, but it does not mature in a child until they reach puberty. Ego and selfishness seems to be exactly what they meant by the loss of childlike innocence."

The conversation at the table was deep. All were interested, and the consequences of Tim's hypothesis were profound.

Alicia blurted excitedly, "I can't wait to go over this with Peter tomorrow!"

Brenda stood up from the table and started to gather the cleaned plates. Tim quickly joined in, taking his plate to the sink, running it under the faucet to pre-clean it for the dishwasher.

Alicia joined them by the sink, opening the dishwasher to discover cleaned dishes inside that needed putting away. She removed the silverware and then started placing plates in the cupboards. Tim was waiting patiently with his cleaned plate to place it in the washer. Alicia then asked Tim, "What are you going to do tomorrow when you're asked to find out about the Peter Shaw story?"

Tim answered, "I don't think that's going to be a problem. The editor holds a briefing in his office at 8:30 a.m. every Monday to make sure we are all on the same page. That means going over any news that might have accrued over the weekend and also tying up any loose ends. Peter's story has become very much a loose end. None of the local news stations are working it as it has gone into hibernation until Peter has to pay the piper for his crimes. Peter's lawyer has put a lid on it; until it comes to court everything is speculation. Sir Peter Shaw still has enough clout in this town to make speculation a risky business. I think he will want to drop it until Peter has a court appearance."

Brenda turned the conversation back to food. "I have some apple pie and ice cream if anyone is still hungry."

Tim blurted out, "Yes, ma'am," and quickly returned to the table.

Alicia looked over at her mother, grinned and returned to the table to take her place next to the expecting Tim. She was starting to like Tim more and more, and he certainly had been able to make himself at home.

Brenda heated the apple pie, filling the house with aroma that was obviously having an effect on Tim. Alicia noted he would stop his conversation and keep turning his head to watch the progress of Brenda and the apple pie. Living the life of a bachelor meant that his normal meals were designed around bulk, not flavor, and speed rather than presentation, mainly sandwiches or some fast food. Homemade apple pie was a treat and the expectation was disturbing. Brenda arrived at the table with three plates of apple pie with the vanilla ice cream melting over the top. The conversation was minimal until the pie eating was done.

Alicia finally asked a question. "Who wrote the book of Genesis?"

Brenda answered, "It was believed that the Book of Genesis was written by Moses. Many assume that the book of Genesis was made up of oral traditions; just a bunch of stories passed on from one generation to the next or that Moses borrowed from the pagans. The views are starting to change. Many people are starting to realize that Moses did not plagiarize these accounts of creation and the flood. Instead, there is evidence that Moses took the earlier documents of Adam, Noah, Abraham, Enoch, Isaac, and Jacob. These are documents that were passed on from one generation to the next, and Moses put them together into one book called the Book of Genesis."

Tim complimented Brenda on her answer and said, "You really did attend bible study. Good for you."

"I am absolutely intrigued by the similarities between Peter's story and Genesis," said Alicia. "It will be interesting to see what Peter has to say about it."

Tim asked, "Where do you think this is going Alicia? Do you see it as a book, or what?"

Alicia answered, "I am doing what my mother told me. I am going to let the story decide where it is going. Peter has chosen me to help him get what happened to him down on paper. A lot of people would find it hard to believe. I have experienced Peter's abilities. He knows what I am thinking and if I am upset he senses it. He can communicate with me. The other thing is that he said he felt I was the one to write it down."

Tim said, "He actually said that?"

Alicia went over it in more detail. "I wanted to know why he was talking to me. In fact, I told him I was very new to reporting and that you would be better at it than me. He told me he had a very important story to tell and he felt I was the one to write it down. He said I was the one he needed to tell the story to."

Tim answered with a grin, "The chosen one."

Alicia responded, grinning as well, "Piss off,

Tim."

Dinner was finished and they all left the table, seating themselves in front of the television. Alicia and Tim were on the large leather sofa and Brenda in her recliner. Watching television together, Alicia raised her legs onto the ottoman and rested her head against Tim's arm. Tim, realizing an important step in this relationship had been achieved, and being pleased with the progress, slid his butt forward to a more reclined posture. They all watched TV together until Brenda decided it was time to retire with a good book, leaving Tim and Alicia to enjoy each other's company.

Tim left before midnight, kissing Alicia and asking her to call or text him the following day before he loosened his arms. She promised, kissing Tim once more before they separated. She stood by the door until Tim had reached his car. He looked back at Alicia waving one last good night before the door was closed.

Chapter 12

Alicia arrived at Peter's house to find the door ajar. Popping her head around the edge of the door, she called out, "Peter?" She paused a moment, then called again "Peter?"

Peter finally responded, "Come in Alicia, I am in the library."

Alicia walked down the hall to find Peter sitting behind his desk with a copy of the Harper Study Bible opened to the Book of Genesis. She grinned. "How did you know?"

"Let's just say I had a hunch; and that's what it was, honestly, a hunch," said Peter.

Alicia remained standing, placed most of the items she was carrying on the corner of Peter's desk, and then showed him a covered plate she was holding. "My mother sent you this, some homemade apple pie."

Peter responded, "How did she know?"

Alicia asked, "What?"

Peter grinned. "That I love apple pie and it's been too long since I have had some."

"Oh, it was just a hunch," responded Alicia with a matching grin. "Shall I put it in the fridge for you?" Alicia moved towards the door of the library before Peter could confirm with an answer.

"Yes, please, to the fridge; and yes, I really would like to meet your mother."

Alicia responded, "She would like to meet you too, Peter."

"We need to make that happen. Maybe she could come over some time this week," Peter said.

Alicia shouted from the kitchen. "I will tell her when I get home." As she returned to the library she asked, "Well, what did you think of the Genesis hypothesis?"

Peter looked down at the bible, put a pair of reading cheaters on, and placed his index figure on chapter two, verse sixteen and started reading. When he finished, he sat back, removed his glasses, paused then said. "It really could be a warning against inbreeding. The consequences for the sin: death and the loss of childlike innocence. I heard a report once of a Pygmy tribe that took it upon themselves to stop breeding because of inbreeding problems within the tribe. The children were being born terribly mutated and weak. I am sure it had been going on for a long time, their reduced stature being a sign of a genetic mutation caused through inbreeding. However, I thought it was an amazing selfless decision they made as a tribe. I don't think modern man, as a group, could make such a selfless decision. The desire for a male to produce a descendant is one of the strongest desires in nature. Modern man thinks he is above these primal desires. The advertising industry knows different. They rely strongly on that desire to move product. Convince

Joe Blow he can improve his chances with the opposite sex and you have a winner. At the end of the day, it comes down to that basic desire. The serpent in Genesis is that desire, and inbreeding could quite possibly be the original sin."

He remained quiet, and then looking up at the ceiling, said, "Hawk, how long have you been trying to let the world know?" His gaze returned to the bible on the desk in front of him, both his hands unconsciously came up in a praying position with the thumbs under his chin. He closed his eyes, expelling a long breath, and then lowered his hands.

Peter pushed back from the desk telling Alicia he needed to go and get some of her mother's apple pie that she had just placed in the fridge. Alicia stood and asked him, "Would you like me to get the pie for you?"

Peter grinned as he answered, "No, that's okay I could do with the exercise."

Both of them walked into the kitchen and Alicia proceeded to get a plate from one of the cupboards and a knife and fork from a small drawer to the left of the kitchen sink. She then went to the fridge and removed the pie. Peeling back the silver foil and cutting Peter a large slice, Alicia joined him at the kitchen table.

Peter looked at the pie. "You really must bring your mother around so that I can meet her," he said, spooning the first large bite into his mouth. He placed the fork down on the table, sat back and savored the moment.

Alicia asked, "Peter, I have another question

that I would like you to clear up for me."

"What is it?'" he asked.

Alicia went and sat down, and then looking directly at Peter asked the question that she knew he had been asked before. "It's about the hand prints. Why did you leave all the hand prints?"

"Alicia, you did not read me my Miranda rights," he said as he grinned. They both laughed, and then he continued.

"Modern man has no idea why most ancient civilizations left painted handprints on cave walls. Those handprints were, and still are, very important. The prints are a connection to the person who left them. The best way to describe it would be like a USB port in a computer. Connect to the handprint and you have access to the person's knowledge and memory base. Hawk showed this to me. When I was with him, he would connect to a handprint that belonged to an elder, long passed. I could feel the presence. It was like a controlled dream. Think about this. Antiques often exceed their perceived value if it can be ascertained that a certain famous person owned or used it. Not because it is made better or made from a more valuable material; it's the fact that a certain person held it or used it that gives it the value. The buyer wants to feel that connection, a connection to the person who is now long passed. They will pay many times the value of the item just because of that. I think deep in our pre-birth learning, in the knowledge we gain at the moment of conception; we are made aware that we are able to gain knowledge by touch. A handshake or an exposed palm can say a lot. You can transmit so much, negative or positive, by the way the hand is presented."

Alicia, trying to clarify what Peter was telling her, asked, "So, the Neanderthals would use the handprints as a source of intelligence?"

Peter answered, "Yes. If Hawk had a problem, he would go to the wall in the cave, place his hand over a handprint, and connect. This was not only a source of comfort; it was the way information was transmitted from generation to generation. The handprints were a very important part of the tribe's lives. They were revered much like modern man would revere a religious relic. Hawk gave me knowledge that I have to pass on, so I did what they did. I left my handprints to connect to someone. I was aware that it was illegal, but I knew I would attract the attention of the person I needed to tell the story. That person, Alicia, is you.

Alicia, digging deeper, asked. "What makes you think I am the one?"

Peter grinned and answered, "It was a hunch."

They both returned to the library, Peter reclining on the coach and Alicia taking her place behind the desk. Peter went straight into telling the story where he had left off.

When Wolf had killed Death Dog's troops that had been pursuing them, he was able to focus on getting his young hunters back to unite with what was left of the tribe in the cave. Hawk warned Wolf not to go directly to the waterfall and to take a route that was far longer and more hazardous, but it would make it harder for anyone to follow.

The direction Hawk would lead them was going to be far more dangerous, leading them through thick unforgiving undergrowth and a sheer dangerous climb to get to the cave entrance. This approach would hopefully lose any further pursuers, securing the secrecy of the cave and the tribe's survivors.

Wolf instructed his troop, quickly hiding the bodies of Death Dog's soldiers. They then silently moved off in perfect synchronicity.

As the light of the rising sun cast its long shadows across what remained of the village, Death Dog was standing back from his screaming troops as they burned and plundered, slinging the contents of the huts outside before they set the huts on fire. The hairless ones had corralled the captured Neanderthals into a tight circle and bound them. He moved forward to inspect his prisoners, all now sitting with their heads lowered, staring at the ground beneath them. They were a beaten group, all of them realizing the dire situation and their posture showing their hopelessness.

Death Dog reached forward and grabbed for the hair of the elder, Cloud, who was his biological father. He yanked back his head so their eyes met. He dropped to his knees, still holding the hair of Cloud, and he pulled a knife from his waistband. He then pushed the razor sharp flint deep into Clouds chin. Blood flowed down Death Dog's knife and hand. He then snorted phlegm and spit into his father's extended face. It hit directly into Cloud's left eye and slid along his cheek into his open mouth. Cloud, with phlegm covering his face, looked at his spawn and regretted that he had not listened to Hawk and killed his son several years before.

Releasing his grip from his father's hair, Death Dog stood and grabbed the young Neanderthal who was bound by cord to Cloud. The young Neanderthal was whimpering with fear as Death Dog pulled his head back and slashed the young hunter's throat. The young hunter was shocked, the pumping blood now covering Cloud. He turned and looked into the victim's eyes, offering comfort as the life surged from the young hunter's body. Death Dog's eyes never left the face of Cloud, enjoying the hate he could read in his father's face.

Death Dog finally released the young hunter, who slumped against Cloud. The lonely cry of a hawk flying high above the burning village attracted the attention of both Cloud and Death Dog; Cloud getting comfort from what angered Death Dog, who raised his head and screamed towards the hawk, knowing he was being watched.

Hawk was watching and comforting the passage of the young dying fighter. The situation was dire; he could feel the hopelessness and guilt in his manacled brother.

Death Dog screamed orders for his troops to gather and prepare to return to their encampment. His troops were loaded with furs and artifacts, which would slow their progress. They had to move quickly as the return with spoils and prisoners was a good day's march. The Hairless Ones loaded down the Neanderthal prisoners with their new possessions like pack animals, taking advantage of their massively muscular bodies.

Death Dog was aware that the two troops he had sent to track down the escaping Neanderthals had not yet returned. He was confident they would not return unless they had captured the runners. He waited and looked up again at Hawk circling above them, and then glanced to the direction his troops should have returned from for any signs. He then turned and started to lead his troops away from the now deserted and burning village.

Wolf was leading his troop along the slow and arduous trek devised by Hawk. He was continually backtracking to attempt to cover the troop's tracks. He kept warning his troops to tread lightly and to attempt not to break any saplings or flora, but the lumbering Neanderthals were unable to move through such denseness without leaving signs. The thick undergrowth ripped at their skin as they forced their way through the un-trodden ground. It was difficult for Wolf to cover the tracks they were leaving, the path still reaming obvious for the skilled hunters of Death Dog.

Wolf decided he would lead the small group back towards the river. It would increase the danger, but it would allow his group to use the river to hide their tracks. This would add to the time it would take to get to the cave, but Hawk was watching and agreed with Wolf's action. Keeping the cave secret was vital for the survival of what remained of the tribe. The going was difficult and slow, but finally they arrived at the river. Wolf, leaving the group, went ahead to check for any signs of Death Dog's troops. The riverbanks were deserted and safe. He mentally called for his troops to come forward and they appeared on the side of the river as one. They all walked into the river and headed downstream, floating silently along. On several occasions they emerged from the river and headed into the jungle, then backtracked to the river leaving false trails, which would confuse any pursuers. Wolf felt he had left enough tracks and decided it would be safe to leave the river. He instructed his troop to tread carefully as they left the river at an area that was covered in small rocks. The tracks they left, if any, were few and time would soon get rid of any signs.

Carefully moving through the thick undergrowth, Wolf continually backtracked and checked the trail for Death Dog's troops. Their progress was slow, but finally they arrived at a cliff face, a massive black rock structure rising out of the jungle. The troop looked up at the obstacle and the fear rose up in them immediately. One of the younger troops, Spider, was a renowned climber. As a child, Spider's long limbs and hair covered back resembled a spider as he scurried up trees and rock faces. Always climbing, his vertical agility became a valued asset to the hunters and he soon became a key member of the tribe. His birth name was Earth, but his name was appropriately changed to Spider, which he cherished, for climbing was his gift.

Relishing the opportunity of leadership, he sized up the cliff face. Going forward, raising his arms and grabbing up at a slight divot, he tested it. He then dropped his arm and moved away from the cliff inspecting and planning his attempt. This was his forte and he was in no hurry to start the climb without the showmanship of his consideration. He knew that this climb would become an important part of a great story. This was his moment and he was not going to take it lightly.

He stood back looking, moved to the left side of the open cliff, reached up and grabbed at a root that was exposed. Then, with three stretching and rapid movements he was twenty feet off the ground, his body motionless against the cliff. All of his limbs were stretched to the maximum. He leaned back from the cliff and was again surveying, looking for his next angle of attack. It was not long before he was on the move again, moving across the face of the cliff. The pre-planning of his next move was what made Spider such a gifted climber. He did not move until he had carefully worked out the direction and the progress of his assent five or six moves ahead of his current position. Within minutes, he was a small speck on the side of the cliff. He would stop to plan, and then there was a scurry of activity, his powerful arms extended to the maximum taking advantage of any handhold or rock crack that would support his grip.

Spider was unsure as to what he would find at the top of his climb, but Hawk was with him leading him upwards. At one point, the cliff face looked like polished slate with not the slightest sign of handholds anywhere. He lay back on his outstretched arms, trying to assess his next move, when the high pitch twittering of a perched hawk showed him the way. The hawk was perched on a small divot and remained that way until Spider's hand slid under his warm crop, and then it lifted into the air on its outstretched wings then swooped away. Once he had gained this hold he could clearly see his next move; the cliff face lay slightly back and the climb became easier. He continued up what appeared to be a small ledge. He extended his right hand up towards the ledge. As he did, he was surprised by the powerful, yet friendly grip of Hawk, grabbing his arm and supporting his weight as he swung up over the ledge to a cave entrance.

Hawk pulled him up and greeted him with a silent, friendly embrace. Spider was breathing heavy, sweat trickled down his face. He released Hawk and went into the shade of the cave and rested his back against the cool cave wall. He could feel the power of the cave enter him, refreshing his tired limbs. Hawk handed Spider some water and dried meat.

Spider sat chewing and was now able to reflect on what he had experienced. The sadness filled him and Hawk was able to feel how the experience had inwardly injured Spider. Spider looked at the handprints on the cave walls, aged and still portraying a power that, although he was tired, gave him an overwhelming desire to make his way across the cave and lay his hand on one of the prints. The handprint's power came to him, reassuring him and filling him with hope.

It was not time to reflect. Hawk had to instruct Spider on how to get Wolf and what was left of the hunters up to the safety of the cave. Those left below were not capable of ascending the sheer cliff face as Spider had done. Hawk went back into the cave and brought out a massive rope, which was anchored to a large rock. He laid the rope at the entrance of the cave and kicked it over the edge. The falling rope unwound itself, ending at the ledge Spider had climbed over earlier. Hawk then leaned over the edge and pointed out to Spider that he must follow the ledge across the face of the cliff where he would find a large root sticking out of the rock, where he would secure a second rope long enough to reach the ground where the troop were waiting.

Spider placed the massive rope over his head and squeezed his muscular arm and shoulder through the center of the coiled rope so it hung bandoller style, allowing freedom to climb with both hands. He reached forward, grabbed Hawk's hand and used it as a support as he lowered himself over the ledge. Holding the rope with one hand, he released his grip of Hawk's hand and started his descent.

It was many years since Hawk's father had showed him this way of getting back to ground level from the cave if the other entrance became unusable for some reason. Hawk had never thought that he would ever need to use this entrance, but obviously his father had known better. He looked over the precipice at Spider who was making good speed. He had soon reached the ledge and was making his way across the cliff face. The ledge was small and narrow, and one had to walk sideways with both arms extended. It was a good one hundred sideways paces until Spider reached the root, which Hawk said would make a good anchor for the remaining rope. He quickly secured the second rope, and then lowered himself over the edge. The hunters below could now see Spider as he descended and their excitement spread quickly.

Spider was soon on the ground and one of the younger hunters was the first to grab the rope. He started to make his way up the face of the cliff, his powerful arms overcoming his massive Neanderthal weight. They all soon found themselves in the cave where Hawk gave each of them water and food. They sat against the wall of the cave, enjoying the cool rock and the safety the cave provided.

The march back to camp had gone well. As Death Dog walked back into his disheveled camp the sun was still three fingers high on the westerly horizon. The women began whooping and taunting the prisoners as they were led shackled through the village towards holding posts at the north end of the village.

Each prisoner was removed from the chain of prisoners. They had their hands tied behind their backs and the other end of the rope was then passed over the top of the post holding them. On the loose end of the rope was an attached skin that held heavy rocks. This pulled the rope tight and kept the prisoner's arms under pressure. This at first forced the arms of the prisoner up behind them against the joints. After a short time the arms would dislocate under the weight of the rocks and the prisoners own weight. As the arms dislocated, the head of the prisoner would come up. That was how Death Dog wanted them. The prisoner's head up and immobilized by his own dislocated arms. The ankles of the prisoners were tied firmly to the post also, immobilizing the prisoner and preventing any movement that might help to relieve the pain of dislocation and immobility.

After the prisoners had been secured, the Hairless Ones gathered by the campfire in the center of the village. All gathered to share in the heat and a meal of pilfered dried meats. It was soon dark, but all were enjoying in the sharing and the telling of the battle earlier that day. Even Death Dog was enjoying the excitement while both of his women were doting over him, preening and making sure he had plenty of food and water.

The secured Neanderthals were all watching and wondering what would come next. They felt escape was impossible and the pain of the tethers and dislocated arms focused their thought on the present, preventing any sleep. In an attempt to calm himself, Cloud started to meditate. This resulted in a healing, purring sound that was soon picked up by the other prisoners. They were soon all in a deep meditation, synchronized in dream outside of their body, and for the moment free of the situation.

As the party quieted, Death Dog walked with his two women over to inspect his prisoners. As he approached, he recognized that the Neanderthals were deep in meditation. He walked up to Cloud and quietly stood in front of him, looking closely at the features of his face. He then spat again in his father's face as he turned and walked away. Cloud made no recognition of his presence or of the phlegm that was now running down his haired chin as the purring continued. During the night, Cloud came out of his meditation, craving water for his parched lips. He looked around the camp, which was now quiet. The captors all appeared to be asleep and the fire's flames in the center of the village had diminished, but were still providing warmth for the half dozen young warriors who snoozed in the light of what remained of the fire. As he cleared his mind, he focused on the fact that Hawk was communicating with him, letting him know that Wolf had made it to the safety of the cave with what was left of his troop. Hawk was reassuring but was unable to offer much hope as escape was hopeless and they were both aware of what was going to happen. Hawk helped Cloud calm again and return to his meditation, offering relief from the situation.

Hawk, watched from the cave entrance as the sun came up over the canopy of the forest below. The low mist hanging from the crowns of the trees carpeted below. His options were limited. His brother's capture and imminent torture played heavy on his thoughts. As he sat watching the light of the day race across the canopy, Water joined him, sitting beside him and crossing her legs. Silently their thoughts joined, calming and enjoying the gift of warmth and light the arriving morning gave them. Hawk's hand slipped from his lap finding her hand, holding and comforting her. Wolf stood quietly inside the cave watching the pair of them, gaining a little pleasure from the beginning of the day. Hawk and Water felt the presence of Wolf and turning towards him Hawk beckoned him forward to join them.

Cloud was awake and watching. One of the female Hairless Ones appeared, bringing the prisoners water. Cloud gulped at the water, relieving the parched dryness that had been tearing at his throat and mouth. The young female had strict instructions to make sure they all survived and gave them all enough to quench their thirst and stave off any chance that any of them would not be fully aware when Death Dog arrived to begin his tormenting. It was mid-morning before Death Dog made his appearance to the prisoners, ignoring his father and choosing one of the younger ones to be cut down and spiked out on the ground. The prisoner was forced to lay on his back as both arms and both legs were stretched out and tethered to pegs that had been in place and firmly buried. The prisoner was held firm, only able to move his head from side to side. He looked up at Cloud and the panic became clear in his face and he began a pathetic uncontrollable whimpering, emphasizing his fear.

Death Dog had brought embers from the main campfire and built a small fire near the prisoner. The young Neanderthal's gaze fixed on the fire and the skinning knifes that Death Dog had carefully placed in the embers. The omen was horrific. The concept of what was going to happen just as terrifying as what was about to begin. Turning the blades, Death Dog held them towards his lips then spat on them to judge the temperature of the searing flint. When the blade's temperature was sufficient, he then replaced them into the glowing embers to retain the heat the blades had gained.

He walked over to the prisoner, looking down as if pondering his options. Then taking his large razor sharp flint knife from his belt, he quickly removed any clothing from the prisoner, leaving him naked and totally exposed. Kneeling beside him, he pondered his next action. Part of this was for show. He wanted the other Hairless Ones to see that he thinks his actions through. The other part was to add to the horror and suspense of his victim.

He returned to the fire and removed one of the heated blades. He looked up at his father and at the same time reached forward, grabbing the young

Neanderthal's testicles with his left hand. Pulling them away from the prisoner's body he hacked them free, the hot flint searing the flesh and cauterizing as he cut. The young man, normally quiet, let out a screaming roar, his head thrashing from side to side. He was hopeless, but the panic and pain rose in him as he arched his body in a vain attempt of escape and release. He was still screaming as he watched Death Dog toss his manhood for the camp dogs to race forward, grab and fight over. Cloud's face remained motionless; he was watching and sharing in the agony of the young Neanderthal, but refused to allow his son, Death Dog, to enjoy any stress that might show on his father's face.

Death Dog repositioned himself and continued expertly in the torture of the young capture. He proceeded by opening the abdomen and grabbing the intestines. He called the dogs forward and they snarled and tore long strands of gut from the boy's body, arching backwards and forcing their powerful legs against the resistance the guts offered before they were released from the cavity of the tethered prisoner. The boy was still conscious but had drifted into a stage of silent acceptance. The torture was continued until the life force of the young Neanderthal defied Death Dog's expert techniques and allowed the spirit to escape. He stood, kicking the tormented corpse and instructed his guards to drag it away.

Death Dog tortured two more of the captured Neanderthals that day, each uniquely. On the second he used cold knifes and started with the removal of the eyelids. He placed the captured man's head between his legs then he carefully removed the upper lids, making it impossible for the prisoner to close his eyes or divert his stare from the preparations and actions of Death Dog. Death Dog's stare was focused on the prisoner's face, not missing any signs of the distress that gave him the satisfaction he craved. His torturing always continued until the spirit left and breathing ceased. The body would then be released to the tribe where it would be dismembered. They would keep body parts as a talisman, often removing a hand that would be tethered to hang around their waist. The larger muscle areas were removed for eating and what was left over would be fed to the camp dogs. This was also done in front of the remaining captures, increasing their apprehension and fear.

The situation was hopeless and Cloud was in full acceptance of his fate. He glared at Death Dog as he gathered his implements of torture, then stood and turned to look at the face of his tethered father. Walking towards him, his face covered in sweat and blood, he grabbed his father's chin, his grip deforming his father's mouth as he pushed the point of his skinning knife up to his father's eye. Cloud's face and eyes showed no emotion as the blade dug into the skin below the eye and separated the skin to the bone as he dragged the knife downwards. He stepped back grinning. Cloud, blood dripping from his haired chin, amassed what spit and phlegm he could inside his parched mouth and then spat it with all his force into the face of Death Dog.

This shocked Death Dog, as he did not expect this open defiance from a prisoner. He stepped backwards, wiped his face, and then leapt forward as if going to attack. With the blade held high, he grabbed his father by the hair and brought the knife to his throat, then halted. The temptation to kill him was great but he had the willpower to halt the attack. He stepped back, grinned, and again wiped his face and walked away, leaving Cloud bleeding and trapped.

The doorbell rang, surprising Alicia. She looked up from the desk directly at Peter. Peter, totally un-phased, continued in the same pitch and without changing his recumbent position on the coach, asked, "Alicia, would you be so kind as to get the door for me?"

Without speaking, she switched the recorder off and made her way from behind the desk towards the front door. She pulled it open and peered around the slightly ajar door. Standing back from the door was detective Granger.

"Good afternoon, Alicia," said Detective Granger, who then remained quiet, waiting for a response before he said anymore so that he could judge her demeanor. He was pleased that her response was in a friendly tone.

"Hello detective. How can I help you?" Alicia was confident in her place at the house, but still remained mainly covered behind the massive mansion door, just her head showing.

Detective Granger asked, "Is it possible to talk to Peter?"

Alicia said she would go and ask Peter if he wanted to talk to the detective, closing the door behind her and leaving the detective standing outside, facing the closed door. As she walked to the library, she questioned herself over closing the door in the detective's face, but agreed she really was not quite sure about Detective Granger and if he was not more intentionally involved in her separation with the Austin Statesman. This thought removed any concerns about the closed door or Detective Granger standing on the step outside.

Peter was still lying on the coach totally unconcerned as Alicia arrived to tell him who it was at the door. Alicia found herself whispering as she informed Peter it was Detective Granger.

"Oh, okay, show him in," he said as he struggled to right himself, to make himself slightly more presentable. Alicia made her way back to the door and the waiting detective.

"Come on in Detective. He is in the library."

Before the detective actually went through the open door into the library, Peter was greeting him. "Good afternoon, Detective."

The detective continued his entrance and opened the conversation with an apology. "I have been trying to find out how the Austin Statesman found out that Alicia was at your home when I interviewed you, leading to Alicia losing her position." He then continued as he turned to Alicia. "I am extremely sorry this has happened. Since I found out, I have gone over it many times. I have arrived at a conclusion, but it is one I can't prove just yet.

We have had a problem in the department of leaks to the Austin Statesman for quite a few years. Leaking is frustrating but it is not a crime, so my level of investigating is limited. I have to take the answer of a person to a question at face value. I can't sit them down and apply pressure to them. I cannot apply consequences. This makes it difficult to get a confession, especially when you are dealing with a group that is trained in interviewing and the tricks involved in getting people to confess. They just stay quiet and you have to prove it way beyond any doubt. I'm afraid it would take a confession to pin it to anyone.

I know the leak came unintentionally from me, and I am so sorry this happened. Only a few people were in hearing distance when I spoke of talking to you here and the fact that Alicia was here also. I said it without thinking and had no idea of the consequence. I have a strong idea of who the person is, as he seems to be the only person I can think of in the department and in a position to pass the information to the paper. He is a senior member of the department. The problem is that I can't prove it. I will have to wait for the proof. Alicia, I am sincerely sorry for the loss of your job. The last thing I would have wanted was to hurt you in any way. I am responsible and I am sorry. I have learned a serious lesson and will be far more careful in the future."

Alicia's head dropped and she reached for a hanky she had tucked in her sleeve. She wiped her nose, raised her head and sobbed that it was okay. She hated the fact that she was showing emotion. "The job was not that important, but it was my first job," she said, blowing her nose before she finished the sentence. "I did not want it to end like this."

Peter interjected, "I understand and accept your apology. I will make the necessary phone calls to let people know that I am more than happy."

The detective remained quiet for a moment, then feeling a little uneasy informed Peter and Alicia that he had other pressing appointments and would have to leave. He thanked them for the time, finishing again with an apology. Peter remained seated and accepted the hand of the detective, shaking it and at the same time saying, "Thank you Detective."

Turning and walking towards the door, Alicia followed the detective. He stopped a few paces from the door, allowing Alicia to open it for him. He again apologized to her, offered his hand which she accepted and said goodbye. As Alicia closed the door behind her, she leaned against it breathing in deeply and adjusting her demeanor before returning to the library and Peter.

Peter was still seated but showed concern by asking Alicia how she was. Alicia confirmed she was okay and apologized for being emotional.

"Alicia, I understand. Take a seat; I have something I want to ask you," said Peter.

Alicia went and reseated herself behind the desk. "Would you consider working for me?" he asked.

Alicia was taken aback by the question. "Doing what?" she asked.

Peter had been thinking about this since he heard that Alicia had been fired from the Austin Statesman, feeling a bit unintentionally responsible. "As you know, Alicia, I am not in the best of health and I really think it is important for you to get the story down before I'm gone. I'm not sure how much time I have left. I could do with help keeping this rambling estate in order. I just do not have the time or the inclination. It's dropping to bits since the accident. There is a lot of history to this building. It can be traced back as far as to before the First World War in 1910. It deserves better. We, the estate and I, need someone to look after us, like a manager."

Alicia remained quiet, going over the offer before she spoke. "Peter, I would love to work for and with you. The story is something I am going to do, and you do not need to pay me. As for managing your estate, I think we could come to an agreement that would not be too expensive for you. I would love to help, but let me talk it over with my mother, as she is the one paying most of my expenses."

"Alicia, I have no living siblings and several millions in the bank. I earn more on interest in one week than most people will earn in a year. I need someone to help me. I like you and that's why I am offering you the job. Why don't you talk it over with your mother? I am offering you a job managing the estate and at the same time writing my story. I will cover all your expenses, fuel and vehicle repairs, plus $40,000 per year, paid monthly. I will ask my accountant to make sure you have complete medical coverage. Alicia I hope you take it."

Chapter 13

Bursting through the door, Brenda knew Alicia was in a good mood. She had a smile on her face and was moving quick and easy as she put down her stuff and moved towards her mother to kiss her. Brenda was wiping her hands and standing at the sink. She turned her head over her left shoulder to bring it into range of Alicia's welcome.

"Well, what are we so happy about?" asked Brenda.

"Peter has offered me an amazing job," Alicia replied.

Brenda finished wiping her hands and, taking Alicia by the hand, led her towards the couch, both sitting down together. "Tell me all about it."

Alicia went over the details of the job offer and all the benefits that went with it. "Forty thousand dollars a year! I'm rich," she exclaimed.

"Well?" Brenda commented.

"Well, what?"

"Well, are you going to take the job?"

Alicia answered quickly. "Hell, yea. I have not got anything better to do since I lost my internship and I will still be writing. It's perfect."

Brenda raised herself from the couch and went

back to preparing dinner. "What are we eating Mom?" asked Alicia.

"Nothing special; just chicken fried steak," Brenda answered, knowing that it was one of Alicia's favorites. This brought a smile to Alicia's face and she then told Brenda that Tim was going to join them and was bringing desert, if that was okay with her. Brenda smiled and told Alicia that it would be no problem.

Alicia then stood to help her mother set the table. Before she could make it to the kitchen, the doorbell rang. Alicia stopped in her tracks, changed direction, and informed her mother that she would get the door. She opened it to the smiling face of Tim. Not waiting to be asked, he made his way in, holding his H.E.B. cake proudly in front of him and kissing Alicia as she held the door. She smiled to herself as she shook her head, laughing.

"Good afternoon Brenda. I hope you like Double Death chocolate cake." Tim stated proudly.

She responded, "Yes, I love it, but you do realize you are sentencing me to some serious road work."

Tim made his way to the kitchen and removed his cake from the box and stood back to admire his choice. He looked at Brenda, waiting for her to comment. Brenda obliged. "Wonderful looking cake Tim! I bet it's going to taste great. Do you like chicken fried steak?"

"Love it," Tim said, making his way to the table before being asked. Tim was really starting to feel at home and if asked would explain how Alicia was his girlfriend and how well he got on with his future mother-in-law. That was how he saw it, confident in the relationship after one kiss and a night out in Austin. Alicia, however, clearly liked him a lot but was not as yet committed to the partnership. She had been involved before and hurt when the relationship 'was not working,' as her ex had explained to her. She later found out that he had been seeing one of her friends behind her back. This had given Alicia a slightly standoffish approach to boyfriends. Brenda thought Tim was a nice young man, a bit nerdish, but with a good heart and not bad looking.

Tim asked Alicia where he should sit and took her instruction, taking his place at the table. Alicia brought his fork, napkin and plate to the table placing it in front of him. As she did, he nipped her leg and received a slap on the hand and a smile.

All were seated and the food was on larger serving dishes in the middle of the table. Tim offered grace and thanks before they helped themselves. With food on their plates, they all started to eat when Tim opened the conversation.

"Well, what did Sir Peter think of the Genesis connection?" he asked.

"We went over it. He was already researching when I arrived and prepared for the question when I presented it to him. He could clearly see the similarity in the stories. He wondered how many times Hawk had reached forward in time to dreamers or shaman; someone to tell his story of mutations through inbreeding that led to the demise of the Neanderthals. He is pretty sure the story in Genesis is his story passed down by dream."

Brenda butted in and told Alicia to tell Tim her news. "Well, tell him," she said.

"What?" asked Alicia.

"About the job," she prodded.

"Oh, that," said Alicia with a big grin. "Peter has offered me a job."

"Doing what?" Tim asked, still chewing a good mouth full of chicken fried steak.

"Managing his estate and writing the story. He made me an offer I can't refuse and it's got full health coverage and vehicle expenses."

Tim stopped chewing and put down his fork and wiped his mouth. "You lucky girl. Talk about landing on your feet. I hope I am around when Kerr, the editor, finds out. He is going to be pissed. That's the sort of job he would have loved in his retirement. Good for you, Alicia. I am so proud of you," he stated honestly.

"Speaking of Editor Kerr, Detective Granger stopped by today to update us on the leak from his department. He was very apologetic and believes he knows who leaked, but he can't prove it. He told us he has to have proof and will not give up on it until he pins the culprit," said Alicia.

"Do you trust him? " Tim asked.

"I think so, and Peter trust's him as well. Peter has an innate ability to tell about peoples' character and he trusts and likes detective Granger. I am pretty confident that Granger will not drop it until he pins it on the culprit. He feels personally responsible for my getting fired. Little did he know what a favor he was doing for me."

Granger arrived back at the department. He knew who it was that had been leaking information, but he could not prove it. As he reflected over the last few years and the leaks that had plagued the department, there was one common denominator and Granger did not believe in that level of coincidence. Not having proof meant Jeffrey would keep digging. That's what made him such an outstanding detective: tenacity. He was pissed and wanted to put pressure on who he suspected. Having to apologize to Peter and Alicia stuck in his craw, and the guilt he carried over the firing of Alicia weighed heavy on him, and it was a negative he wanted to share.

Jeffrey's arms were full as he kicked at the station side entrance door. It was always locked for security reasons and had to be opened manually from the inside. The sergeant could hear the kicking on the door and checked the monitor to see who it was. He could clearly see Detective Granger, arms full and looking up at the camera as he kicked at the door. The sergeant did not move, watching the image on the small security screen. He knew Granger was on to him, but also realized that it would be hard for Granger to pin anything on him. Finally, the sergeant made his way to the door and unlocked the double security bolts. No sooner had the bolts slid to free the door it was swung open aggressively. Granger pushed past Sargent Madden without acknowledgement. Madden flattened his back against the wall and let him pass.

Madden closed the door behind Granger then made his way back to his desk, making himself comfortable and looking over his glasses, not moving his head but watching every move Granger made, very aware of his mood.

The detective made his way to his desk, placed his papers down and took his seat. He turned the computer on, slid his chair back from the desk and placed his feet onto the desk, contemplating as his computer fired up. He waited as the computer slowly went through its firing up process, asking him to enter his password before it would continue its awakening. He provided it with his password then stood and made his way towards the high-tech coffee machine percolating on a table, which also offered several different choices in creamer kept chilled in a plate of ice. Sargent Madden watched and thought he would join Granger to confirm if his cover had been blown without making it too obvious.

Granger had selected his coffee choice and was holding the plastic cup and placed the pot back down on the hot plate; his choice, black with no sugar. Madden joined him and opened the conversation. "Are you doing okay, Jeffrey?"

Jeffrey backed away from the table, sipped at

his coffee, and then answered the sergeant. "I have been better."

"Anything I can help you with Jeffrey? " Madden asked, looking concerned at Jeffrey as he filled his cup.

Jeffrey responded, "I have been investigating the fact that the young reporter, who happened to be with Peter Shaw at his house when I asked him to sign his statements, was fired by the Austin Statesmen later that day. Whoever leaked was from this department."

Madden butted in saying, "Fucking tell me about it. I have been complaining about this for months."

Jeffrey placed his cup down on the table and walked inside of Madden's comfort zone. Towering over Madden and looking directly into his face, anger welling up inside him. Barely remaining in control, he said, "Madden, I was born at night, but not last night. I know who is fucking leaking and I promise you I will make them pay for it." He then turned, picked up his coffee and made his way back to his desk, leaving Madden in no doubt as to the state of his cover.

Madden had been around long enough to realize that unless Granger could get hard evidence he was safe. He smiled as he made his way back to his desk, looking over at Granger who was ignoring him. "Fuck him," thought Madden; reassuring himself and thinking he had better let everything cool before he called Kerr again. He again glanced over at Granger who was staring back at him, feet on his desk, and forcing

Madden's own gaze back to his desk. He knew that he had not heard the last of this.

Tim loved the home cooking and feeling part of a unit. He finished his main dish first, but waited for everyone to finish. He then stood up and collected the dirty plates, taking them to the kitchen and placing them in the sink. He then returned to the table with his pride and joy, the H.E.B. Double Death chocolate cake. He placed it in the middle of the table then again took his place at the table. Alicia thought it too damn cute the way Tim was playing up the cake, enjoying the spectacle. Tim asked Brenda to cut the cake, which she did, placing a large slice on Tim's plate first and then two more for herself and Alicia. The conversation was stifled as they all enjoyed the first spoon full. Tim, mouth full and smiling, nodded his head yes, looking at his fellow diners. Alicia swallowed and said, "Awesome." Then she returned to silence as she continued eating her plate of cake.

Once they all finished, the table was cleared and Tim pointed out it was still light and plenty of time for a walk around the park. They made their way to the park and began walking and talking and going over the day. The conversation soon returned to the job offer Alicia had decided to accept and the details of the day's telling by Peter. Alicia was wondering more about managing the estate and getting everything back in order, saying she had to remember that the story was the most important part of the job offer. She explained the torture and suffering of the captured Neanderthals and how Peter seemed as if he was feeling the pain. He had to stop the telling several times to wipe his aged eyes. She could tell how personal the story was to him, which emphasized the importance of her reporting. She pondered her situation then decided to ask him if Tim could help her to review her notes and compile them into a story.

Texas sunsets are massive and full of color. The Starlings weighed heavy on the electrical cables, noisily chattering before the inevitable silence imposed by darkness. They all linked arms as they finished the walk, chatting and laughing at some of Tim's quick comments. Brenda loved the walk and would stop the group to point out certain flowers or plants that a casual stroller might have missed. The Bull Bats flying low over the flora started to take over the evening, feasting on the clouded mosquitos as they swooped low, calling out to each other as they fed. They arrived back at the car and made their way back to the apartment. Tim joined them without being asked. All three got a large glass of water and sat down to watch the local news.

Tim was able to give the inside on some of the headline stories. The arsonist whose bankrupt furniture business had miraculously gone up in smoke had at the same time had ended up in the emergency room with third degree burns to his arms and face, saying it happened when he was trying to light his barbeque pit. Tim exclaimed, "Some people are so stupid."

After the news, Brenda excused herself saying she was going to bed to read her latest Wilbur Smith novel, an author she loved. She kissed Alicia good night on her cheek and then did the same to Tim. As she left the room, Tim kicked off his tennis shoes and maneuvered over to the recliner where Alicia was sitting. Squeezing into the chair, they both sat cuddling as Tim flicked through the channels, feeling at home.

In the morning, Brenda was up before dawn to go for her two mile run. She was not surprised to see that Tim's car was still there. She liked Tim, and as she ran was hoping that this time Alicia would not get hurt. Although she was now in her twenties, she was still her little girl.

Her run through the neighborhood was as much a part of her day as brushing her teeth, and some of her neighbor's routines had entwined with hers. Not knowing the names of these other early birds was okay, as the sharing of each new day had, in a way, bonded them. The raising of a hand or a verbal good morning as the lady in her nightgown collected her freshly delivered paper, recognizing Brenda, but only as the lady that runs every day. Just as she turned the corner, the massive, but friendly, Golden Lab goes through her routine of letting everyone know that it's her yard as she is guarding the property. She will run along the fence line beside Brenda, barking until she reached the gate, preventing her from running out into the street. Brenda would then stop and share a few moments rubbing the dog's damp head, which easily reached over the gate. "Good morning Sunshine. Are you being a good girl today?" The lab loved the attention and ear rubbing that Brenda gave her and would remain with her head over the gate as Brenda left to continue her run.

Tim and Alicia heard Brenda leave. Alicia seemed very casual about the fact that Tim had spent the night, but Tim was apprehensive about how Brenda would react. What concerned Alicia more was the fact the she felt Peter knew everything she did. Before going to bed the previous night, she mentally tried to close her mind down and made a point that she would ask Peter about that when she saw him next.

As Brenda made her way back to the house she could see that the young couple was up. She walked up the drive and collected the paper, which was lying on the drive. She walked in and kicked off her shoes. She greeted them with a very open and pleasant, "Morning children," as she made her way to the kitchen to top up the coffee cup she had left beside the pot at the beginning of the run. "Going in early today?" she questioned Alicia.

Alicia said, " Well, I start my new job today and I wanted to get there early to let Peter know that I am going to take the job and have a look around to see what I need to start on and to prioritize my duties."

Tim was eating a piece of toast and sitting at the table. His hair was a mess, but he looked comfortable. He looked at Brenda who was glowing after her run, answering Brenda's greeting, "Morning

Brenda." He then commented, "Prioritize? I think the story is the priority."

Alicia paused before answering. "Um, yes," enforcing the yes. "I know that Tim, but I really am not sure as to what extent Peter wants me to get involved. Peter's day is pretty well laid out. He can't work a full day because of his health, so he likes to take a nap at midday to recuperate. That's the time I hope I can take a look around and find out what needs doing."

Brenda offered, "I am pretty good on Quick Books and could soon set up an accounts system for him, like I did for you Alicia."

"That might be a good idea, but let me first find out what needs to be done," said Alicia.

Tim was the first to finish his breakfast and the first to leave the house. Before going to work he had to go home and get changed. He kissed Alicia who was still sitting at the breakfast table, then went over to Brenda and gave her a peck on the cheek. "I will give you a call later today, Alicia. Thanks for the meal last night Brenda, and may you both have a great day."

As soon as Tim left the house Alicia asked Brenda, "Well, what do you think of our Tim?"

Brenda grinned, looking up from her morning paper answering, "He seems really nice. I like him."

"That's great. I am glad you like him. So do I," said Alicia, as she stood from the table, grabbed her plate to place in the dishwasher, and went to get ready for work.

As Alicia arrived at Peter's she found him again

sitting by the front door, on the floor, door ajar. "Good morning Alicia. How are we today?"

Alicia, overloaded with her things, closed her car door with her foot then pointed the remote key at the car and pressed the lock button, the beep indicating she had locked the door successfully, allowing her to then turn to Peter and answer his greeting. "I am feeling great Peter. It's a beautiful morning." She made her way to him and placed her stuff on the ground beside him. "Peter, let's get you up from the floor before we find ourselves in the same situation as yesterday. One of the first things I am going to do is to take you to Home Depot and get a bench delivered that we are going to put by the front door so we can sit and enjoy the mornings together, without the drama of trying to get off the floor." Peter smiled and realized that in her comment was the acceptance of the job. Alicia offered her hand again, but could not stop herself laughing as she helped Peter to his feet. By the time he was standing, they were both laughing.

They made their way to the kitchen where Peter asked, "I am assuming that you are going to accept the job offer I made you Alicia."

"Yes, I am. It's a wonderful opportunity and I thank you for offering me the position."

"Let me top up my coffee and I will show you around and let you see what you are taking on."

"Okay, let me just unload my stuff in the library and then you can give me a tour."

Alicia was soon back and waited while Peter

finished his coffee. The tour Peter gave her around the house was a sad look into Peter's past, since the accident. Most of the house was unused: 6 bedrooms, four with attached bathrooms. A complete apartment, fully furnished with its own kitchen, lounge, bathroom and massive tastefully decorated bedroom. Although the house was unused, it was clear that lots of money had been thrown at the décor. It looked like a time capsule, slightly dusty, but nothing that a good clean would not put right. The building itself did need some repairs. For example, a tree limb had fallen at the back of the house destroying the green house. It had just been left.

The small area Peter lived in was in need of some TLC. Peter was doing all his living down stairs, as the painful trip up the staircase effectively cut off the upper levels. He had converted a small room on the ground floor to his bedroom. Peter had kept a cleaner on staff that would tend to his laundry, shopping and basic cleaning. Other than that, everything had been left untouched.

Alicia soon realized she had plenty to do on the cleaning and some maintenance that would require a budget. Peter took his place on the large sofa and Alicia took her place behind Peter's large desk. "Peter, we are going to need a budget and we are going to need to prioritize. I will go over each room and prioritize what we need to do to get everything ship shape. In the meantime, I think we should continue working on your story first thing every day. Then, when you go for your midday rest, I will start getting what needs to be done down on paper."

Peter agreed and told her, "I will get the bank manager to open an account for you to use. I will put some money into the account, which you can draw on as needed. If you need more, all you have to do is ask."

Alicia wanted to assure Peter. "I will have my mother set up a set of accounts on Quick Books so we will have a record of spending and it will help us budget."

Peter grinned. "Alicia, I trust you. I will be here for a while to help you get the old place back into shape. The money is not a problem."

Alicia realized that Peter had developed a power where he could certainly tell whether he could trust a person or not, but that brought up something that she needed to clear up with him, but she was concerned how to broach the question. She wanted to know if Peter was able to know everything she did. Was he aware, for example, that she and Tim had sex last night? She had to ask as it was creeping her out. Before she could ask the question, Peter started to explain.

"Alicia, before we get into the story, let me go over how the transfer of information works. It is much like the article that you found on the Aborigines. If a person wants to send a message over a long distance, first they light a fire, which sends up the smoke. Then the person, seeing the smoke signal, has the responsibility to clear their mind so they then can receive the message. For me to be able to communicate with you, you have to be transmitting, broadcasting if you like, then and only then can I receive. I can sense certain things, like if you feel you are in danger or distressed. I will pick up on that. Other signs that I can pick up on which are involuntary are if someone is lying to me, and equally if they are being sincere, but that comes over more as a hunch."

"Well, how did you know that was what I was thinking?" asked Alicia.

"I don't know Alicia. It was just something I thought I needed to go over with you. I do think the more time we spend together our thought transfer will get stronger, which means more detail and certainty. We will never reach the level of the ancients. Their transfer was perfection in communication, so detailed and precise."

"So, you think if someone was to practice the techniques, you could improve communication between two people who had this gift?" Alicia asked, wanting confirmation.

"I am not sure, as I have not been able to work with anyone. However, I have picked up noise and have communicated back with them," said Peter.

"Let's make a point of practicing and see if we can improve our ability. I would love to be able to do it," said Alicia.

They went over some of Alicia's concerns. Peter called his bank to make an appointment later that morning to open an account for Alicia and make her a signee on the account. Peter showed her his Rolodex that had his contacts for her to use for certain repairs and other needs.

The appointment at the bank was for 10:30 a.m. and by the time they had got Peter in the car and made their way across town; there was very little time to spare. Alicia hated being late, but it did not seem to bother Peter. America Bank was waiting for Peter to arrive, the manager coming outside the bank to hold the door for him to exit the small Toyota. Holding Peter's arm as he climbed the few stairs into the bank was a bit over the top, but showed how valuable his account was at this branch.

Alicia could see the way the manager was acting and thought to herself what a creep the manager was and what power cash gives you. She was sure that if Peter arrived at the branch dressed as he was with no cash in the bank the manager would not be giving him the red carpet treatment or the offer of the manager's arm to climb the few steps into the branch. As they entered, the manger led them both to a small glass office with a massive desk where he took his place, seating himself into a massive leather throne. Peter and Alicia seated themselves in the two chairs in front of the desk. On the manager's desk was the standard set of family photos. His loving wife was holding his arm, fronted by two children, both looking immaculate. The picture was positioned for the benefit of the visitor, as was the bible that looked just as pristine; again for the benefit of the visitors. Once they were all comfortable the manager asked, "Would you like a coffee or anything?"

Peter responded, "No thanks, I am coffied out."

Alicia never said a word as she felt the question was not for her and was surprised when the manager turned his attention to her and asked, "Would you like a coffee?" Alicia completed the coffee rejection with a simple no refusal.

"Okay," said the manager, "Let's get down to business. I have opened an estate management account with ten thousand dollars to start. All withdrawals over eight hundred dollars will require two signatures. I have arranged that Alicia will be a signatory on the account and I need you, Alicia, to sign these documents."

He slid the documents across the large desk, turning them so Alicia could read each document and sign where marked by a small plastic tab. It was explained how the documents were for samples of her signature, and then he also explained the account structure and information. With the account came two debit cards, one for Peter and one for her, which she had to sign on the back. Once signed, she passed the card back to the manager and he produced a card reader that would lock her four-digit PIN to the card. The manager made sure to mention the fact that only she would know the number. Peter went through the same process and slipped his card into his pocket. Peter then looked at the manager and thanked him for setting up the account. He stood to indicate his intention to leave. The manager then said that he would like to make an appointment for one of his staff to come over to Peter's house to go over some of the benefits and potential of appointing an investment manager to his account. "You have considerable funds not earning what they could; a bit of guidance from one of our young money managers could be very profitable."

Peter grinned. "I really don't think so. My investments are long term and safe. Thank God I stopped playing the markets when I did. With what happened to the markets, my lack of investments and not earning turned out to be the best bet."

The manager quickly agreed with Peter, standing, and at the same time dropping the subject. He realized that Peter was still very capable of handling his accounts and had not been described to him as having lost his marbles.

Peter and Alicia both made their way towards the door, telling the manager that they would see themselves out. The manager had made his way to his office door, opening it for Peter and offering his hand, which Peter accepted. Alicia and, arm in arm supported him; they made their way down the stairs towards the little Toyota. Alicia helped Peter squeeze his long and increasingly ungainly legs comfortably in before closing the door for him. They made their way to Home Depot, going to the garden section and sitting on three different benches. They sat side-by-side imagining the sunrise and the Mocking Bird singing as the day unfolded before Alicia made the decision on which one to purchase. When paying for it, she had included in the price the delivery and set up, fifty dollars well spent.

Chapter 14

Plenty lay on a mattress made from skins wrapped around dry grasses that had been collected from the plains below. The fire in the center of the cave entrance, which had burnt down to a few embers, was small comfort now compared to when sleep finally relieved her of the torment and anguish the capture of Cloud put upon her. As she opened her eyes, the reality and the sadness of the situation returned, tearing into her heart.

She buried her large head deep in the skins and breathed deeply, the aroma of the dried grasses taking her mind back to the hunting trips she and Cloud had taken together before she became heavy with their child. She had been in love with Cloud from when they were young children together. He had always been with her it seemed, and the thought of him captured and in danger felt as if part of her was being torn from her body.

As children, they spent many hours together being watched by the elders. The children would be bathed together in the river, and then dried with a hard rubbing of dried grasses, which would always make the younger children scream and sob. The kindergarten environment allowed the young parents to hunt and gather, the couples working as a team and being gone for days at a time. The elders would love this time, having the children to themselves. The teaching the elders gave would be remembered throughout life. They were taught how the tribe was more important than self; every action was for the betterment of all.

As Plenty started to awaken, her first thoughts were for Cloud. She focused her thoughts, clearing her mind as she transmitted her love and wishes. "Good morning my Cloud, I love you."

Cloud was quietly watching the darkness as it weakened to the onset of a new day when he realized Plenty was communicating with him. He started sharing his view and thoughts with her, trying to remain positive.

Her mind went back to share again with Cloud the day she had given birth to their eldest child, who was now known as Death Dog. When he was born, both of them were so happy that their first-born was a male. Cloud commented about the lack of hair to Plenty as she held the helpless child in her arms, but the fact he had no hair was of little consequence. They had no idea they were dealing with a mutation that would threaten not only her family and tribe, but also the existence of her and her kind as a species. The love they had enjoyed would become bittersweet; the unknown chromosome mutation identified by the lack of hair. The lack of hair itself offered no threat. It was the development of an ego and the far more developed voice box combination that allowed the mutation to proliferate and eventually dominate. As their child grew, they realized he was aggressive and different. They had no idea their love was the cause of the difference, the inbreeding and its consequences beyond their comprehension.

Hawk had dreams, vivid dreams, showing a young couple of the tribe copulating and then both being trapped by a massive restricting snake. The snake slowly slid around the copulating couple, unnoticed as they were locked in each other's embrace. The snake's massive body coiled around them both then started to restrict, its deathly coils squeezing the life from them. They were unaware of the danger until it was too late. Hawk realized it was an omen of an evil that was growing and hidden by the couple's love and passion for each other.

Hawk could not understand the warning or message in the dream and it was only later, once the mutation had become dominant and the offspring showed the signs, did he comprehend the message. His only defense was to eliminate the hairless children, a practice he enforced upon the tribe. It was difficult for the new parents to take it upon themselves to kill their newborns who showed the signs, and some of the young parents chose to leave the tribe and keep the child, which increased the numbers of the Hairless Ones. The Hairless Ones were gregarious. The voice and aggression of the individuals would unite them into marauding groups as young adults.

Cloud remained in thought with Plenty as the camp started to awaken. He slowly came back to presence and the flood of pain from his bonds raked through his tortured body. His dry blood-filled mouth remained silent, the jaw hanging open with its extended tongue dry and exposed. His focus moved to a young girl who was prodding at what remained of the campfire, hoping it would reignite some of the un-burnt embers to warm her against the chilled, still morning air.

Slowly, the camp came to life. One of Death Dog's women came to check on Cloud, looking up at his lowered head. She detected movement in his eyes, and taking a leather strap from her waist she drenched it in water and placed it to his mouth. The water felt thick and cool, refreshing his parchedness. She knew that Death Dog's anger would be furious if the prisoner was allowed to escape torture through death.

As the sun started to clear the horizon, Death Dog made an appearance. He came out of his hut, throwing the skins hanging over the entrance to the floor and walking across them. He made his way towards the still-sleeping troops lying near what was left of the fire. As soon as the first one came within range, he started to rain down kicks making them aware of his presence and quickly waking them. In seconds, they were all awake, standing and wiping the sleep from their faces and wondering what he would want of them, trying to read his thoughts to prevent his anger from focusing on them.

He sat by the ashes of the fire as his women brought him food and drink. As they did, he instructed one of the young warriors to take fire and place it near the prisoner, Cloud. He fed himself on cold smoked meats, ripping at the deer ham and barely chewing as he swallowed large mouthfuls of the succulent protein. When he had finished, he tossed the bone into the ashes of the fire. A camp dog, braving Death Dog's boot, approached tentatively. Death Dog watched as the young dog tested the heat of the fire, leaning forward and trying to reach the bone that was just out of reach and protected by the still warm embers. Death Dog found amusement in the dog's struggle and as the dog reached forward he kicked it in the rear, sending it into the embers. The dog yelped and quickly escaped the fire. Whimpering and running, he quickly stopped to remove the hot coals that continued to burn into his hide. Death Dog watched and found the suffering amusing and the young warriors standing near him joined in, also laughing at the suffering mutt.

Cloud opened his eyes to the young warrior building a fire in the ashes near his feet, the fire that Death Dog used the previous day to torture his young companion. The young warrior was a skilled fire builder and soon had the fire rekindled and a clean flame leaping from the fresh fuel. He also stacked extra wood for when Death Dog needed to add to the embers.

The young warrior turned to look at Cloud, tethered and helpless. Their eyes met and Cloud stared deep into the young warrior's face. He felt the power of

Cloud's gaze and lowered his stare. Even bound and immobilized, Cloud's power was evident and the guilt of what Death Dog was about to do to him weighed on the young warrior.

Death Dog finally arrived where Cloud was tethered and members of the tribe, who had come to watch him at the work he so thoroughly enjoyed, followed him closely. He laid out his various bone-handled flint and fine obsidian knives. The flint blades he placed in the fire so that he could cauterize any bleeding that might prematurely end what he had planned. As the flint blades heated, he squatted at the feet of Cloud, sneering and looking up at him. Cloud had his head lowered and his eyes closed. He knew what was about to happen.

When in pain or sick, the Neanderthals would meditate. This was induced by what is best described as a purring sound; a low, barely audible rhythmic mmmmm on the outward breath. This meditation would allow the body to self-heal, letting the Neanderthal to separate them selves from the presence of the pain. It was a focus on the now of any situation. The pain circle was not allowed to live in the past, so all pain became only in the present and fleeting. Death Dog was aware of this ability having dealt with it before. His objective was to break the focus of his victim, so he could enjoy knowing the pain he was inflicting was being felt to its fullest. This was his greatest challenge.

He instructed two of his warriors to place twine around the forehead of Cloud and to force his head back, then to tether it to the post, immobilizing it. Once this had been done, Death Dog removed one of his finest obsidian blades from the pouch, inspecting it for sharpness and form. Holding it, he approached Cloud, his father, and raised himself up and proceeded to remove Cloud's upper eyelids. Cloud remained silent; his lower jaw still wide open with both his eyes exposed and staring.

Death Dog backed away looking up at Cloud, walking from side to side to see if he could detect any movement in his father's eyes. He could not, but he could clearly hear the low, audible purring on every outward breath.

Still holding the small, very sharp blade he again approached Cloud. With the skill of a modern day surgeon, he removed a six-inch wide strip of skin from across Cloud's chest. Then reaching down to the fire, he removed one of the heated bone handled blades so that he could sear and cauterize the wound. Still, Cloud was deep in his meditation.

In Cloud's thoughts, Hawk had joined him and both were high above the torture that was going on below. Cloud could see far across the canopy of the forest, enjoying the maneuvers that Hawk was sharing; lifting on thermals, circling upwards, and then breaking from the lift into an exhilarating dive. The wind noise easing only as Hawk leveled out and again began to be lifted by the gentle up current. Hawk joined Cloud in keeping his focus away from what was happening to his body below.

Death Dog was frustrated, as he could not break Cloud's meditation. The torturing went on for two more hours; Cloud's body tortured to the extent the life force was starting to fade. Death Dog became aware that he was being watched. He looked around himself, scanning the village for the presence of what he was feeling. He then looked upwards to the sky. Circling high above him he could see the hawk. His anger raged inside him. He removed one of his heavy blades from the skin on the floor. Looking up at Hawk he moved close to Cloud, striking the blade deep into his sternum and opening up the chest cavity. Reaching in, he grabbed the still beating heart and ripped it free. Holding it above his head he screamed up at Hawk, the blood still pumping down his arm as he screamed upwards. He threw the heart of his dead father to be eaten by the snarling camp dogs who fought over the morsel, pulling and tearing it apart.

Hawk could feel the release of Cloud's spirit, the light taking over his vision. Then, there was a feeling of relief as the brilliance raced from Cloud, taking him back to his source. Hawk circled, watching from high above and looking down as Death Dog turned his back on the corpse of his tortured father. He was sweating and covered in blood as he walked towards the water sack hanging by his cabin's entrance. He removed the bag and lent his head back to take a large mouthful of the cool water. He closed his eyes and waited for the water to enter his mouth.

Hawk watched, circling. He started to see an opportunity, and closing his wings he entered a powerful dive. His hawk eyes focused on the target below. The speed of his dive rapidly increased. His target raced towards him, and at the last moment, flaring back his head and opening his wings, he extended his talons in front of him.

Death Dog instantly became aware of something hitting his face, fleeting and painless. He lowered the water sack and started to comprehend that Hawk had attacked him. Hawk had slashed his face and ripped one of his eyes from the socket. The bird lifted from his face, and Death Dog brought his hands to his face, feeling the wound and the void where his left eye used to be. The deep rip to his right cheek poured blood that now mingled with the dried blood of Cloud, still covering his hands.

Hawk lifted from the affray still holding the eye as he climbed away from the camp and finally perched. Then, ripping into the eye, he ate it.

Death Dog was still trying to comprehend what had just taken place, probing his face with his bloody hands and trying to assess the damage. He started to scream for his women to come forward and dress his wounds. They, along with the warriors who had witnessed the attack, had retreated away from Death Dog, not sure of what it was that had attacked. In the years to come, the bird would grow in size, as would the wounds it inflicted. Eventually it grew to a size in the telling where it picked Death Dog up and was flying with him. According to the legend, Death Dog pulled a knife from his belt and killed the bird.

His screaming and ranting finally over, the fear of those present subsided and they helped him dress and clean his wounds, covering them with healing herbs. The tribe was convinced it was the spirit of Cloud that had attacked and that the killing of his father had crossed some unwritten line.

The healing to Death Dog's face was a slow process. He would spend many hours with his head covered by a dampened skin over a small fire, allowing the herb-filled smoke to do its work. His image had, in fact, been enhanced; the scar down his cheek was wide and jagged, and the closed empty and sunken left eye added to his fearsome appearance. These wounds helped to make his mood fouler and his constant demeanor uglier than ever.

His desire to kill the rest of the Neanderthals was feverishly fueled. He knew the power of Hawk and that what had happened to his face was clearly the work of the old Shaman. Every day, Death Dog would send out hunters to look for signs of the Neanderthals, scolding them on their empty-handed return. He knew they were hiding, holed up close. They would make a mistake, relaxing their diligence. He would be ready, never relaxing until he had tracked them down and made them pay.

Plenty had felt the separation as Cloud's tortured physical form released his spirit to return to its base. She was devastated, a terrible feeling of being alone consuming her every thought. She could only ever remember having Cloud with her, either in thought or being together as one.

Throughout the next few days her mourning increased and she moved to the wall away from the entrance of the cave. On this wall were many handprints. Cloud had never left a print, which could have given her comfort just to touch, a connection that she craved. She placed her back to the wall deeply depressed. From that moment, she never again let water or food pass her lips.

The other tribe members tried in vain to comfort her, sitting beside her. Young Water would spend many hours stroking her face, offering her food and touching water to her lips, which she ignored. It took fourteen days for her to pass. She never spoke, only sitting cross-legged, silent, hands palm up and deep in meditation. She had closed herself down so that telepathic communication was not possible. She stayed like this until she joined Cloud in death. On her passing, her body was taken from the cave and laid out under the sky so it to could return to its base.

Peter was deep into his telling when the sobbing and sniffling of Alicia got his attention. Alicia was clearly disturbed by the violence of the telling and the passing of Plenty.

"Are you okay, dear?" Peter asked.

Alicia apologized. "I'm sorry, I could not help myself."

Peter dropped his legs from the couch to the floor, and then relying heavily on the arm of the couch, he attempted to stand. Even with the help of the chair arm, he was unable to make it in one attempt, getting to the half-standing position then dropping back to the couch. "Getting old is tough," he said. He refocused his energy and again attempted to stand, which he achieved. Finally, he was able to walk towards Alicia who was wiping her face and blowing her nose.

He stood next to her, placing his arm across her shoulder and again asked her, "Are you okay, my dear?"

"I'm okay," she sniffed. "It's just so sad that poor Plenty had to go through that. She loved Cloud so much. The torturing was so horrific. Why would anyone do that to his own flesh and blood? It's awful."

Peter responded, trying to explain and at the same time reassure Alicia. "Death Dog is an ego-based individual that will do whatever he must to remove any threat to him or what he perceives as competition. You can see it taking place even today; prejudice and insecurity often leads to genocide. During the last century we, as a species, killed more Individuals than in any other time in history. The Buddhists have a saying that, if you give it a name, then you can kill it. In any society, the enemy within can be created by intimating a difference, and then identifying it with a name. That de-humanizes the individual and then you can kill it without guilt. Some names used to identify groups, Jew, Nigger, Wop, are all very dangerous and have been used to initiate killings and torture. Even in our politically correct and liberal Austin you can soon stir up a prejudice with both political names being used as an identifier: Republican and Democrat. You have given them a name; you have in fact de-humanized your opposition and now, if the situation arises, you can kill without guilt. Most of the killings that were done in the last century were by people thinking they were doing good, killing someone that the society considered a threat or different.

Darwin's observation identified the assent of species, or as I prefer to call it, mutation. A mutation that gives an individual an advantage in the geographical area it finds itself continues to be dominant and takes over. Nature is always looking for an advantage to capitalize on and there will always be winners and losers.

Death Dog had developed ego backed up by self-serving aggression. His mutation provided him with the motivation and cunning to dominate and replicate in his own image. We might be heading finally to end of aggression being the key to success. In the words of Jesus, 'The meek will inherit the earth.' That can only be achieved by a spiritual awakening on a global basis; so don't lose faith Alicia. That, my girl, might be your calling. Come on, let's take a break and get a cup of coffee."

Alicia, still wiping her face and blowing her nose, started to follow Peter towards the kitchen.

Chapter 15

Over the next six months, Alicia worked hard to get Peter's house cleaned and into shape. He had given her the guest apartment which she would use two or three times a week. At times, her mother and Tim would come over and her mother would cook for them all. The meals were entertaining and enlightening. Peter was really enjoying his new family. The house grounds were looking good and this again allowed more time for Alicia to spend working on Peter's storytelling.

One evening when they all were enjoying a meal and get together, Tim pointed out that he had come across an article by an anthropologist, Dr. Jim Zeallow. He was working in Spain and had been studying the meaning of handprints in a cave known as the El Castillo Cave. The cave included handprints and art that dated back between forty to fifty thousand years. This period is known as the end of the Neanderthals; the modern humans started turning up around this time. Tim quickly added, "El Castillo is the name of a conical limestone mountain in the Cantabrian region of what is today Spain." Alicia laughed at Tim's nerdish detailed quotes that he loved dropping into conversation. Tim removed from his pocket two sheets of paper he had downloaded and continued to read the article word for word.

When he finished, Tim continued. "What was interesting about these prints and the cave they were in was the artwork that accompanied the handprints. The artwork was carbon dated to the same period, yet depicted animals and weapons from different parts of the world. One part of the cave had artwork that, for all intents and purpose, was Australian, Aboriginal, in form. They are starting to believe that the ancients had a joint knowledge source. At present, the migration of the early humans is the most popular belief of how knowledge spread. The speed of which knowledge of weaponry and tools became globalized does not validate this hypothesis under closer investigation. Remote Pacific Islands have been discovered with similar tools found in what is now Europe. It all points to a knowledge that was shared between the ancients by dream or telepathy, a Google of the ancients, if you like." Tim grinned, satisfied at his nerdish comparison.

Peter was very excited by this information and asked Tim to repeat some of the story and if it would be possible to contact Jim Zeallow, the anthropologist. He then went over his understanding of the painted handprints that had been left by many of the ancient civilizations, explaining that the handprints were used as a teaching aid, much like a USB port on a computer. "If you wanted to know how to hunt a particular animal, you would meditate to clear your mind, and then carefully place your hand upon the print of an ancestor that would have had that knowledge. Through the handprint, you would receive the knowledge from that past ancestor on how he would have gone about the hunt. Through contact with the print, you will receive the information you require."

Alicia asked Peter "Was that why you left handprints all over the monuments? If someone had taken the time to meditate and clear their mind, would they have been able to get a message that you had left?"

Peter grinned, "Maybe we should try it sometime." He then continued, "The information the hand can transmit is much underestimated. Most cultures even today will unconsciously evaluate an individual by the information gained by a hand gesture or touch, as in when we shake hands. The Native American's would raise a hand to indicate peace, but maybe the information was subliminally sent: this is my hand and this is who I am. You can trust me.

This, however, was only part of the methods they used to communicate. Much knowledge was shared by dream. The dreamers were a very important part of the ancient world and any individual that had this ability was valued amongst the tribe members. They would receive dreams that they felt were sent to them. Often the meaning of a dream would be hidden in a riddle within the dream. The dreamer would share the dream in detail as experienced, transmitting his dream to the elders of the tribe. Many hours would be spent working out the true meaning or message hidden in the conundrum.

An easy example would be how they began burning flint to make it more workable. The dreamer received a vision of a toolmaker knapping some low grade and difficult flint, with many misshaped and broken flints surrounding him where he sat cross-legged. He is depressed by the problems he is having working the flint, so he throws the flint rock into the fire. Later, he returns. The fire has burned down and the blackened rock lies in the ashes. He picks up the now cool flint and holds it towards the sky. The flint transforms into a perfect spear point, the napped parts of the blackened flint dropping to the ground. After the dreamer had shared the dream, one of the elders suggested they heat the flint by fire before they try to work it. They did and found that it became far easier to get the flint to flake as desired. From that date, the tribe's flint was heated before used for making tools. That's what intrigued me about Genesis and the story of Adam and Eve. It is how a warning of inbreeding would have been given in dream. This is how knowledge was spread between the ancients."

Peter questioned Tim as to how he had come upon the information. Tim explained that he had been listening to a podcast called Radio Lab that was doing a series of stories on art. Art is a determining factor in deciding if a society is civilized. They then went on to interview Dr. Jim Zeallow. "I thought you would find it interesting so I noted his website," said Tim. Standing, he left the table to retrieve his laptop from his car, bringing it back to the table. He showed Peter the cave art and handprints and then went to Google Earth to show the region of the cave location.

Peter was intrigued and he asked Tim to navigate around the region of the cave, looking closely at the topography. Taking over the mouse from Tim, Peter zoomed in and out, going down and following the track of the river. It was the location of the cave to the river that intrigued Peter. It was set in a due east direction which would fill the cave with the rising morning sun. The river track was different than what he remembered, but it was very similar in distance from the cave. Peter looked for a waterfall and asked Tim to assist him to track the river on the laptop. Tim zoomed in and guided the mouse over the river, looking for the waterfall. Peter commented, "No waterfall," sounding a little disappointed.

Tim interjected, "Look, Peter; rapids. Over the course of forty thousand years, the waterfall could well have been worn away to become what is now this valley with rapids racing through it; the water having worn away the limestone over time."

Peter wanted to look at the website of the cave again. It had a panoramic view of the cave walls, showing the painted handprints and art. He took control of the mouse and sat quietly, studying the images on the cave wall. Alicia stood beside him looking over his shoulder as he passed through the images. Finally, he turned from the computer saying, "Amazing."

Alicia asked, "Is it the cave you were in Peter?"

Peter appeared slightly confused, walking away from the table to refresh his coffee. "I am not sure. It could be. The location of the cave to the river certainly makes it possible, but the cave art and handprints I can't be sure. I really need to do more research."

He then asked Tim to read the text of the website and what Dr. Jim Zeallow was basing his assumptions upon. After Tim had verbalized the content of the website, Peter, who was sitting at the table sipping his coffee, commented, "He is one smart dude. We really must get in contact with him. Tim, would you be kind enough to help us set up a new computer and network for the house? The one we are using is a bit dated now and should be replaced. I was very impressed at the speed and graphics of your laptop. Being able to fly over that cave site was very impressive. Why don't you take Alicia to Best Buy and get me a set of up-to-date computers?"

"I would love to do that. What's your budget?" responded Tim.

"Alicia will help you decide what we need, and as for budget, just get me the good stuff."

Alicia said, "Let's go all Apple: Desktop, MacBook Air, and you, Peter, need an iPad. You will love it."

"Let's go," said Tim. "I can't think of anything I would enjoy more than going to Best Buy and spending someone else's money." Peter and Brenda stayed behind, Brenda cleaning up from dinner and Peter taking a much-needed rest.

Three hours later, Tim and Alicia returned with her car loaded to the hilt with box upon box of Apple computers and peripherals that Tim had deemed necessary. It took two days to get the old computer packed away and the new ones working. Tim spent the next couple of days after work showing Peter how the new Apple system worked. He also showed Peter how to play Words with Friends on his iPad. Peter and Tim spent many hours playing the word game, trying to outdo each other. Tim was surprised how quick Peter was at picking up how to use his iPad and about the amount of words he had at his disposal to equally match Tim on the game.

The storytelling hit a hiatus as Peter and Tim played with the new equipment, allowing time for Alicia and her mother to work on the décor of the house and do a little spring-cleaning. Once all the new computers were up and running and Peter was efficient using them, they settled into a routine that always started with a cup of coffee on the front porch swing watching the day begin, with the dominant Mockingbird joining them. After the coffee and the day had been greeted, they would retire to the library and Peter would continue with the telling.

After Death Dog consumed the body of Cloud, he had his skull cleaned. He then placed it at the entrance to his hut. It was stuck on a large stick buried to the left of the skinned entrance. Every time he would leave the hut he would stop, turn and look at the skull. He would then rub his fingers over the scar that Hawk had left on his face. This refocused his hatred for the Neanderthals and he would commence to scream instructions for his hunters to find what was left of the clan.

His hatred for the Neanderthals and his desire for revenge had become an obsession. Hunters were scared to return to the camp each night as they knew that they would be questioned and beaten for not finding them. One of the hunters had returned, saying that he had found a fresh killed Moose that had been killed with stabbing spears, like the ones used by the clan. Death Dog questioned the young hunter in detail, finally resorting to torture of the young hunter. The result was the death of the young hunter for not finding the location of the Neanderthal camp. He screamed that the track just disappeared and begged for Death Dog to stop. He sobbed his innocence, explaining that he followed the tracks for several hours but they disappeared in the river below the waterfall. He explained how he had walked both sides of the river, checking to find where they exited. This was not enough for Death Dog and the pleading of the young hunter was not enough to quell the temper and hatred inside him.

Wolf was very aware of the persistence of Death Dog and the danger they all faced if discovered. He spent many hours going over the defense of the cave with Hawk, planning together and putting in place traps for anyone trying to get to the cave. They both, however, were aware that, if discovered, the chances of survival were slim. At the moment, the cave was still their best option. Hawk had gone over with Wolf the potential of escaping from the cave and leading his group away from the constant threat.

The range of mountains to the north potentially offered freedom from the threat of annihilation at the hands of Death Dog, but it was a three-day march for a fit, well-prepared hunting group. The prospect of doing this march with the elderly and young was not practical. The group was out of balance in that too few were effective at hunting and gathering. Too many needed looking after, and too few could hunt and soldier. However, with all the danger, to leave the cave was the only hope of long term survivability for what was left of the tribe, and Hawk knew he would have to make a decision to set out before long.

Wolf and Hawk planned for the eventual move of the tribe. Resting places would have to be well hidden and stocked with food and water. To put all this in place with so few capable of going out and achieving the required objectives while remaining undiscovered was difficult.

Daily excursions for food and firewood were necessary just to sustain the remains of the tribe. The few hunters that were left realized they needed a big kill and that was why they killed the Moose. The need to quickly dress and return to the cave without leaving signs meant leaving a lot of the Moose skeleton behind. The remains contained a lot of the marrow so high in protein. Normally, the group would have taken the time to pack and bag the bones in the skin of the Moose, but the hunters could not afford time to properly dress the magnificent beast, as they feared discovery. Wolf would constantly remind all of them the importance of covering their tracks and not to be caught in the open if at all possible. The location of the two groups and the overlap of hunting and herb gathering grounds were too small and had to lead to eventual discovery.

The collection of herbs was a task best done by the females with their more dexterous and delicate hands, but it was also dangerous. Some of the plants you needed to treat very carefully, and the pollen itself was all you wanted in other plants. You needed to leave the plant undamaged to produce more for future use. The women would remove the pollen with a feather and place it into a dry leather buckskin bag for return to the camp to be used for medicine. The pollen was used to treat wounds and had excellent healing properties. They would search for the plants they needed on the high grounds, Hawk sharing with them some of his own ancient and well looked-after gardens. The young females would join the female elders in the collecting of herbs and pigments from high on the flat lands, which was reached by going through the back of the cave. Hawk would not allow the women to hunt these herbs and plants in the low ground, where Death Dog and his troops continued to look for signs of their presence.

The constant fear of being discovered started to have its effect upon the remainder of the tribe. The children were petrified to go outside in case they were seen and often would awake during the night screaming, dreaming that Death Dog's savages were attacking them. The loving parents would try hard to reassure the children, but the children were able to pick up on their parent's concerns and fears, perpetuating their misery. Hawk realized that this situation could not be sustained. A mistake would be made.

The tribe settled into a day-to-day routine to help quell their fears. The elders would entertain the children, involving them in the cleaning of the cave, making of fire, cooking, and even playing games or learning skills they would need when grown. Using flint to make tools for shaping wood and cleaning skins was something the young males enjoyed, smashing the large flints onto the cave floor, shattering the flint. They would run forward, digging through the splintered fragments for particles that could be used as knifes or scraping blades.

One of the elders was an expert flint knapper who enjoyed teaching the young ones how to handle and master flint correctly. Laying a skin across his crossed legs, he would demonstrate how to look for the grain in the flint. With a few grunts, facial expressions and body language, he was able to entertain and teach the young boys, his enthusiasm infective. All sitting, they would each be given a piece of rock and shown how to hold it. He would orchestrate the first blow of the hand-held striking rocks, all impacting perfectly at the same time. The excitement of the young boys as they quickly went through the flakes, holding up for inspection and for all to see the tool they had just created, was infectious. Some were so excited they could not remain seated and would rush around the group, showing everyone the perfect knife or point for a stabbing spear.

The elders also showed the children how to build a fire, and then carefully place Birch bark near enough to the fire to sweat, but not close enough for it to combust. This would create pitch that would be used as glue. They needed a lot of heat to sweat the pitch from the bark. This required an oven that would generate enough heat to extract the valuable pitch needed to make the first synthetic glue. When the pitch had been collected it would be used to hold weapons together, the precision-made flint spearheads being tethered and then covered in the pitch that would harden. The elders shared these practices with the young and used the results to prepare knives and spears for the coming, inevitable, battle.

Another pastime the children would love was looking at the pictures of animals and hunts from the past painted on the cave walls. Hawk would point out certain elements of the art that represented some person or story, entertaining the children for hours. The children themselves were shown how to make the paint from pigment and how to use the charcoal from the fire. One part of the cave had nearly been covered in the handprints of the children and the elders. The gift the handprints held were not at first apparent to the young as they did not have the ability to clear their mind and accept the information held in the prints.

One day, a young hunter and his girl friend approached Hawk. She was the one to communicate using hand gestures and thought that she requested permission to go with her young mate to the low lands to collect stinging nettle for her mother who suffered badly from joint pain. The Neanderthals would take long sprigs of nettle and swat the affected joint, trading joint pain for the sting of the nettle. The sting produced by the nettle causes the body to manufacture chemicals that have anti-inflammatory and pain reducing powers. Because of the damp living conditions, joint pain in the elderly was common and the desire for nettle treatment popular amongst them. The root of the plant was boiled also to make a soothing lotion. The nettles have high levels of boron in them and can be used to treat arthritis. The nettles that were needed only grew in the lowlands in irrigated earth that can be found near the river.

Hawk let them know that he wanted time to think about it, which he did. He took council with Wolf and between them decided that, as she was so proficient in the collection of herbs, she would be allowed to go to the lowlands. She would have to go with two hunters to guard her as she collected the specimens. The young hunters were again instructed how important it was to make sure that all tracks were covered.

The next day, the three of them set off to the lowlands. The excitement of the young female at the opportunity to escape the confines of the cave was obvious in her gestures and expressions. Slowly, they made their way down the cliff face, through the waterfall, and then down the cave, which led them to the low grounds below to where the river slowed. Hawk was above, watching and searching the area for any signs of Death Dog's troops. He could see no signs of them. He flew over Death Dog's camp and all was normal, reassuring Hawk.

The young female soon spotted the nettles she was looking for. She carefully wrapped her hands in soft deerskins to protect herself against the stinging hairs that covered the stem and underside of the leaves and began selecting her specimens. She carefully removed the nettle from the ground, including the roots that she needed to make the lotion.

She was instructed by Wolf not to remove too many from any one spot, spreading her collecting out so that it was not noticeable that someone had been harvesting the nettles. The two young hunters spread out, each taking one side of the river to look for signs of the Hairless Ones. All looked clear and the girl's mate returned to sit and watch his young love carefully harvesting the nettles. The other hunter stayed out of the way on the other side of the river, allowing the two of them to have some time together alone.

The young hunter waited until she had gathered a large armful of nettles. She knew he was watching and was orchestrating the moment when she could ask him to come and help her carefully wrap the collected nettles into skins for transporting. It had been too long since they had been able to get away together and they were both excited with anticipation.

He approached her and she knew what was about to happen. She handed her large armful of collected nettles to him, and then indicated that she needed to go to the bathroom before they made love. She walked away from him to a large Raspberry bush that was just to the side of the nettle patch. Making sure she was not in view, she bobbed down and peed. When completed, she dried herself on a Dock leaf before standing and straightening her skin clothing and returned to her lover. He dropped the nettles to the ground, the collection no longer his focus. His hormones were controlling him and the matter of safety faded in importance as his desire to make love to her raged inside of him. She felt the same and reached out and grabbed his hand. She pulled him towards her, then down to the ground where they made love. It was, by design, that their emotions were able to take control. The fear of being discovered meant nothing, nor did the consequence of inbreeding. They were cousins, but the lust for each other blinded any consequences. This is the snake talked of in Genesis. This is the uncontrollable desire that has tainted the perfect bloodline, a genetic bottleneck that threatened their existence as a species.

They made love passionately, physically and mentally becoming one. It had been too long. They needed each other.

Hawk sat silent on the cave floor deep in meditation. Young Water had joined him, placing her back next to his, feeling his calmness and power. He circled above the loving couple watching what was happening below, making sure they were safe from being discovered.

The young couple laid beside each other looking at the sky, both feeling satisfied and deeply in love. The young hunter noticed the hawk in the sky. He felt safe as he turned and, holding her head, kissed her softly.

The other young hunter decided it was time for them all to return to the group. He crossed the river noisily to let the couple know that he was approaching. He saw the two heads pop up above the vegetation like two MeerKats and so felt comfortable to continue his approach.

The couple stood and continued with the wrapping of the collected nettles for transportation. The young girl also insisted on taking some Raspberry leaves, again being careful not to collect too many from one spot. The Raspberry leaves were used to treat nausea, bowel problems and inflammation of the eyes. The collecting was done and carefully they covered their tracks back to the cave entrance that would lead them back to the waterfall and the long climb up the narrow path to the cave entrance. The young hunter in the lead made sure to replace the traps as they went past. Wolf had constructed small pads of clay that had shards of obsidian baked into them. If anyone were to stand on one of these it would cut the foot badly.

Later that day, one of Death Dog's hunters was checking holes in the riverbank for catfish. The bottom of the waterfall was a well-known area for the catfish it produced. Working his way along the river and checking the bank for holes, he came across a place where he could see that something or someone had climbed out from the river and up the bank. On closer investigation, he could see that it was a person who not only had climbed from the river but had also tried to cover his tracks.

Climbing from the river, he placed his captured catfish down carefully. He had strung the catfish on a vine rope and he used a branch to hold them in place so as not to fall back into the river. He moved slowly, observing every twig and blade of grass for signs. With his trained eye, it was soon evident there had been people here not very long ago. He moved purposely, every step measured and carefully placed so as not to destroy the signs that he might need to track the direction of whoever it was had taken.

He dropped to his knees; moving forward to the area the nettles had been collected. He slowly moved around the area. Then, he could clearly smell urine. Still moving cautiously towards the place the young girl had relieved herself, he found the exact spot and lowered his head and breathed deeply to confirm this was the place. He could clearly see the footprints on either side of the place the urine had landed and knew that it was a female that had relieved herself at this spot.

His heart was bounding with excitement, but he had to control himself and remained diligent of every move he made. He knew that no woman from the Hairless tribe would be this far from camp, confirming he was tracking Neanderthals. He continued investigating the area and could clearly see the depression where the couple had made love. He again lowered his head, sniffing deeply to confirm what his eyes were telling him. He rose up and started to move in circles: slowly, diligently, determined to find the place and direction the Neanderthals had taken. He was on the tracks, the signs so weak that he often had to go back to confirm he was on the spore.

If he found where the Neanderthals were, he would be elevated within the tribe. Death Dog would almost certainly give him a woman of his own. However, if he lost the track he would never be able to tell anyone, as it would lead certainly to his torture and demise. This thought chilled him and re-focused his mission. The tracks led into the forest across a game trail that headed towards the waterfall. The Neanderthals had stayed off the path, being a good ten paces into the dense forest vegetation. He was able to see how they had made sure not to damage some of the larger plants, but in the process left subtle signs in the lichen and moss that covered the damp forest floor. Taking his time, he was able to track them to the hidden cave entrance, which again had been covered with vegetation. The casual observer would have completely missed the entrance, but to his trained eye it was obvious this was the track they had taken.

Slowly, he entered the cave, which headed up an incline. Water ran down the center of the cave towards the entrance, but dispersed before the exit through large fishers in the bedrock. He stepped slowly and carefully deeper into the cave. The light was difficult to see by, but he could feel the updraft of the wind on his back caused by the chimney effect of the cave. He realized there must be an exit in that direction. Feeling his way along the wall of the cave he headed up, finding Raspberry leaves which the group had dropped. This reassured him that he was on their trail and they were unaware that they had been detected.

It was not long before the roar of the waterfall filled his ears and the light in the cave improved. He found himself behind the waterfall and in front of another cave entrance that the Neanderthals had taken. He stopped to take in what he had discovered. He could taste Death Dog's pleasure with him and the fact that he would be held so high among the hairless ones. The thought of him having his own woman excited him, and he walked backwards and forwards laughing out loud and rubbing his crotch.

He refocused and proceeded into the cave entrance. Before long, he came out of the cave and could see the small ledge that the group had taken and decided it was a good time for him to return to inform

Death Dog that he had found the hiding place of the Neanderthals. His excitement was almost uncontrollable as he ran down behind the waterfall and finally down the last cave to ground level. As he exited the cave, he took the time to again cover the entrance. He did not want anyone else to discover what he had learned. He raced back to the river, collected his drying catfish that he tied to his waist, and slid down the bank. He then jumped into the river to head down stream towards the camp and his speculated rewards and admirations.

The young girl and two hunters returned to the cave to be greeted by Wolf. He helped them place down the collected herbs and the group gathered around as they all showed excitement at their return. Hawk walked forward and placed his hands into the hands of the young hunters. He felt reassured they were comfortable and that they had not been discovered and had covered their tracks.

The elders sorted through the gathered herbs, each thanking the group with hugs and smiles. The elder women took on the cleaning of the herbs and preparation. The roots were removed from the nettles without damaging the sting hairs that would relieve the aching joints. The center cave fire was rekindled and water gathered in large leather bags was then placed into clay-covered wood pots that would allow them to heat the water to make a tea from the Raspberry leaves and an ointment from the roots of the nettles.

Chapter 16

Detective Granger's telephone burst into life, bringing him quickly down to earth from the latest local murder scenario he had been working his way through in his head. He looked at the caller ID and could see it was the chief. He picked up the phone. Holding the phone to his ear, he stood and turned to look over the top of the dividers that separated the room. He made instant eye contact with the chief who was looking back at him through his open blinded window.

"What's up, Chief?" Jeffrey asked.

"Jeffrey, would you mind stepping into my office for a moment? I have something I would like to go over with you."

Granger responded, "Certainly, Sir. Be right with you."

He scanned his desk wondering if he should take with him any of the case files he was currently working on. His caseload was heavy but nothing seemed to be out of the ordinary. As he approached the chief's office, he took advantage of the opportunity to top up the cold quarter-cup of coffee he had left with steaming hot fresh coffee. He sipped the coffee, smiled to himself, and proceeded towards the chief's door.

"Morning Chief, what's the problem?" he asked.

The chief responded, "Take a seat, son. I have got something I want to chew over with you."

Jeffrey took himself over to one of the chairs in front of the chief's desk. As he sat, he removed a notepad from his rear pocket and a pen from his shirt pocket.

"You won't need that Jeffrey," the chief said. Jeffrey sat down and made himself comfortable.

The chief began, "Jeffrey, you have been with me since I took over this department. I have grown to respect the work you do. You are always diligent and thorough. The truth is, Jeffrey, its time for me to move on, to retire. As you know, Sylvia and I have been married now for two years and we would like to go south and settle down near Mazatlan, Mexico, near her parents. The fishing is good there; the climate and life style fit our plans nicely. Also, my pension will stretch further. I would like you to consider taking over this department. I don't need you to make a snap decision, but I would like you to let me know as soon as you can so that we can start tying up loose ends."

Jeffrey stood back up and walked towards the chief, putting his hand out. "Chief, thank you for your confidence. I don't need time to think it over. I, of course, am honored than you would consider me to replace you, and yes I will take the job."

The chief smiled, shaking Jeffrey's hand vigorously. "You will need to get some of your own loose ends sorted over the next couple of weeks. I would like you to shadow me so the transition is smooth. Follow me around and see what the job entails. We will need to get the press office to work out the best way to handle the announcement. I will give Marie a call and ask her if she can come over."

Jeffrey stood quietly as the chief pressed a three-digit number on his desk phone and waited before he started talking. "Morning, Marie. Could you come down to the office as I have something I want to go over with you?"

Jeffrey and the chief spent their time on small talk while waiting for the arrival of Marie. The chief told Jeffrey about the massive Rooster fish that can be caught from the surf in Mazatlan. Jeffrey could see the chief's bright eyes glowing with excitement as he spoke and replied that one day he might be able to bring his family down for a holiday.

Marie arrived and was not surprised by what the chief was telling her. She had heard rumors in the staff lounge of the chief's desire to retire.

Her first comment was, "Has your choice of Jeffrey replacing you been cleared up stairs?"

The chief said, "Yes, but we still have to publish the fact that I will be retiring and that people who are interested need to apply; just a cover-our-ass thing, Jeffrey."

"I understand Chief."

Okay, so when do you want the world to know that you are retiring Chief?" Marie asked.

"Well, I was thinking of making it at the

beginning of next month. That gives us nearly four weeks to get everything in place and for me to transition young Jeffrey here."

"How do you feel about it, Jeffrey?" asked Marie.

"I'm excited and looking forward to the challenge. Chief will make sure I have everything I need before he leaves."

"Okay, I will work out a press release and get back to the chief later today. I will be sorry to see you go, Chief. I have enjoyed working with you." Marie turned her attention to Jeffrey and went over to shake his hand. "Congratulations, Jeffrey. You will make a fine chief."

"Thank you, Marie," replied Jeffrey as he let her hand go. She turned to leave the office, and as she reached the door Jeffrey asked, "Did you ever find anything about the problem we had with someone leaking to the press?"

Marie stopped and re-closed the door, so that what she was about to say never went any further than the three of them in the room. "No, I tried to put pressure on the editor, but got nowhere. I do know that since that incident with that young reporter, it's all gone quiet. No more leaks, so someone was getting edgy and thought they had better lay low for a while. What about you? Did you find out anything?"

Jeffrey answered slowly, "Oh, I found out who it was, but there's not enough to pin it on him. My time will come; he isn't off the hook yet."

Returning to his desk, he removed his cell phone from the clip on his belt and called his wife to let her know of the promotion he had been offered and what it would mean to them as a family. Her first question was, "Will you get any more time to spend with us and the kids?"

Jeffrey answered, "The schedule should be more predictable, but I would think it will mean handling more of the day to day stuff on the fly; twenty-four seven."

She immediately wanted to know more detail about the twenty-four seven comment.

"Well, I will have the responsibility of several detectives that will require permissions and guidance, mainly phone calls at the house I would think. I will just be needed more overall, but less time in the field. The job is more organizational and political than what I am currently doing and there is a considerable increase in salary."

He could hear her yelling, "Whoo-Hooooo," on the other end of the line. "Congratulations darling, you deserve it. I will go and get some nice steaks and some good wine to celebrate this evening. Maybe I can even get my parents to keep the kids!"

Jeffrey replied, "That sounds great. You get it sorted out. I've got to go. Love you loads." He pressed end and looked at his phone to make sure the call had ended and then placed it back on his belt.

He immediately started to go through the files on his desk. He sorted them into the varying stages of the process, and those that could be filed away as completed. Looking at the files, he realized the suffering they represented. Every one of them represented some form of loss. The departed that had been left lying on the side of a road or burned in a car had, at one time, been someone's child. Hopefully, at sometime, loved by his family and friends. His job had been to find the reason behind the madness and clear society's guilt and responsibility for the corpse that they cared more for when it was dead than alive. He moved the files into heaps that he would later make separate decisions on.

Finally, he came to the file of Peter Shaw, still uncompleted. He grinned to himself as he opened the file and quickly reviewed the notes he had left when he had last worked on it. He had passed the file to the prosecutor who had chosen to procrastinate on any further actions. He smiled to himself and then remembered how embarrassed he had been over the leak. That was personal, and he would make sure that part of the inquiry did not join the cold case files for review.

Within a couple of weeks the word was out. It was time to empty his desk and move into the chief's office. Marie worked closely with both of them to make sure all of the i's were dotted and the t's crossed. The actual passing over of the job was done live and was well covered by the local television stations. Peter, seeing it on the local news, smiled to himself. He liked Jeffrey Granger and thought he would make an excellent chief. He wondered if, in his new position, he would pursue the case he had pending against him or if, as time passed, it became more irrelevant. He figured that his young lawyer, Scott, would soon get in touch with him if it did come to the surface.

Jeffrey settled into his new job and the department soon got the feel for the rhythm that Jeffrey liked to get things done. He was a good boss that had come up through he ranks. Everyone liked him as long as you took care of your duties. Have a problem, share it with him. That's all he wanted. It was a couple of month's before he felt comfortable enough to deal with the leak issue and Sergeant Madden.

It was late on a Friday afternoon. Jeffrey had been sitting in his office listening to Madden cursing up a storm and shouting at some young rookie when he finely could not take it anymore. He had Madden's file pulled and started to go through it. He had twenty-six years of service with the department, which he joined straight from the Marines after serving in Vietnam. He had got a suspension with pay back in 2002 for being over-enthusiastic with a stun gun. Apparently, the person he was stunning was a drunk and harmless, but did approach Madden when he pulled the stun gun and zapped him with it. The drunk went down, but Madden kept hitting him with the shocks so that an ambulance had to be called and, of course, someone had it on video. It made the news and Sergeant Madden's days of leading a patrol group was done. He was given the option to resign or stay inside. Reluctantly, he took the desk job. Jeffrey picked up his phone and called the front desk. Sergeant Madden answered, "Madden."

"Sergeant, when you get a few minutes I would like you to step into my office. I have a couple of things I would like to go over with you."

Madden did not like Chief Granger. As far as he was concerned, Granger was a brown-noser that had kissed enough asses to get him the captain's job. He did not like him and at every opportunity he would tell everyone that he only had nine months to go and he was out of there, retired. As he approached Granger's office, Granger stood and closed the blinds. He did not want anyone to see or hear what he had to say to Sergeant Madden.

Madden knocked on the door, but did not wait to be asked to enter. He walked in saying, "How can I help you, Chief?"

"Well, take a seat Madden. As you know old Mike who runs the car park security is about to retire and we need someone to fill his place."

Madden answered, "So, what can I do about it?"

Granger lay back in his chair, dropping his eyes to the tin of tobacco he was rolling in his hands. "Well, Madden. You remember the problems we had with someone leaking to the press in this department?"

Madden answered hesitantly, "Yes."

"Well, that problem seems to have gone away since we had the leak that got that little girl reporter fired."

Madden said, "Well, that's good Chief."

Granger added, "You know why that problem went away, don't you sergeant?"

"No, Chief," said Madden.

"That problem went away because the person that was doing the leaking was starting to feel the heat, the sort of heat that can get a man in trouble." Madden never said a word. He just sat looking at Jeffrey, wondering how much he knew and where this was going.

Jeffrey continued, "That particular leak that got that young reporter fired and me accused of being the only person to know that she was with the senator really pissed me off Sergeant. It pissed me off so bad that I made a point of finding out who was doing the leaking. Who it was that was phoning his friend John Kerr, the Editor."

Madden remained still and quiet, and stared directly at Jeffrey.

"We both know who it was that was doing the leaking, Madden. I can prove it. So, Madden, I am now in the position where I can offer you a change of position. You can finish your time with the department running security in the parking lot, nine months I believe, or I will ask you to resign. I can't have you inside my department. I'm going to give you until Monday to let me know what you want to do. When you leave this office, I want you to empty your desk and not talk to anyone about what has been said, and that includes Kerr. You no longer will be required inside the department. I will have someone fill in until we can appoint someone your old job. Okay Sergeant, you can leave now, and I look forward to talking to you on Monday." Madden stood up without saying a word and made his way quickly for the door and left.

Jeffrey did not like doing it, but it had to be done. He made a call to his wife to let her know that he would soon be heading home; she asked how his day had been. Jeffrey replied, "Just tying up a few loose ends."

Over the next couple of weeks, Madden accepted his fate and set about his new job with enthusiasm and vengeance. Everyone entering the vicinity of his car park had to show his or her identification, and of course that included the chief. Not only would he check the photo ID, he would also check the registration of the vehicle against the photo, no matter how many times you had been through the gate and how long he had known you. It was his way of pissing you off, which was his objective. Chief Granger did not mind as he accepted it as enhancing the security of the station. As for the department, it had taken on a whole new demeanor since Madden had accepted his new job. Everyone was working as a team as Jeffrey thought they should.

It was early one Wednesday morning when he thought he would take a short detour and drop in on Peter Shaw. The sun was still low in the east and the shadows of the trees were heavy across the driveway up to the mansion. As he arrived, he could see Peter, still shoeless and wearing what might have been the same jeans as the last time he saw him. Alicia was sitting beside him on a new porch swing, drinking coffee and watching the day begin. Jeffrey parked his car and made his way up the steps to join them. Peter greeted him, "Beautiful morning, Chief." Alicia stood and asked if Jeffrey would like to join them in a fresh cup of coffee.

Jeffrey looked at his watch. "I think I can afford a bit of time for a cup of coffee. Yes, please Alicia; black, no sugar."

Alicia made her way to the kitchen, taking Peter's cup from his hand without asking. Peter and Alicia had been practicing telepathic communication as they sat together each morning. Both were amazed and impressed at how Alicia's ability was improving. Daily, she would grow stronger in her understanding and was sending and receiving clearer transmissions.

Peter asked Jeffrey to join him on the swing seat, which he did. Alicia returned with a tray with three coffees. She gave Peter and Jeffrey theirs, and then very easily sat crossed legged on the deck. Jeffrey noticed that Alicia had stopped wearing shoes, her pretty hair allowing the morning sun to shine through. 'She looks almost hippy- like,' he thought to himself.

"Well, Jeffrey. Have you come to lock me up?" Peter asked.

"No, Peter. I have come to again apologize for the leak that caused Alicia to lose her job, and to update you on the conclusion of my investigation into who it was that was leaking information. I was finally able to pinpoint who it was that cost Alicia her job."

Alicia commented, "I hope you gave him a medal. He did me such a favor!"

Jeffrey laughed and continued. "I wish it was that simple Alicia. We had a major problem with leaks in the department over the last few years. It was getting seriously worse and in a couple of instances it had compromised investigations. It had to be stopped. Your incident had a timeline to it and an exposure that I was involved in. I was able to identify the offender because so few people had been involved. This put my suspect at the top of a list I had already created. When I went back over the leaks that had happened over the last couple of years, he was the common denominator."

Peter chimed in. "Did you fire him?"

Jeffrey responded, slowly and thoughtfully. "No, I checked on his background. He had been with the department a long time. Prior to the Police Department, he had served well in Vietnam. This man has served our country and us all his working life and has only nine months to go to retire. It was bad what he was doing, but I did not want it to affect his pension. I gave him the choice to resign or take a job that has less exposure to sensitive material. He took the less sensitive job."

Peter sat quietly and sipped his coffee. Then he said, "That's good Chief."

He never asked who it was or what the job was. It was finished as far as Peter was concerned. Jeffrey was impressed by Peter's empathy, as most people would want to know who it was and gloat in the suffering of the accused, but not Peter. He changed the subject, pointing to the Mockingbird who was again chasing the cat across the well-groomed lawn. The cat stopped to swipe at the bird, and then continued its escape to the cover of the hedge.

Jeffrey commented on how nice the place was looking, which Peter quickly attributed to Alicia. He finished his coffee, thanked them both, stood and gave his empty cup to Alicia. "You two have got it made," he said. "When I get the time, I am going to make a point of stopping by. Just to step off the merry-go-round for a few moments does one good." He bid them goodbye and made his way to his car and away down the drive. Peter and Alicia both agreed that they liked Jeffrey and he would make a great chief for the city.

Alicia's cell phone rang. She looked at the screen and transmitted to Peter that it was Tim. "Good morning, darling," she answered. "What's up?"

Tim, excited, said, "I got a response to my email from the anthropologist, Dr. Jim Zeallow, in Spain. He is interested in what Peter has to say about the cave and the art."

Alicia repeated the news to Peter. He commented, "That's great that he got back in touch with you."

Tim continued, "In the email I had sent him, I told him that Peter said that the handprints were used as a knowledge base and by touching them with a clear mind it was possible to download information. I think the fact that I also said Peter was a senator and I was a reporter might have had something to do with it." She could almost hear Tim smiling smugly to himself. "Anyhow, I have arranged a Skype meeting with him. I just need to confirm a time with Peter, and I will set it up. We need to remember that they are six hours ahead of us, so if we are going to do it, it will need to be between 8:00 and 10:00a.m. our time. I think that would be the best for them; between 2:00 and 4:00 p.m. their time."

"Okay, let me fill Peter in on what you're suggesting and lets see what time will be best for him," responded Alicia.

Alicia went over the details of the proposed Skype conference with Peter. He was excited that Tim was able to arrange this and confirmed it would be okay to make it that early and on any day that would suit the doctor.

Chapter 17

Fisherman drifted down the center of the river, his stringed catfish bobbing along with him as he made his way towards the camp of Death Dog. He had found the Neanderthals and he could hardly contain himself, occasionally letting out a loud whooping which reflected off the surface of the water then diluted itself into the thick forest. As he approached the curve in the river where they were camped he could see several others paddling across the river supported by a large log. Fisherman could not contain himself and recommenced yelping and whooping, which soon got the attention of the people on the shore as well as the hunters making their way across the river.

They all turned and looked his direction, thinking that he must have caught a monster fish. He began shouting, "I found them. I found them." At first, no one seemed to understand, staring his direction with puzzled faces. One of the young hunters soon clicked as to what Fisherman was shouting and wanted to be the first to tell Death Dog. He ran quickly towards Death Dog's hut, dust flying from his uncovered feet as he raced through the camp from the river.

Death Dog lay inside his hut, comfortable on the

thick skins supporting him. He was aware of the noise going on outside, but he did not move. His one eye stared at the hut roof as he waited. The young runner stopped by the hanging skin that covered the entrance to the hut. He knew there could be a dire consequence for disturbing Death Dog and he started to second-guess himself. He stood motionless, not saying a word, when Death Dog shouted from inside the hut. "What is it?"

"Fisherman has found them," the young hunter blurted in a breathless exhalation.

Death Dog rose from the floor without putting his headdress on that he normally would wear when outside his hut. He ripped the skin back from the entrance. The young hunter was standing sideways to the entrance so as not to be in Death Dog's way and did not raise his eyes or face to look at him. He was still unsure how Death Dog would react to the news.

"Where is he?" screamed Death Dog.

"He is down at the river," replied the hunter.

Death Dog, without saying a word, made his way towards the river. The young hunter, his gaze remaining low, followed closely. Everyone went quiet as Death Dog joined the group, waiting for Fisherman to pull himself from the river. The large stringer of catfish had tangled around his legs and he was wrangling them free so he could move forward and onto the bank. He finally stepped out of the river and with a huge grin shouted, "I found them!"

Death Dog screamed at him. "Shut up, you

fool!" He then turned to the crowd gathered around and booted the nearest one to him in the rear end, telling them all to go. Then he struck out and hit a woman in the head with a hard backhand and sent her sprawling. The group quickly broke up, scarpering as quickly as possible to follow Death Dog's instruction and to reach the safety of their huts.

"You piece of dog shit. We are being watched. Come to my hut where we can talk," he demanded.

Death Dog made his way back to his hut, scanning the sky with his one eye for any signs of Hawk. Fisherman scampered behind Death Dog, head lowered and dragging his fish behind him. Finally, he handed the leash to one of the women who took them to begin processing the meat.

He followed closely behind Death Dog, secretly wishing he had kept his mouth shut. 'No one would have needed to know,' he thought to himself, as the excitement quickly faded to fear.

Death Dog pulled the skins aside and made his way into the hut, dropping cross-legged onto the skins he had moments earlier been lying. Fisherman followed, holding the skins to the side as he pushed his way inside. When his eyes adjusted to the darkness, he was surprised to find two women laying to one side of the hut on skins several layers thick. They were watching him quietly and one was obviously heavy with child. Fisherman stood just inside, lowering his head so he did not have to look directly at Death Dog.

Death Dog was calm. He wanted to know what

Fisherman had found and asked him to explain everything. Fisherman, feeling slightly more at ease, squatted and started to draw in the sand as he told his story.

"I was working the river bank near the waterfalls looking for catfish in holes along the shore. I noticed signs that something, or someone, had left from climbing out of the river. I know how important it is for you that we remain vigilant, so I checked out the track more closely. There were no animal tracks leaving the river so I decided it must be a person. It was soon evident that several people had been collecting herbs and had tried to cover their tracks. They had done a good job, but I was still able to find signs, small ones, but enough for me to establish the direction they had left the river. I followed the tracks to a hidden cave entrance. The cave took me behind the waterfall and then up to a small ledge that goes along the cliff wall. They were on the ledge and were no longer worried that anyone might be following. They started to leave signs that were obvious. There were three of them, one female."

Death Dog asked, "How did you know one was female?"

"I found where she had pissed and I could smell it. It was definitely from a female. I could also tell by the pattern where she squatted and left footprints. They had been collecting herbs, nettles and Raspberry," Fisherman explained, starting to feel more and more confident in Death Dog's demeanor.

Death Dog sat quietly a while before he spoke. "You have done well, Fisherman, but now I need you to do more. We need to plan an attack on the hiding place, but we must not show a sign around the camp that we are planning or that anything different is happening. Hawk is constantly watching and will know something is wrong if we are not careful. I will explain our plans this evening once it is dark. The camp is being watched during the day. Do not speak of this to the others. Leave from here now and go about your day, preparing your fish like any other day. Do not let others gather around you. If you tell anyone, I will kill you and them as well. Now leave."

Death Dog waved him away, a sneer on his face. Fisherman stood, keeping his head bowed as he made his way to the door, pulling the skins to one side. The light burned itself into his skull as he quickly stepped away from the hut.

People started to come towards him to find out what Death Dog had said, but he quickly shunned them away. Keeping his head lowered, he made his way to the fish he had given to the woman. He took over the cleaning and ignored anyone who attempted to talk to him. The tribe soon got the message and realized talking to him would probably be dangerous. They gave him quarter and let him go about his day, cleaning and drying the fish.

Hawk was uneasy, the apprehension making it

hard to focus. He did not know why, but there was something eating at him. Taking himself to the back of the cave, he placed his back against the cave wall. This filled his body with a feeling of belonging and calm. He started his deep breathing and his spirit lifted to his familiar, the hawk. Lifting high on the thermal heat generated off the canopy of the forest, he was soon over the camp of Death Dog. Soaring over the camp, he focused on details that would show that the Hairless Ones had found the location of the Neanderthals or were planning an attack. Everything was calm and Hawk lifted on the upward current of a small cumulus cloud. The height he was able to achieve laid out the lands his people had hunted, fished and lived in peace for generations. There were clear tracks below that had been honed from the thick forest by the constant use of his ancestors. They were now inaccessible to his people, and this saddened him.

The evening light faded and the followers of Death Dog gathered around the large fire in the center of the camp. Death Dog appeared from his hut, again donning his headgear. As he stepped out he turned and looked at the cleaned skull of his father, feeling the scar on his face and refocusing his hatred for the Neanderthal. He approached the fire, his two women walking close behind him. He found a place upwind of the smoke. The other members of the tribe would not take their place around the fire until he was seated and his women had brought him large leafs filled with fresh cooked catfish and herbs.

The tribe started to join Death Dog in the meal. First, the young hunters made their way from the huts, then the women and children. Soon all the camp was gathered around the fire, the fish and fresh herbs were shared and no one was talking. Death Dog finished his meal, and wiped his oil-filled hands on his bare chest. He then threw what was left over his shoulder to the camp dogs patrolling just outside the circle of humans.

His first words were to Fisherman. "Tell them," he instructed.

Fisherman, his mouth full, started to tell how he had found the Neanderthals. He was at first inaudible, having to stop and swallow. He then managed to get the story out as Death Dog wished. The excitement of the young killers was apparent. It had been too long and the thought of another raid, especially on Hawk, had their hearts racing in anticipation.

Death Dog told the women and children to leave the warmth of the fire. Most had finished eating and returning to the huts was not a problem. Once they had left, Death Dog turned his head to check who was remaining and raised his head to the now darkened sky, just to reassure himself that Hawk's blinds had been closed.

He laid his plans out for the young killers that remained. "We will leave tomorrow after the evening meal, under cover of darkness. We will take the forest track to the cave Fisherman has found. We will then go through the cave to the ledge and track them to their lair, where we will kill them. I will kill Hawk! No one is to touch him; he is mine. It is important not to show any signs that we are preparing for a raid, so go about your day tomorrow as normal. If Hawk feels something is different, it could give them time to run or prepare against us. We are being watched every day. I have seen Hawk, the eyes of the Neanderthal, always watching. I will be watching you all closely. If you show signs we are preparing I will kill you instantly."

The next day, as planned, the Hairless Ones spent their time on the mundane: gathering, hunting, fishing and cooking. The camp gave off no signs of its preparations for the attack, everyone knowing the consequences. Most of the young soldiers had stayed awake during the night, knapping extra spearheads and selecting shafts they had collected for trueness and strength. These they kept hidden in their huts. They were excited, the anticipation of the attack slowing the daylight hours.

The group gathered by the fire as the evening shadows started to lengthen and the day began to wane. The tribe shared in a meal of a large Mule deer that had been killed and dried a few weeks prior. There was plenty for all. Death Dog sat eating, quietly watching the sky and making note of the massive Cumulonimbus that were gathering in the west, the deep rain bands highlighted by the setting sun. The weather was heading his way, but he would not be deterred from his plans. He had waited too long for this night. Feeling the scar on his face, he watched as lightning raged inside the massive approaching cloud.

Hawk was watching as the children gathered around the fire, the parents feeding them and everyone enjoying the lightning show that was now going on at the cave entrance. The uneasy feeling was still troubling him. He looked around at the cave wall paintings and handprints. The art and the feeling of being gave Hawk comfort. He stood, went to the fire and removed a large burning log that he held above his head as he made his way back to the cave wall. He played the light on the art of his ancestors, the movement of the shadow and light bringing the art to life.

As the lightning flashed, his eyes focused on a painting that he had never paid much attention. It was a drawing of a young hunter throwing a spear at a nest of young birds. The mother bird was flaring her wings and, with an open beak, was screaming at the approaching spear. The image never made sense as the Neanderthals did not throw spears and would not hunt a nest of birds that would be high and hard to get for very little reward.

The lightning raged; the Instant flash followed closely by a massive thunderclap. It felt like the oxygen was being removed from the cave, and the young children screamed and ran to be comforted by the elders. This added to the image as it burned into his brain. His closed eyes clearly showed the image against his closed lids. He knew suddenly what the image was telling him. It was a warning from long ago that showed the inevitability and consequence of staying in the cave. He realized then that he must take the risk and move his people.

The sky darkened and the air was filled with static moisture, which added to the fearsome appearance of Death Dog as he appeared from his hut. He threw the hanging skins covering the door to one side as he stepped into the open. The rain, lightning and thunder added to the tenseness amongst his gathered group. The young soldiers were keen for the attack to begin, the excitement and readiness showing in their bravado.

Fisherman was instructed to lead the group, taking the jungle path that would lead to the entrance of the cave. The massive thunder claps and driving rain caused some of the young soldiers to flinch, affecting their gait as they made their way through the darkened forest. The small burning torches leading them gave little comfort and it was difficult to keep them alight as the massive rain droplets fell from the soaked forest canopy. Death Dog was not going to let this foul weather hinder his attack. He wanted his revenge.

Fisherman slowed as he approached the area of the cave entrance, but he was unable to find it in the dark. Death Dog was getting angry and they were all standing back, not wanting to be near Death Dog if Fisherman could not find the bragged-about cave. Death Dog started screaming at Fisherman, making it harder for him to focus. He decided to return to the river and see if he could pick up the tracks that led to the entrance. Death Dog and the group waited as Fisherman, trying to keep the torch alight in the now-driving rain, desperately tried to find the signs.

He was finally able to pick up the dissolving tracks he and the Neanderthals had left, slowly and methodically making his way towards the group. They had unknowingly walked past the entrance, and it was right behind them. The wind had increased, testing the foundations of the massive trees and adding to the noise of the forest. Fisherman shouted to the group who were only a few feet away, but the rain, wind and thunder made it difficult for them to understand. "Come back. The cave is here. We passed it," he said, smiling and trying to add some humor to lighten the situation.

Death Dog forced his way past the standing group to again take his place behind Fisherman as he led them into the cave through the small entrance. Although the cave protected them from the driving rain, the water on the floor, which had been but a trickle, was now nearly knee-high and raging. Finally, the entire group was in the cave and the few torches that had remained alight were refueled with dry Silver Burch bark which, even when damp, was soon afire, adding needed light to the inside of the cave.

They followed Fisherman through the cave, the deep, rushing water slowing the progress of the group. Finally, coming out behind the waterfall, Death Dog checked to make sure all were present, screaming at any stragglers, "Keep up or you'll be the first to die!"

All of them were soaked and starting to feel the strain of the forced march in such dire conditions. The storm was raging, the lightning illuminating the racing waterfall, almost consistent in its rapidness. The energy of the thunder was audible over the roar of the water. Fisherman made his way into the second cave that would lead the group to the narrow ledge where he last saw the signs of the Neanderthals.

As they exited the cave the storm had started to ease, but the conditions were still severe along the narrow path that now faced Death Dog's troops. The storm moved to the east and the time lapse between the lightning strike and the thunder became separated as it moved away. Death Dog told Fisherman to continue leading the group. Fisherman became more apprehensive, as now he was leading them into the unknown. He wanted to slow his pace to make sure every step was well placed and to look for further sign, but Death Dog was behind him, prodding him with his armful of light throwing spears.

Fisherman made his way along the ledge, leading Death Dog and the following group. The ledge narrowed and the drop-off became more severe. He was soaked and was afraid of slipping over the edge. All the troop's handheld torches had now been extinguished by the water rushing down the side of the cliff and the smoky smell was still heavy in the air. The progress was slow and blind, with the wall of the cliff rubbing Fisherman's left shoulder.

Fisherman continued forward with Death Dog forcing the pace. A pain raged through his leg. At first he did not realize what was happening as his leg collapsed under him. He fell to the ground, screaming out in pain and holding his foot. Embedded into the sole of his foot were a clump of clay and several shards of obsidian that the Neanderthals had set as a trap. One shard of rock was buried deep and the point could be seen trying to escape the top of his foot. He raised it up so that Death Dog could see the problem as he continued to cry out.

Death Dog removed a massive antler-handled flint knife from his belt, and pushing Fisherman's leg to one side he dropped on top of him and sunk the blade of his knife below the ribs of Fisherman's chest and then up into his heart. The shock on Fisherman's face mocked the silence that came from his screaming mouth. Death Dog laid on top of him, using the weight of his body to force the blade to rip away his life.

Death Dog felt the energy flow out of him and when Fisherman finally calmed, Death Dog pushed back from him and removed his knife, which he wiped across Fisherman's bare stomach. Cleaned, he placed it back into his belt then pushed the now lifeless body over the edge of the narrow path, tumbling to its resting place below.

Wolf, who had been sitting by the fire in the center of the cave, thought he heard something. It was enough for him to rise up and make his way to the entrance of the cave, which was still being illuminated by the lightning that was finally easing. He stayed inside the cave entrance, not wanting to go outside into the still-consistent rain. The massive clap of thunder reassured him about the noise he thought he had heard. As he stood in the darkness, he remained still and aware. No other sounds bothered him and soon his alertness and his tension flowed from him. He continued to watch the lightning dance across the massive storm clouds rolling eastward. Wolf had an amazing amount of respect for the power of nature that humbled and held him as he watched.

The strike of the thrown spear did not register at first. Wolf looked down and wondered at the shaft that was protruding from the right side of his chest. He reached around himself to feel the shaft with his left hand and at the same time looked around to try to comprehend what it was and where it had come from. The narrow shaft of the throwing spear had forced the sharpened flint deep into Wolf's chest. It had ripped itself between his massive ribs then easily passed through the soft lung tissue. The energy stored in the shaft continued forcing it deeper into Wolf's chest cavity, finally settling and severing the life giving tissue of his massive heart. The wound was a kill shot. Death Dog remained quiet as he watched Wolf become aware. He loved watching the shock of his victims as they comprehended the inevitability and consequences of their realization.

Hawk sat watching Wolf silhouetted by the lightning at the entrance of the cave. Wolf turned to look back at Hawk, and then dropped to his knees. He tried to support himself with the massive stabbing spear he held in his right hand, the effort supporting him enough to sit him back on his haunches as his life force vacated its current vessel.

Hawk remained seated, his back to the cave wall watching as the nightmare unfolded. Death Dog ran forward from the shadows into the cave, screaming and followed by his troop. The screaming of Death Dog's killers quickly woke the women and children. The children jumped from the skins they had been asleep and wrapped in, running with arms extended for an elder to protect them. The women gathered the children and ran to the tunnel that led to the back entrance of the cave and possible escape.

The few Neanderthal hunters that were left had been sleepily gathered around the fire watching the storm. The sudden horrific appearance of Death Dog slowly forced itself upon them. Before long they were all standing, some running to the cave wall to recover their massive stabbing spears. Death Dog unleashed his second spear from the throwing stick, the spear racing forward and burying itself deep into the back of one of the young hunters. He fell to his knees then slid into the stacked weapons, adding to the confusion.

Quickly, Death Dog's troops came out of the

darkness, soaked from the forced march but ready to revenge the effort they had put into finding their enemy. They unleashed a volley of spears from the atlatls, quickly felling any of the other young Neanderthals that were making for weapons, putting down any resistance that might have been a threat. The four Neanderthals left standing formed a line across the cave, hoping the distance between them would close so that the superior strength of the Neanderthals could come into play.

The twenty paces between Death Dog's killers and the Neanderthals were enough to give the throwing spears the edge. The hairless killers moved ahead of Death Dog, holding their spears ready to hack down any of the remaining Neanderthals. The killer's spears were notched into the throwing aids. Death Dog gave the word and the young killers unleashed the spears that would quell any remaining resistance.

As they fell, the young killers of Death Dog raced forward past the fallen hunters and down the cave in pursuit of the screaming children and women. It did not take long before the screams of panic could be heard coming from deep in the cave as the killers set about killing any they came upon. Worse than the screams was the silence that followed; the muffled sounds of the killers as they mutilated the bodies. One of the young killers returned, brandishing the head of one of the young Neanderthals. He held it high for the rest to see and was laughing and whooping with excitement.

Finally, the young killers gathered around Death Dog, watching him as he paced up and down in front of Hawk. Young Water was between them, restrained by the fear that gripped her. Hawk did not move. His concentration was on Water, trying to hold her focus to calm her. She was staring into his face; both her hands spread open and down turned, shaking almost in unison. Her bladder had let go; she was petrified. In her mind, she could hear Hawk, his slow, calm hum coming from deep inside her. Calm slowly came over her as Hawk took control of her fear. His deep, repetitive humming reassured her and put her into a trance that removed her from the presence of the situation.

Death Dog remained directly behind Water, realizing that Hawk had control of her. The young killers went silent; waiting to see what Death Dog was about to do with the young girl and Hawk. They knew they must not interfere. They remained silent, watching Death Dog pace up and down behind the young girl. Hawk's gaze never left the face of Water, his deep breathing and purring becoming more audible to those in the cave. Death Dog knew that Hawk had control of the young girl, raising the anger inside him. His pacing became shorter; a few steps either side of the young girl, until finally Death Dog stopped close behind her.

He began to touch her skin-covered back, but he could not get her attention. Death Dog's gaze was firmly fixed on the face of Hawk as he reached for the razor sharp skinning knife on his belt. He grabbed Water from behind, pulling her hair back and exposing her throat. He then slashed deep into her fragile neck, the obsidian blade scraping against young Water's spine as it slashed through.

Still, Hawk remained unmoved and continued with his control of young Water. Hawk released her hair as she slumped sideways, a plume of blood spurting high into the air, covering Death Dog. His gaze did not leave the face of Hawk. He stood silently behind Water, looking for some sort of reaction from Hawk who remained silent and calm. Death Dog kicked the now lifeless body of young Water, shoving her away with his leg and smearing her blood across the cave floor.

Hawk remained with his back against the cave wall, his legs crossed, breathing deep and purring, robbing Death Dog of the fear he craved. Death Dog again started to pace backwards and forwards in front of the seated Hawk, who he had not touched. He felt the scar deep on his cheek, closing his good eye for a second to remind himself of the loss Hawk had caused him. The anger raged to a high pitch inside him, cursing and pacing as he decided on his next action.

The young killers remained silent; no sound was uttered as they waited in anticipation for Death Dog's next instruction or action. They were keen to go through the belongings of the Neanderthals, to pillage and collect their valuables. The rewards would go to those that found the treasure; so waiting for Death Dog to finish his little game of revenge was playing on the attention of some of the younger soldiers. The fear of Death Dog was greater than the desire to start the pillaging, however, so they remained silent and watchful.

Death Dog had closed in on Hawk, barely missing his crossed legs as he paced. He turned his blind eye to Hawk and started to walk past him once again. As he became level with Hawk, a massive flash of lightning illuminated the entrance of the cave, and for a second, got the attention of Death Dog's troops, who turned away to look at the cave entrance.

Hawk made his move. He sprang from the seated position, wrapping his massive arms around Death Dog's upper body and pinned them to his side. His massive head turned sideways and bit deeply into the neck of Death Dog, silencing him as he ripped away the center of Death Dog's neck from his body with powerful Neanderthal jaws. He remained locked on Death Dog, both of them doing a strange, silent, deadly dance.

Death Dog's young killers had been watching the light show that had grabbed their attention. Turning, they were shocked at the scene unfolding and were having a problem comprehending what was playing out in front of them. When the seriousness of Death Dog's situation was realized, they sprang forward and started stabbing at the back of Hawk, who would not release Death Dog from his powerful deadly grip. They continued stabbing until, finally, Hawk's legs started to buckle, the pair of them still locked in the embrace. Hawk and Death Dog finally collapsed to the cave floor, but their entanglement remained. They had represented the opposites in life, so different that they could not exist on the same plane. Suddenly, both men's souls left their bodies. The flicker we call life did not separate as it vacated their entwined bodies. It became the yin and yang of a double helix that extended upwards towards the brilliance of light they both raced towards now in death, as one.

Peter then described to Alicia how he slowly started to awaken from his coma, unsure of where he was. He could feel a cold dampness of his face, which he thought might be the blood of Death Dog. In his confusion, he started ripping at the tubes he had going into his nose and arms. The brilliance of the light slowly formed into a masked face that was talking to him.

"Hello, Peter. We have been waiting for you to regain consciousness," said a female voice. She continued wiping his face, holding his hand and using her reassuring voice to help relieve Peter's confusion. He soon started to realize he had returned to modern time, going over the last thoughts he had of the crash and of his wife in his mind.

A young doctor explained how his wife had died at the scene of the accident and was dead upon arrival. He assured Peter that she would not have known anything about the accident and certainly did not feel anything. Peter realized this was supposed to make him feel better, but the feeling of absolute loneliness continued washing over him. The pain of the loss joined with the loss of Hawk and Water, forced itself upon his conscious mind. The only relief he would get from the three losses was the morphine-induced sleep that he craved. After a few days, he started to go over in his mind the experience and to ask himself why this would have happened.

"I started to feel I had purpose. I began to understand that I had a message I had to share. That idea is what motivated me to get better. Daily, I would push myself and I felt myself getting stronger, finally reaching a point when I was able to be released from the hospital and totally get off the drugs that fogged my mind."

Alicia was clearly upset. Looking at Peter and pouting her bottom lip she said, "Poor Water." The slight attempt to lighten the mood could not hide the tears in her eyes.

Peter strained to get off the coach. Alicia came from behind the desk and pulled on his extended arm. He stood, saying, "Alicia, let's go to the kitchen and have a coffee. The telling, my dear, is done."

Chapter 18

It had taken Tim two weeks to arrange a Skype meeting with Dr. Zeallow in Spain. They were all excited and Brenda arrived with Alicia and went about preparing a light breakfast for them all. Alicia joined Peter on the swing with a cup of coffee while Tim made sure all was working with Skype before the call was made.

Peter had made several notes to make sure he did not waste his time with the doctor, a habit from his past life that he had not deemed necessary since the accident. This was different; it could prove a vital link to the Neanderthals and his dream. Alicia looked at the note pad and pen Peter was nervously fumbling. 'Sweet,' she thought.

"Are you ready to talk to the anthropologist, Peter?" she said as she turned, holding her coffee to take her place beside him on the swinging bench.

"I'm ready; I just need to make sure it's the same cave," Peter said, pushing against the ground and starting the swinging that he found so relaxing.

Peter had spent many hours in front of the massive Apple computer screen, trying to establish if the cave in Spain was the same one, but time had played its trick on the visual. 'Which it does,' he thought as he felt his own sagging face, wondering how many of his past associates would be able to identify him in a line up.

"The cave is so similar, but it's not the same, of course," he told Alicia. "I remember the paintings and handprints being far brighter than the current pictures. The wall directly to the right of the entrance had been covered in designs from Hawk's ancestors, but that wall was exposed to the elements and now there's nothing. The children would love it when the elders, in the low evening light, would move a lighted torch to cast shadows across the surface of the paintings, bringing them to life."

Peter digressed. "My wife took painting lessons and the most important thing to remember when painting is the position of the light. It's the light in a picture that gives the picture its link with reality, its depth and shadow. Light itself is the vital part of any art and as important as any color. Light itself becomes destructive and in time it will destroy and fade the image it was once a vital part of."

Alicia sipped her coffee. "I never thought of it like that. Talking about images," she continued. "I found one of your handprints on a large piece of thick flat glass beside the green house. I cleaned it up; it's an awesome image. I would like to have it mounted and hung in the hall, opposite the entrance, so it's the first thing you see as you enter. Would that be alright with you?"

"Alicia, what you found is not glass. That is

Block Crystal. I ordered it from Italy. I wanted it for the handprint. I had found a local supplier of the pigments I felt I needed to make the print authentic, but the crystal had to be ordered special."

Alicia chimed in. "I bet that was not cheap."

"Don't ask," Peter answered with a grin.

Tim came to the door telling them that everything was ready for the Skype conference. He helped Peter get off the swinging bench, and then they all went to the library. Tim positioned Peter in front of the computer. Leaning across him, Tim grabbed the mouse and clicked the blue and white Skype logo. The program fired into life with a loud pitch note that indicated the program was ready to use. Tim checked the image of Peter on the screen.

"Okay, we're all set. I told them we would call at 9:30 our time, so that gives us some time to enjoy some eggs and bacon Brenda's been working on." They all moved to the kitchen and enjoyed the breakfast that Brenda had prepared, going over the meeting. Alicia asked Tim how he had got time off from the paper.

"I told them I had an appointment at the dentist; no problem," he replied.

"Liar," Alicia replied, smiling and taking a mouthful of breakfast.

Tim answered playfully, "Oh, it's okay for those that don't have a job."

Alicia finished chewing, then responded, "I have a job, don't I, Peter?"

Peter was busy enjoying his eggs and ignored

the back and forth bantering between Alicia and Tim.

Brenda chimed in, "I am not going to miss this. Hell, no! I'm as excited as the rest of you, and I'm not being left out."

Peter assured her, "We would not leave you out. You're part of the team."

They all finished and returned to the library. Brenda was the last to arrive, still wiping her hands with a dishtowel as she stood in the entrance, watching as they all got into position.

Dr. Zeallow prepared himself for the Skype call, wondering why an American senator would be contacting him over the art in the caves. The young reporter had tried to explain in his email, but it really did not make any sense. How could the Senator possibly have any information of importance about the cave? The doctor's program was always short of funding and the opportunity of talking to an American senator had possibilities. This was the real reason he was bothering with this Skype call. Maybe he could get his team some additional funding.

As the time showed precisely 9:30 a.m. in the corner of the Apple monitor, Tim slid the mouse pointer over the name of Dr. Jim Zeallow highlighted in the Skype program and clicked it with his left mouse button. The screen quickly transformed into a picture of Dr. Zeallow, a man of about forty-five with a full head of dark curly hair, wearing a white coat and sporting a small Vandyke beard. The image transformed in front of their eyes to what appeared to be the top of someone's head. It was clear the doctor was trying to adjust the camera so that his face would come into view. The camera again missed the desired target and showed an image of the doctor's chin. He reached forward again and repositioned the camera, this time showing his face. "That's better," the doctor said, dropping back into his chair, satisfied with the image he was transmitting.

Peter opened the conversation. "Good morning Dr. Zeallow. Thank you for taking the time to talk to me."

Dr. Zeallow answered. "Just call me Jim," he said in a strong Spanish accent, but in perfect English. "Now, how can I help you, Senator?"

"Just call me Peter, Jim," Peter responded.

He continued. "Doctor, I mean Jim; I have had an experience that I believe might have taken place in the cave that you have been studying. You first came to my attention when our researcher, Tim, showed me your work."

Tim slid his head around the side of the computer screen so that his face came into the focus of the camera and waved. Alicia thought how stupid he was and chuckled to herself. Tim returned to his chair with a big self-satisfied grin on his face.

"Please continue," said the doctor.

Peter went on to briefly explain his story, from the accident forward, describing how the demise of the

Neanderthals was through inbreeding.

The doctor commented, "We have been investigating a similar hypothesis as the latest research shows that most Europeans do, in fact, have traces of Neanderthal DNA in them. It's under six percent in most cases, but it proves that the Neanderthal and Homo Sapiens, or Cro-Magnon, could breed and produce a child that was able to reproduce; not just a mule. However, the concept of the Homo Sapiens being a mutation of a Neanderthal due to inbreeding has far reaching consequences."

Peter interjected. "The mutation showed itself as the development of an ego. Ego was unheard of in any mammal prior to that mutation, I understand. The desire was for self rather than the group, and with that came speech and the improvement of weapons. There was a change from the stabbing spear of the Neanderthals that had sufficed for thousands of years to the throwing spear using the Atlatl. The reason for the change was the desire to kill someone who only had a stabbing spear from a safe distance. Funny, even today most developments are through war. It motivates the minds of men."

The doctor listened to what Peter was saying. He certainly seemed sincere. The idea of the mutation was interesting, but it did not prove anything. He asked Peter, "What makes you think that this is the cave you were transported back to?"

"It's the handprints; the formation of them and the location of them in the cave. A lot has changed though." Peter went on to explain about the drawings that were missing off the right hand side of the cave entrance.

The doctor pushed back from his computer and placed his hands behind his head. "That's interesting. We know there were originally paintings on that wall, but they faded long ago. We were able to find minute traces of the pigments used to create the handprints trapped in the texture of the rock, but the images have faded and disappeared over time."

This started to give Peter the credibility he craved. He smiled at Alicia, transmitting the word 'maybe'.

"I have one other thing that would help us to establish if this was the cave," Peter said.

The doctor dropped his hands from behind his head and slid closer to the camera and the screen. Folding his hands in front of his mouth and resting on his elbows, he waited in anticipation for what Peter was about to reveal. Peter then began describing the cave and asking questions: "If you go back into the cave about two hundred feet you will find a tunnel that goes off to the left."

The doctor interjected, "That's correct."

Peter continued, "In that tunnel you should have found the remains of a baby Homo Sapien. When left there, it was wrapped in deer skin and placed there by the Neanderthals."

The doctor again interjected. "That's amazing! That is correct. We have not told anyone about this and we are currently doing quite extensive carbon dating and DNA analysis on the remains. They do appear to be human and not Neanderthal, but from around the same time period as the art, which definitely is Neanderthal. Peter, I am amazed that you know this. We have been very careful not to let this out as it could affect the whole project. Some of our sponsors would not like the fact that our research is leading us in this direction."

Tim, being the reporter he is, could not let this pass without asking for clarification.

Popping his head around the side of the Apple screen so that he came into view, he asked, "Doctor, would you mind clarifying your concerns and please be assured this is off the record?"

The doctor paused. "Tim. It is Tim?" he asked in a very concerned Spanish accent.

Tim confirmed and the doctor continued. "A lot of our sponsors are religious based. The Mormons are heavily involved in lineage research, sponsoring us considerably, as are the Catholic Church. They will not like the fact that we are the mutations of Neanderthals. It does not tie in with their doctrines and we are not in a position to continue our research without their backing."

Tim returned to his seat and Peter reassured the doctor, "We understand, and please be assured we will not do anything to knowingly affect your research. As for funding, I might be able to help. I still have some clout and feel sure that I will be able to raise a few bucks to assist you."

The doctor thanked Peter, and then asked, "Have you got anything else that might surprise us Peter?"

Peter thought for a minute. "Only the fact that the paintings themselves were used for teaching and reference, as you had figured out from your research. Some of the images I would need to explain; the spirals, for example, are a form of calendar that defines a timeline, not only of the past, but also the future, as they saw it in dreams. The beginning of the spiral would represent a point in time that a certain thing happened, the present was represented by a line breaking the spiral, and from that point forward in the spiral was future. This would give them a timeline of a prediction. Another thing that might help you is to know that they depict the movement of time through their art from east to west, as in the movement of the sun. Not like us from left to right."

"That is very good, Peter," said the doctor. We had figured out they were working from east to west, but I am very impressed with your insight.

Peter continued, "The handprints are another thing. I would like to come to the cave and make sure it is the one. Would that be possible?"

The doctor was excited by this. "It would be wonderful if you were able to come here. I will personally show you the cave and some of the work we have been doing."

Peter detected the enthusiasm in the doctor's voice. He confirmed he would look into the planning of a trip and get back to him with the details when the trip had been firmed up. He then asked the doctor, "Would you mind sending us information as to the nearest airport, the best hotel, and other details?"

The doctor answered in his very Spanish-sounding accent, "No problem."

Peter then started to close the Skype meeting down. "Doctor, thank you again. We know how busy you are and we appreciate you taking the time to listen to what we have to say. We will be in contact with you soon. Before we confirm our flight we will make sure you are available. Again, thank you, doctor." The doctor responded in kind, and then hit the red telephone in the corner of the screen, finishing the call.

Peter sat back from the desk and Tim exhaled, "Wow."

Brenda took a seat next to Alicia and said, "Peter, it's just as you said it was."

Alicia, folding down the Macbook Air she had been taking notes on, was beaming.

"Well, we going to Spain, Peter?" she asked.

Peter said, "Have you got a passport, Alicia?"

"No," frowned Alicia. "I have never needed one before."

"I've got one," blurted Tim.

Peter smiled, commenting, "Well, I suppose we will need our researcher, won't we Alicia."

Alicia commented back, "Not sure, Peter. Not sure."

Alicia, taking charge of the situation, said,

"Okay, we need to get some things sorted out and then we will be able plan when we are going. Mom, would you mind staying behind and looking after Peter's house?"

Brenda, always helpful and understanding, said, "Of course I will. You will have to make a list of everything that needs doing and bills that will need paying. I will move into your apartment while you are all in Spain."

Alicia quickly flipped her iPad cover off and researched what she had to do to get a passport. "Okay, it's simple. I just have to go to the main post office and they have a passport place there. They can take the picture and send in the paperwork. They also offer an expedited service if we need it."

Chapter 19

The first part of the journey started from Austin Bergstrom airport at 9:55 a.m. Peter was taken aboard in a wheel chair to his business class seat. He was looking tired, as he had been working hard over the last few weeks. He had left the trip organization to Alicia. He had focused on hustling, and convincing some of the oil companies that were operating locally removing oil using a controversial technique called fracking, a method of oil extraction by pumping water into the porous rock and forcing the oil to the surface, to commit to some funding. Water in south Texas is a guarded resource and the oil companies had not had it easy trying to convince the public that the technique was harmless and for the betterment of all; energy independence being used as a keyword in their defense.

Senator Peter Shaw was doing the asking and, with the bad publicity the technique of fracking was getting, it was easy for Peter to raise support for Dr. Zeallow and his research. The cash rich owners craving respectability were an easy touch. People might have thought Peter had lost it, but he still had an amazing ability to organize and raise money when needed. Dr. Zeallow was ecstatic to find that Peter had raised enough to fund his research for the next two years in such a short time; relieving a lot of the pressure the religious sponsors had been putting on him.

"It will allow me to be more truthful towards my research," he had explained to Peter. Dr Zeallow and Peter had become quite close, spending several hours talking over Skype in the last few weeks and both equally excited to finally get to meet.

The journey was tiring and especially wearing on Peter, having to change flights in New York and Madrid before finally arriving at Bilbao, Spain thirty-six hours later. Traveling for thirty-six hours, though comfortable in business class, was still traveling, and it worried Alicia. She constantly asked Peter how he was and kept asking him to stand awhile and stretch as this should help prevent any thrombosis she had read about; blood clots the common result of sitting too long.

Once they had cleared customs and immigration, they collected their bags from the carousel and left the secure part of the airport to be greeted by the doctor who was holding a sign in front of him with Peter Shaw clearly written across it. He came forward, greeting Peter first with a warm hug. Peter was still seated in a wheel chair the airport had provided him, but knowing he would feel a lot better if he could lie down.

Tim and Alicia stood back waiting their turn to be greeted by the doctor. He greeted them both then escorted all of them outside to a minivan that was waiting. The driver was unable to speak English, but smiled politely and was helpful.

On the side of the minivan were the words Gran Hotel Balneario, Puente Viesgo. On the way to the hotel the doctor explained that due to the humid, rainy climate, the countryside in the Cantabria region is very lush. "There are lots of forests where you can see many different types of trees". He went on to name them. "There are Oak, Chestnut, Beech, Elm, Maple and Ash. In the mountains, the forests consist mainly of Pine and Eucalyptus trees. Cantabria has lots of beautiful green valleys, too. There are also several National Parks and nature reserves that are very popular." As the minivan sped towards Puente Viesgo, the doctor pointed out several cave locations that had handprints and artwork in them, especially the most famous of them, The Cueva de El Castillo, or the Cave of the Castle. It was, at best, only a twenty-minute walk from the center of town and the beautiful hotel where they were staying.

They arrived at the hotel and Peter looked and said he was exhausted. He told Tim and Alicia that he would see them in the morning as the hotel staff pushed him into the elevator. They used the chair to take him up to his room, where he would stay until morning. He showered up, had room service bring him a small snack, and took to his bed to rest up for the coming days and excitement they would surely bring.

Alicia and Tim spent the night exploring after they recuperated with a massage and then a soak in the hotel's natural spas. For decades, the mineral/medicinal properties of the springs in Puente Viesgo brought fame to the village in Cantabria. Tim commented that as far back as the eighteenth century, people would take advantage of the benefits by visiting the town's spas. "Nowadays, the Puente Viesgo Spa Resort is one of northern Spain's best-known thermal centers. In fact, its modern facilities have often been chosen by athletes and sportspeople to get in shape and to improve their physical and mental condition. Its new Water Temple, for example, is a leading thermal-recreational installation," Tim reported, as if reading it from a tour guide.

Alicia commented, "Nerd."

Tim answered, "It worked. I feel great."

Both were very impressed over the beauty of the area. Walking through the ancient town, they joined the locals at one of the small coffee shops, enjoying tapas and a few beers. Traditional music filled the air from a bar down the road, which they decided to move to for the rest of the evening. Lots of the patrons were from other countries in Europe and one couple, who introduced themselves, were from California. They quickly made Tim and Alicia aware that it was obvious that they were from Texas.

"I would never have guessed they could figure out where we are from by our dress," said Alicia.

Tim commented, "It might have been the cowboy boots that gave it away," with a big sarcastic grin on his face.

"Shut up, Tim" Alicia commented and then sat

back to enjoy the cold beer, Spanish guitarist, and the general ambiance of the bar.

They returned to the hotel at just before 11:00 p.m. local time, the tiredness now reminding them of how long the journey had been and how it had taken the strength out of them. Alicia had booked the room for them and Tim was pleased to see it was a single.

The jetlag had them up early. Tim woke up at 6:00 a.m. and was fumbling around in the dark for the coffee pot and trying not to awaken Alicia. She lay there quietly, not letting him know that she was awake and hoping that he would find the coffee pot and bring her a coffee to complete her awakening. They had been sharing the apartment at Peter's house for some time now and Tim knew how she liked her coffee first thing in the morning.

Tim let out a stream of profanity. "Fuck, fuck, fuck."

This finally made her give up and let him know she was awake. "What's up, Tim?"

"I just broke my fucking toe on that stupid damn fridge. I bet I will need hospital treatment. It fucking hurts like a mother. Have a look and tell me how bad it is."

She climbed out of the bed and walked over to Tim who was now lying on the floor and holding his foot in the air with his eyes closed. She cradled his heel with her hands and said, "It looks bad. I bet they have to remove the nail before they resent the compound fracture."

Tim rose up on his elbows. "Really? It's that bad?"

"No, you great baby," she said as she wiggled his toe.

He pulled the foot back screaming and rolling on his back for a few moments. He then started to realize it might not have been so bad. He carefully inspected it himself before he wriggled the toe, then tested it by standing up and adding his weight a little at a time.

Alicia had lost interest and had slipped on a pair of jeans and a t-shirt and was making her way to the door.

"Where are you going?" Tim asked.

"Coffee and breakfast," she said as the door shut behind her.

Tim rushed to get dressed and raced along the hall to join her as she walked into the dining area; apparently the toe was now the last thing on his mind.

Peter looked at the clock that slowly came into focus and 8:45 realized itself upon his waking mind. The banging on the door that had awakened him was again repeating itself. This time he was able to realize what it was and recognized the voice of Alicia asking if he was okay. He cleared his throat, and then answered, "I am fine. Thanks Alicia, I just over slept."

"Would you like me to get you a cup of coffee?" Alicia asked.

"Yes, please," he answered gratefully.

Twenty minutes later, Alicia arrived back at the room with a breakfast tray and coffee for them all. Peter had got up, had a shower, and donned some nice clean clothes. He let Alicia and Tim in and they both went to the veranda, which opened onto the beautiful view of the wonderful part of northern Spain where they were staying. The temperature was in the low seventies and the air was full of the smell of fresh cut grass. The sun was washing the hills and mountains in cloud shadows, unveiling the amazing textures and colors of the rock and vegetation as the clouds raced by. The small table and four chairs were a perfect place for Peter to enjoy his first breakfast in this beautiful place.

Tim commented to Peter, "You look so much better."

Peter answered, "I sure feel a lot better after a good sleep. That journey was tough." He then took his place at the table and before he sipped his coffee he feasted his eyes on the beautiful view. "This is a very picturesque place. I look around here and I feel like I belong."

Alicia smiled, reached across the table and squeezed Peter's hand. It was around 10:00 a.m. when the telephone in Peter's room burst into life. Alicia stood, leaving the table, and answered the phone.

"Hello."

"Good morning. This is Dr. Zeallow. How is Peter this morning?"

"Good morning, Doctor. Peter is enjoying his

breakfast on the veranda and taking in the beauty of this area."

"Ah, that is good."

"Hang on and I will let Peter know it's you," Alicia replied.

Alicia, out of habit, placed her hand over the mouthpiece of the phone. The doctor could hear the muffled, "It's the doctor, Peter."

Peter wiped his mouth and placed the napkin over his plate showing he had finished and then stood, assisting himself with the table. "Good morning, Jim," Peter said as he placed the phone to his ear.

"How are you feeling this morning, Peter?" Jim asked.

Peter replied, "I feel a lot better, thank you. That journey was tough on this old man, but it's amazing what eight hours of sleep and a strong coffee will do for a man."

"That's good, Peter. I thought I would let you rest this morning, then take you to our lab this afternoon after Siesta time," said the doctor.

"What time is Siesta time?" Peter asked.

Jim answered, "It is between two and five p.m."

"Five p.m.? Normally, that's when we are getting ready to call it a day," replied Peter.

"The rest will do you good, Peter. Everything will be closed around that time, so it's a good time for you to get some rest. Then I will collect you at five and we will go to the lab for a couple of hours so I can show you what we have found and the research we have been doing before we go to the caves in the morning."

Peter answered, "That sounds great. I would like that."

"Okay, I will pick you up at five," said the doctor.

Peter put down the phone then turned to Alicia and Tim. "Well, we have got some time to waste. Let's go and have a look around the town." Tim had done some research and was quick to inform Peter and Alicia. "The Catholic Church, San Miguel de Puente Viesgo, was on the top of the list if you typed Puente Viesgo, places of interest, into Google."

Alicia, quick as a flash, came back at him, "Well, that's it then. Let's go."

They made their way down to the foyer of the hotel where the desk clerk was able to show them how to get to the church and also gave them a small map with the church and several other things, including the caves that tourists might find of interest. The region relied heavily upon the income from the tourist industry; Mother Nature had been kind to them. The spectacular location had been a desired residence since man had discovered it, giving the region a balance of nature and history that would be hard to match anywhere in the world. They decided to take a short walk to see the church, which was as spectacular as described in the tourist book.

They arrived at the church to find it open and the three of them proceeded inside. The heavy rock structure kept the inside cool, and the visuals and atmosphere were heavy with history, forcing the quiet to scream in your ears.

Tim, in a low whisper, looked up at the ceiling and said, "Amazing." The masonry and art was breathtaking. Alicia had never seen anything as beautiful and made a mental note that one day she would bring her mother there to share in the beauty.

There was an old lady kneeling between one of the pews, quietly praying. Her eyes were open and staring at the gold encrusted alter and statue of Mother Mary. The rosary beads she had in her hands were passing between her index finger and thumb; each one an offering, a link to a perceived, yet unseen, plane.

The three of them quietly took their place in the pews behind the praying lady, trying desperately to do so quietly. Each lowered their heads and began praying, overcome by the power the structure had upon them. Peter was the first to get back up, Tim and Alicia following. Tim stood and made the sign of the cross, mumbling the words that went with the motion, "Father, son and holy ghost." He then kissed the hand he had made the cross with before moving to let Alicia out of the pew.

This surprised Alicia and when they were outside she inquired about it. "I did not know you were Catholic."

Tim looked perplexed, "I'm not".

Alicia just bit her tongue. Peter overheard them and grinned as he exited the large oak doors into the brilliance of the day. They made their way through the center of town, walking slowly, Alicia and Peter's arms linked, enjoying the old buildings and enjoyable temperature. Tim was fifty yards ahead pointing at a café that was open with outside tables. He made a gesture like he was drinking coffee and at the same time pointed to the restaurant, into which he disappeared. Alicia and Peter joined him at a table he had selected. They ordered a midday snack and watched the world go by, relaxing and enjoying the scenery. When the meal was done, Peter told them he would like to join the locals in taking a **siesta** before Jim picked them up. They returned to the hotel where Peter disappeared up to his room, getting into the elevator and reminding Alicia not to let him oversleep. Alicia and Tim continued on their sightseeing tour of the town.

At 4:15 p.m., Alicia called Peter's room. He answered immediately as he was already up from his nap. He greeted her then said that he would meet them in the foyer in a few minutes. They all gathered downstairs and had another coffee while sitting in the large couches as they waited for the arrival of the doctor.

The doctor arrived a few minutes early, greeting them in Spanish, "Buena tarde."

Peter answered in English. "Good evening to you, Jim. Are you ready to take us on tour?"

"I have the van outside," Jim said.

The group stood and Alicia did a quick double

check to make sure they had everything. Peter reached into his wallet and left a tip in American dollars on the table. They made their way to the van waiting for them outside. The same driver greeted them, again very helpful and assisting Peter into the van. Peter took the seat next to the driver for ease and comfort.

They pulled away from the hotel and Jim explained that the lab was twenty minutes outside of town, but on the way they would pass the cave they had been researching.

After a few miles, Jim told the driver to take a very narrow dirt track that led along the side of the massive cliff. They came to an area that had two portable buildings with a massive scaffold going up the outside to a cave entrance approximately two hundred feet from the base of the cliff. They all piled out of the van as Peter wanted to stand and take a look at the face of the cliff and what they could see of the cave entrance.

Jim pointed out the huts that were for the watchman and also used as a canteen for the volunteer workers who were helping in the research and excavation of the cave. Peter stood quietly looking up and then turned to put the cliff behind him, not saying anything, but taking it all in.

Jim told them, "Okay, all aboard," his strong Spanish accent heavy in the statement. He had heard it in a film a long time ago, but it had stuck in his mind and was one of the first sentences he had learned as a teenager. He remembered repeating it, trying hard to sound exactly as he had heard it in the Spanish subtitled film that he could no longer remember the name.

They all piled aboard and soon arrived at a large fenced-in area with a security officer at the gate. The van pulled up at the gate and the security officer, recognizing the van, did not get out of his small office. He just pressed the button that opened the gate, the driver talking friendly to the security officer through an open window as he proceeded to the large single story office.

They again vacated the van to line up at a large door. Jim turned his head to make sure all were present, and then pressed the button that allowed him to talk to the camera mike to the left of the entrance, again in Spanish. The door unlocked and Jim pulled it open and then asked the party to proceed into the building.

Once inside, Jim's assistant, Henry, greeted them. He was a young Spaniard with a dark complexion and was good looking enough to prompt Tim to stand closer to Alicia, putting his arm around her shoulder. Alicia walked forward letting his arm slide down her back to a more normal position. Henry greeted them all and made a special fuss of Peter, telling him the doctor was very excited he was able to visit.

Jim then led them into a massive area with tables laid out with artifacts in various stages of identification and reconstruction. He took them to a table and asked Henry to show some of the different artifacts they had found. Peter was very excited and went forward to the table. Henry showed many flint objects, from skinning knifes to the two styles of flint spear points, which he passed to them so they could hold.

Peter commented to Alicia and Tim, "Look at the difference in the size of the spear points from the stabbing spears of the Neanderthals to the throwing spears of the Homo Sapiens."

Then Jim moved over to another table and picked up an object that had a small white tag attached and a number. He passed it to Alicia. "Have you any idea what you are holding, Alicia?" asked Jim.

Alicia carefully inspected the artifact she was holding in her hand, rotating it and looking at it closely. She recognized that it was a vertebra. She had seen many when she was growing up in the country, sometimes watching a bit of road kill decay over a few days, the fire ants making quick work on the protein, exposing the skeletal structure that she had always found interesting. She commented, "A vertebra which has something stuck in it."

"Very good, Alicia," said the doctor, reaching forward and taking the artifact from her and pointing to the object protruding from the bone. "It's part of an atlatl which is from the Cro-Magnon period, the very earliest Homo Sapien. It is stuck into the vertebra of a Neanderthal, proving they were interacting, which had, until recently, only been a hypothesis."

Peter pushed his hand forward reaching for the artifact, which Jim gave him. Holding it Peter asked if it was from the cave. "Oh, yes. All of the artifacts are from that one cave," replied the doctor.

Peter went quiet, inspecting the vertebra and going over in his mind the killing and how he had seen the young Neanderthal hacked down as he raced towards his weapons. This artifact could be a direct link to his experience. Alicia watched and shared in his thoughts, aware of what was going through his mind and the relevance. A physical link to a vision would be like finding the tablets the Ten Commandments were written on. 'Powerful stuff,' she thought.

The doctor returned the vertebra to the table he had got it from and then reached across the table and picked up a larger bone, which turned out to be a tibia from a Neanderthal. The first thing they noticed was the size and denseness of the bone. Jim pointed out, "We inspected these bones carefully for growth lines and structural defects caused by hunger when young. These bones show no signs of such deficiencies. This particular bone is from an old man, over 50 years old, who, when younger, had an accident breaking his leg. But, as you can see," he paused. He pointed to part of the bone that clearly showed it had been broken and then fused itself together. "He recovered quite nicely, you would think for it to heal so well he must have kept his weight off of it and it would have been in a splint. This tells us that he was part of a unit that was able to provide for the injured or elderly, a sort of Obama Care." The doctor laughed to himself as he replaced the bone, grabbing another for the show and tell.

He asked the group to follow him to another table that had many bones. He explained to them how the coding of the white tags worked. Pointing to one of the bones, he showed scraping marks. Henry picked up a large rib section, showing how the meat had been removed from the bone, demonstrating with his hands the action of the scraping. Jim commented, "This is a sign that they were eating the dead, quite a common thing when dealing with ancient civilizations." This was not news to Peter. He knew the Hairless Ones would eat a Neanderthal they killed.

Jim continued his showing of the facility, showing how they could do all the analysis of an artifact, including x-ray. They did their own carbon dating of objects, but explained that the DeoxyriboNucleic Acid, or DNA, analysis was done by a large medical university in Madrid.

Henry then showed them to another room. They had constructed a large model of the cave, which covered a twenty-foot by twenty-foot table. The model was a cut away, top elevation, as if looking down on the cave, with pins placed representing the location of artifacts. It clearly showed the main entrance and the secondary smaller entrance.

Peter commented, "There's a lot of the artifacts in one place," pointing to the model and an area midway between the two entrances.

Henry answered, "They are mainly Neanderthal bones. We believe it might have been an area where they processed or butchered them for meat."

Peter knew it was the area the killing of the women and children had happened, but kept it to himself and only shared with Alicia by thought.

Jim came forward and indicated to the small cave that led off from the main cave. "Peter, this pin represents where we found the young one wrapped in buck skin. We have been able to establish that it was a newborn, and at first we believed it was Neanderthal, mainly through the carbon dating we had carried out. However, it clearly has the **FOXP2 gene, which is needed for human speech. Therefore, it is Homo Sapien. It's a very confused time. It is approximately forty-five thousand years ago, the last of the Neanderthals and the beginning of us. Your little one, Peter, could be what we have been looking for, the missing link."**

Tim intervened. "So, it's that one gene that allowed us to evolve?"

Jim answered, "No, Tim. It is just one protein that is different from what we find in the Neanderthals."

"Is it the DNA changing that represents evolutionary development in a species?" asked Tim.

Jim went on to explain. "DNA inevitably hogs the limelight, but it is its' relative RiboNucleic Acid, or RNA, which is actually doing the clever stuff. There are hints that some genes have arisen relatively recently in primate evolution. In addition, a gene may change in sequence during evolution, giving rise to a slightly different protein with altered properties. For example, the FOXP2 gene, which I mentioned, is in the child we found and is needed for human speech. More generally, though, evolutionary complexity may change by using each part in more sophisticated and flexible ways. This, we believe, is where RNA comes in. RNAs are turning out to have important regulatory functions: fine-tuning the activity of genes. In 2006 researchers found that one of the fastest evolving points in the human genome, as judged by comparison with the chimpanzee genome, was in the RNA."

Tim was amazed at the complexity of the answer and thanked him for explaining. Alicia hoped that Tim got what the doctor meant enough to explain it to her later.

The doctor then summed up his explanation on evolution. "Not only does the mutation have to physically happen, it has to find itself located geographically in an environment where it can take advantage and become dominant. Alpha, if you like." He then asked if they would like to see the young one and walked to a massive heavy looking door that turned out to be a fridge filled inside with shelves and small drawers. The doctor knew exactly what he was looking for and removed a large plastic box with a lid, bringing it out from the fridge to one of the large tables. Unclipping the lid, he showed the three of them what was inside the box.

"Please don't touch. We try and not to get any cross contamination on these specimens."

Tim added, "Like a crime scene."

Inside the box, Peter looked down at a blackened object that was about fourteen inches long. You could clearly see the folds in the leather shroud, but were unable to see the child inside. Jim left the table and returned with x-ray slides of the young child inside the shroud, which clearly showed the skeleton, which he held in a position relative to the box. With a pencil, he pointed to the slide and then to the object, so the three of them could see how the child was laying inside the shroud.

He looked at his watch, deciding it was time for them all to go for an evening meal. Young Henry joined them in the van, taking them back to town. They finally arrived at a wonderful, traditional Spanish restaurant. They spent the evening going over what they had seen at the laboratory and asking the doctor and Henry more questions. Peter was starting to get really excited about what the following day might have in store. To finally get to the cave and confirm, for him, that it was the place of his vision, was exciting. They finished their meal, which they all enjoyed and laid out the plans for the trip to the cave the following day.

"I will collect you at 9:30 in the morning. Will that be okay, Peter?" asked Jim.

"That will be fine," answered Peter.

As they all started to leave the restaurant, Alicia noticed that Peter was pressing his hand into his diaphragm. She asked, "Are you okay, Peter?"

Peter answered, "I am fine. I think I must have had too much of the Paella or Sangria. Something has given me indigestion."

The doctor said, "I know of a pharmacy where we will be able to get some indigestion medicine. We can stop on the way back to the hotel."

"That would be great," said Peter.

The next morning, Alicia called Peter's room at 8:45. He answered the phone on the second ring, sounding refreshed. "Good morning Alicia, how are you today?"

"I am good," answered Alicia. "Would you like me to bring you some coffee, Peter?"

Peter answered, "No. I've already had a cup. Shall we meet in the breakfast bar?"

"That will work," said Alicia. "Tim is saying he is starving, poor thing. It's been at least eight hours since we had dinner."

Peter laughed, telling Alicia, "See you downstairs."

They all met in the restaurant where Tim had selected a table and was waiting while watching the weather forecast. Tim commented, "It looks like it's going to be a nice day."

They all made their way to the self-serve breakfast bar buffet. Tim loaded up on the scrambled eggs, bacon and toast, spending the next few minutes looking for the Maple Syrup. It was an item that was not on the menu, but Tim felt sure that he would be able to find some. He was not successful and finally returned to the table with his bacon, eggs and toast covered in ketchup as a Maple Syrup replacement. He commented to Peter and Alicia, "It's hard to believe they don't have any Maple Syrup. If I had known that I would have brought some with me."

Alicia commented as she put down her coffee. "Whatever."

They all enjoyed their breakfast and were sitting in the foyer waiting for Jim when he arrived. He escorted them to the van, which had the same happy little driver who welcomed them. "Buenos días," he repeated to each of them as he helped them load up into the van.

Tim was carrying his camera gear making sure to clear it with Jim. "Will it be okay to take pictures?"

Jim gave him permission, explaining, "We don't normally allow people to take pictures as it might generate unwelcome interest in what we are working on, but today it will be okay."

As they made their way to the cave, Alicia again noticed that Peter was holding his abdomen and was taking more of the heartburn tablets he had purchased the previous night. Again she asked, "Peter, are you okay?"

He responded, "I am fine. I must slow down when I eat." Then he quietly continued to suck on the indigestion tablets.

They arrived at the cave to be greeted by the security officer who appeared from one of the two Port-a-Cabins, small temporary portable buildings. He helped with the unloading and then they made their way to the scaffolding stairs. The security officer came forward and unlocked the large gate that secured the entrance.

The climb towards the entrance of the cave was slow, as Peter could only manage a few steps at a time. Then he would need to rest. Alicia hung back with him, giving him time to recover before doing the next ten steps. The higher they climbed, the more beautiful the view became. Peter was mesmerized by the beauty of it all. Breathing heavy, he told Alicia, "For once in my life, I have a place that I feel part of; it is as if I have come home. Alicia, when we return to the hotel, please look for a small three-bedroom house that might be for sale in the village."

Alicia commented. "You want three bedrooms. Why do we need three bedrooms?"

Peter answered, "The next time we come back, we will bring your mother with us."

Alicia again held Peter's arm and said, "She would love that, Peter. Thanks for being so thoughtful."

Peter responded, "That's okay, Alicia. Your mother is very much part of this team and I think she will love it here."

"Yes, she would, Peter. Yes, she would," said Alicia, as she again soaked up the beautiful view.

They finally arrived at the entrance of the cave. Peter stood with his back to the entrance taking in the beauty of the location. "Beautiful," he commented, still breathing heavy after the strenuous climb.

Tim and Jim were already inside the cave and Jim was showing Tim the wall that had previously been covered in art, but now showed no signs to the untrained eye. The elements and time had removed all traces, requiring a powerful magnifying glass to show the slightest traces of pigments that had been used and had covered the wall.

Finally, Peter turned to walk into the cave, the temperature noticeably dropping as soon as he entered into the shaded entrance. Jim walked ahead to a wall, which had a large electric switch. He pulled the switch, which turned on a single strand of cable hanging from the cave roof that had a light bulb hanging every ten-foot. The light racing along the length of the cave illuminated the massive cavern they now found themselves entering.

Tim and Jim went ahead, going deeper into the cave and heading for the area that had been marked where they found a lot of the Neanderthal bones. Peter and Alicia could see the flash of Tim's camera every few moments as they moved away deeper into the cave.

Peter walked slowly, inspecting both walls as he progressed. Alicia quietly walked behind him, giving him time to take it all in. He stopped looking at the handprints on one of the cave walls. He walked forward, inspecting closely a group of handprints.

He remained stationary and silent, and then placed his hand over one of the prints.

He dropped his head back and closed his eyes. He remained like that for several moments. He then turned; smiling at Alicia, and without saying a word, let her know that this was the cave he had been transported to during the coma.

He finally removed his hand from the wall and walked back to Alicia. He then verbally confirmed what he had been transmitting through thought. "Alicia this is it. We have found it." He started to point out some of the artwork on the wall, telling her the meanings and they finally arrived at the drawing of the hunter throwing a spear at the bird in the nest. He didn't have to explain. She already knew and understood the picture's meaning.

They both proceeded deeper into the cave, where the entrance narrowed from the large cavern to a tunnel that Tim and the doctor went down, their footsteps and voices fainter, but still clear, reverberating against the ancient natural walls.

Peter said, "This is the place that Hawk would love to sit and meditate with his back against the wall." He kicked off his shoes and slowly sat on the floor, shuffling so his back was touching the wall with his legs straight out in front of him. His old legs would not bend, but he was able to get himself in a position where he felt connected, the strength and power of the massive rock he was laying against very comforting. The thought that this was the same place Hawk would sit humbled him.

He opened his hands and placed them palm up on his legs, dropped his head back, closed his eyes, and started breathing deep, beginning to meditate. Alicia stood quietly as she watched Peter go deep into his meditation. She could feel the tranquility and depth of Peter's meditation and quietly moved off, inspecting and admiring the art and prints that covered the wall.

She was transfixed by a large group of prints, many made by children. The position of the prints was low on the cave wall and the prints were small compared to those higher. Her mind went back to the telling of the story by Peter and how the children would enjoy placing prints on the cave wall, mixing the herbs and minerals to make a paint. The children also knew of the importance of the prints, having it explained to them that the prints held the essence of the person that left the print. This made them feel adult and also gave their handprint a purpose.

Alicia noticed a perfect print low on the wall. 'A child,' she thought. She went forward, inspecting the print that had attracted her attention. Clearing her mind, she placed her hand over the small print. She closed her eyes, which instantly experienced a bright blue flash of light. 'I am connected,' she thought. Breathing deeply, she relaxed. Her senses became super keen. She had passed back in time. She felt comfortable in her surroundings, the earthy smells comforting her. The sound of people moving in the cave behind her made her look around. The cave was busy. Neanderthals and their children were going about their day. The entrance of the cave was highlighted with the brightness of the daylight outside. Sitting around the fire were children being shown how to clean and prepare animal skins.

There was laughter and calmness amongst the inhabitants as they went about their day, paying no attention to her. One of the children, however, approached her looking deep into her eyes, bringing her face close. The look on the child's face was friendly and it was she who communicated her name, calling Alicia the name Water. She repeated the name several times, her look getting more concerned. She brought her face closer to look deep into her eyes.

It was then she realized she was experiencing the cave through the eyes of Water. This must have been her handprint. She could also clearly see Hawk, legs crossed, meditating where she had left Peter. The image of Hawk was bright, surrounded by a calm pulsating blue light.

To her surprise, it was from the image of Hawk that Peter appeared. He was emanating from the body of Hawk and looking straight at her; Water. He moved smoothly, unfolding and standing upright and then looking up. He seemed to recognize something that made him smile; then again he lowered his eyes to look directly at her. As he did he smiled once more. He looked up again and reached up with his arms. Then the image started to fade. The last part of the image was his smiling face. She looked again at the image of Hawk and the blue light had gone.

This refocused her attention, bringing her back to the present with the same suddenness that she had arrived in the past. She was back in the present time, removing her hand from the print on the cave wall. She turned to where Peter was sitting.

He was in the same place, slumped to one side.

Alicia ran to him and dropped on her knees, grabbing at his hands. "Peter, Peter," she cried. He did not respond and she pulled him from the wall to lay him down so that she could start CPR. As his body lay flat, she called his name once more, holding his hand. "Peter?" She could feel that life had left him. She lowered her head and started sobbing, realizing it was useless to try and bring him back. She had seen him in death and he was at peace. Knowing this, however, did not stop the sobbing.

Tim and the doctor returned eventually and realized something was wrong, running the last one hundred feet to where Alicia was kneeling beside Peter, who was lying flat on the cave floor. They did not need to ask. Alicia told them between sobs that he had passed. That was all she could say. The doctor reached forward, searching Peter's neck for a sign of a pulse. He dropped his hand away. Peter was already starting to lose the heat of life and there was no sign of a pulse. Alicia was right. He was gone. He placed his hand on the back of Alicia who was sobbing in the arms of Tim, but remained holding the hand of Peter.

Chapter 20

Alicia and Tim arrived back in Austin just after 2:00 p.m. two days after the passing of Peter. They were exhausted. Doctor Zeallow had arranged for the body of Peter to be flown back once the Spanish authorities had time to establish a cause of death. This involved an autopsy and they were certain the findings would show that Peter had a massive heart attack.

The word was out and the local media was waiting at the airport arrivals terminal to get the information from the people who had been traveling with Senator Peter Shaw when he passed. Alicia was still very upset and burst into tears when her mother came forward to hug her in the terminal. Brenda started crying as well, the two of them very upset and both were embracing each other, heads bowed. Brenda was upset with herself saying, "I promised that I would not cry," wiping her nose with a hanky in her free hand.

"I did the same thing," Alicia let out with a small laugh mixed in with sobs.

Tim stood beside them both, his legs either side of the bags on the floor. One of the reporters recognized Tim and shouted out. "What happened to the Senator, Tim?" He ignored the question; just standing with his head down wishing the reporters would disappear. The reporter approached Tim and placed a recorder in front of his mouth and asked, "Well, how did the old boy die?" Tim said nothing and turned his back on the reporter. The reporter moved his recorder over to the girls. "Can you tell us when the Senator's body will be brought back to Texas?"

Brenda looked up, blowing her nose, but ignoring the question. Tim had enough and came forward to the reporter, telling him to fuck off and pushing the recorder away from the girls and placing himself between them.

The reporter answered back, "Just doing my job, Tim."

Tim responded, "You can see how upset they are. Give them time and we will give a press release later." As Tim was talking, a large well-dressed middle-aged man approached. Holding his business card out for Tim, he introduced himself. "Charles Powers; I am Peter's lawyer. I have been waiting for you to arrive."

Alicia heard the man introduce himself and turned. "Oh, thank god you're here. I have no idea what to do or how to handle everything."

Charles turned his attention to Alicia. "Alicia, my dear, you have nothing to worry about. Peter has taken care of everything for you; it's okay."

Charles then turned his attention to the gathered media, raising his hand to get their attention. They gathered around him and he handed them all a small, prepared document that laid out the basics of Peter's demise. He then verbally explained to them all,

"Senator Peter Shaw's body is still in Spain and the cause of death as yet has not been determined. It is believed to be a heart attack and there are no suspicious circumstances."

One of the reporters shouted from the back. "Is it true he was in a cave studying cave art?"

Charles commented, "The Senator did have an interest in ancient civilizations and their art. He did pass away while researching cave art in Spain."

The same reporter then asked, "Did this research have anything to do with the on-going case where the senator was accused of defacing national monuments with handprints?"

Charles ended the conversation. "We have no other comments and as you can see his friends are very upset over this and need some time to mourn the loss of a great servant of this wonderful country of ours, Senator Peter Shaw. Please respect their privacy. We will give you more information as it becomes available. I have given you all my contact information if you feel you need it."

The same young reporter again approached Tim, asking for a comment. He again obliged with his head lowered and a stifled, "Fuck off," as he followed Alicia, Brenda and Charles out of the airport.

Austin Statesman Editor John Kerr had brought to his attention the arrival of the now-deceased Senator Peter Shaw's traveling partners. He had sent a young reporter down there to see what he could find out. J.K. walked in front of the flat screen television in the conference room next to his office, not concerned that he was blocking the view of the other reporters who had gathered to see that Tim was in the group to everyone's surprise. J.K. could hardly believe his eyes. It was him all right. Tim had asked permission to take seven days off for a trip to Europe. J.K. had reluctantly given it to him, but had no idea that he was going to Europe with Senator Peter Shaw and the young intern, Alicia, who had caused so many problems and had to be fired.

He reached down for his Blackberry that was attached to a clip on his belt, flipped through the contacts, and finding Tim's number, pressed the connect button. It rang four times and then went through to Tim's answer phone. Tim's voice was asking the caller to leave a message after the beep and assured them he would return the call.

"Tim, this is J.K. Call me." He paused, and then added, "Now!" J.K. would make that call every thirty minutes for the next three hours, until he finally got an answer.

"Hello. This is Tim's phone. He is not available at the moment," answered a woman's voice.

J.K. was surprised the person answering was a woman. The voice sounded too mature to be Alicia, forcing J.K. to ask, "Who is this?"

"Oh, my name is Brenda. I am a friend of Tim's," she replied.

"Okay, my name is John Kerr. I am the editor of the Austin Statesman. In fact, that is my phone you just answered."

"I know who you are," answered Brenda. "You might remember my daughter, Alicia, who you fired from an internship. Both of them have just arrived back from Spain and are taking a rest, sleeping. Jet lag, as I'm sure you know, is stressful."

"That's fine. Wake him up and tell him I need to talk to him."

Brenda answered back. "I don't think so Mr. J.K. I will tell him you called when he awakens. You have a great afternoon, Sir." She ended the call and placed the phone back on the kitchen table. It was already ringing again and would remain unanswered, muffled by the dishtowel Brenda had placed over it.

Alicia and Tim both remained in bed until early the next day. The sun had not risen when they went outside with a fresh cup of coffee to take their place upon the porch swing and watch as the sun brought the new day with it. Alicia thought about the last time she had sat there with Peter. Tim, sensing her sadness, reached over and grabbed her hand. The swing was rocking slowly backwards and forwards and Alicia could see the image of Peter smiling at her as she had seen it when he passed.

As the morning sun started to light up the day, the Mockingbird again placed itself high on top of the green house and started to claim the day with its calling. Alicia was pleased to see the bird, thinking how much pleasure it had given Peter.

It was 9:30 that morning before Tim decided that he would call the editor. He called the office and had to be put through to J.K. by his secretery. She asked, "Who shall I say is calling?"

"Tell J.K. that it's Tim. I understand he has been trying to contact me."

The secretery recognized his voice. "Tim, watch it. J.K. is smoking hot. He has been waiting for you to call since yesterday."

Tim waited silently for J.K. to pick up and start the conversation. He picked up and began sternly. "Where have you been Tim and why have you not been answering your cell phone?"

The answer from Tim was short. "Well, as you know, I have been on vacation."

"I fucking know that," yelled J.K. He then added, "You and that young intern, Alicia, have been all over Channel Three News. I don't need to remind you that you are the political reporter for this newspaper and should have been covering the death of Shaw, seeing that you obviously have first-hand knowledge of the entire event. I should not have found out about it from other sources."

Tim responded, "I was on vacation, J.K., and your reporter was at the airport. I told him I would give him a release at a later time."

J.K. was not happy with the answer and had to push his authority. "Okay, where are you now?"

Tim answered, "At my girlfriend, Alicia's."

"Okay, I want you in my office within the hour with the full story, Tim."

"J.K., I am still on vacation."

"Fuck your vacation. If you want to keep your job, you better be here."

Tim responded quickly, "I don't," placing his hand over the phone and miming laughter. Alicia and Brenda, seated around the kitchen table, were trying to make sense of the one-sided conversation.

J.K. had fired enough reporters in his time to know that's where this conversation was headed. He needed to get a couple of good shots in before Tim blew him off. "You, young man, will not work for any publication again. I will make sure everyone in the game knows how devious and self serv.." He had not quite had time to get it out before he heard the click and silence that followed, indicating that Tim had dropped the call. He cursed to himself.

Tim turned to Brenda and reached forward shaking her hand. "Hello. I am Tim Green, freelance reporter." He raised his middle finger in the general direction of downtown Austin, then switched the paper's phone to off.

It was 10:45 a.m. before the house phone started ringing and Brenda answered it. "Peter Shaw's residence. Brenda speaking."

"Hello, Brenda. It's Charles, Peter's lawyer. We met at the airport. Is it possible to talk to Alicia?"

Brenda answered, "Sure, I will get her for you,"

Alicia was found standing in the hall, admiring the handprint she had found, which Peter had placed on a slab of Italian Block Crytsal. Prior to their trip to Spain, she had a local jeweler attach a chain to the back of the crystal so she could hang it in the entry.

Brenda called to her, "Alicia, Peter's lawyer is on the phone and would like to talk to you."

Alicia made her way to the kitchen and picked up the call. "Hello, this is Alicia."

"Good morning, Alicia. I hope you are feeling refreshed. Is it possible for you to come over to my office later today? Brenda and Tim should come as well if they can. Peter has left some quite detailed instructions which I need to go over with you."

Alicia said, "Of course, when would you like to see us?"

Charles replied, "I am busy this morning, but will be free around three this afternoon if you can make it."

Alica confirmed, "That will be fine."

"My office is at 5333 Congress Avenue, Suite 230. See you all at three?" he inquired.

Alica confirmed they would both be with her and put the phone down.

At 2:30 they all piled into Alicia's Toyota and made their way downtown, finally finding a parking place that only left them a two block walk to the lawyer's prestigious offices.

As they arrived at the office of Charles Powers, the large polished brass plate clearly showed that Charles Powers was an Attorney at Law and doing well. Tim opened the door for Brenda and Alicia. A secretary sat inside the room they had just entered; large pictures showing fishing and hunting scenes hung from the walls.

Lush carpets, the location, and the polished oak all indicated that Charles Powers was very successful. The secretery asked for their names and then asked them all to take a seat as she disappeared through a large heavy oak door. The door had a security lock, and she tapped the numbers in before the door opened, allowing her through. The door closed behind her and the lock resecured the occupants. The three of them sat waiting for the secretary to reappear, and for some reason were now all talking in a whisper. The large door opened and the secretary, holding the door ajar with her back, indicated for them all to come in. They did and she led them to a large conference room. A massive oak table with several leather chairs filled the room.

She indicated for them to take their seats and told them that Mr. Powers would join them shortly. They arranged themselves around the table, leaving the head clear for the arrival of Charles Powers.

Charles arrived, followed by the secretary who had an arm full of files, which she placed at the head of the table for him. She then excused herself.

Charles sat down, thanked them all for

attending, and at the same time explained what a sad occasion this was for them all. At the same time, he opened a large manilla folder.

"I have been a friend of Peters from when we were at school together. Since the accident that killed his wife, he has been very much aware of his diminishing health. As you know, Peter had no family. In fact, he told me Alicia and Brenda, that you, for all intents and purposes, are to be treated as his family. I have acted as an advisor and estate planner on a professional level, creating a private foundation for the reasearch of ancient civilizations. He transferred over sixty percent of his personal wealth, which was a considerable amount, over to the foundation. The foundation, being private, was headed by Peter. Upon his death, he has arranged for you, Alicia, to take the helm. I am to act as an advisor, for which he appointed me secretary. He recommended that your mother, Brenda, should be given a directorship in the foundation, for which she will be recompensed on a quarterly basis. He laid a loose framework of how the foundation should be operated, but he wanted you, Alicia, to direct it. The foundation has and will continue to support Dr. Zeallow on his research of the caves in Spain. I believe you have met Dr. Zeallow already, as he was with you when Peter passed.

Alicia, the mansion and surrounding grounds, plus forty-four million dollars has been willed to you personally. Brenda, he has willed to you two million dollars and the Mercedes sports car that, he says, you greatly admired. Tim, to you, he has willed one million dollars. He said it was compensation for the reasearch you had carried out on behalf of the foundation. He also would like you to consider a position on the board of the foundation for research and marketing. Apparently, there is a book that Alicia has been working on with Peter and he would like you to assist with the completion and marketing of the said book.

So, basically, it is a very simple will that Peter has created to make sure that the foundation has the necessary capital to continue and also that you all are looked after. I know this sounds strange at this time, but congratulations to you all. Have any of you any questions?"

They all looked at each other, Brenda holding Alicia's hand. They all remained quiet, thinking over what they had just heard. Alicia finally coughed, looking around at Tim and her mother, and said, "I don't think so, Mr. Powers."

"Okay, then the official reading of Peter's Last Will and Testament has been completed. Give me a couple of days and you will all need to come back to the office as we have documents that need witnessing and signing. Before you go, Peter asked me to do one more thing."

He walked from the head of the table to a cabinet that was against one of the walls. On it was a DVD player, and above that was a sixty inch flat-screen, high definition television. He placed the DVD in the player and pressed the button. He then walked back to the table and pressed a button that dimmed the lights in the windowless room.

The DVD opened with Peter walking away from the camera, the shot too close as all it showed was the back of his shirt. He sat down so that he was looking directly at the camera, his face large, filling the high definition screen. He began to talk.

"I am doing this recording for you, but at this time we have not yet met. By the time you watch this, I will have have passed. The story I will share with you is important; important enough to have breached the planes that separate life from death. It is a story that has to be shared. We have been chosen as the vehicles of the sharing of this story. The demise of the Neaderthals, with all their child-like innocence, is the consequences of inbreeding. The Neaderthals were the most successful species on earth at that time, but they did not understand the warning given to them in dream. They were warned by the vision of a snake in the tree of life. The snake was the DNA double helix; the warning of the damage to the blood line through inbreeding remained misunderstood."

Tim looked at Alicia and mouthed, "He knew all along." Alicia, dumbfounded, just looked back at the screen.

Peter continued. "Hawk became aware when it was too late. The seed had been sown and the mutation too powerful to put back into the box. The development of ego was one of the consequences. The mutation itself craved duplication. The Homo Sapiens were unable to control the desire. As in the bible, they had lost their child-like innocence. The desire to replicate was like a virus and is how it secured its progression, killing anything that could possibly threaten it. Ultimately, Homo Sapien will destroy itself. Resources, overburdened with an ever-expanding populace is being driven on by the desire to reproduce in our own image. Seventy percent of pregnancies in the undeveloped world are unplanned, and fifty percent in what we call the developed world.

We were warned about this through dream, but we needed Hawk to clarify what we were being told. It is only now that I know my purpose.

It is said the meek will inherit the earth. If we are to survive as a species, we must eventually become meek and think more as a global tribe, with a global conscience. The ancients were the meek and the desire of the Homo Sapien violently wiped them from the earth."

Peter then reached forward. On a piece of glass that had been placed between him and the front of the camera, he placed his hand. When he removed it, there was a perfect red handprint; a print that Alicia recognized instantly. It was the same one she had hung in the hall. Peter then reached around the Block Crystal to the camera and turned it off.

Alicia sat silent. She realized she would not be able to spend time with Peter again, but felt comforted by the thought of Peter's essence guiding her toward her purpose.